HIDDEN SECRETS
A Whispering Pines Mystery, Book Four

Shawn McGuire

OTHER BOOKS BY SHAWN MCGUIRE

WHISPERING PINES Series
Missing & Gone, prequel short story
Family Secrets, book 1
Kept Secrets, book 2
Original Secrets, book 3

Gemi Kittredge mystery novellas
One of Her Own
Out of Her League
Over Her Head

THE WISH MAKERS Series
Sticks and Stones, book 1
Break My Bones, book 2
Never Hurt Me, book 3
Had a Great Fall, book 4
Back Together Again, book 5

Short Stories
The Door
Escaping The Veil

HIDDEN SECRETS
A Whispering Pines Mystery, Book Four

Shawn McGuire

Brown Bag Books

This book is a work of fiction. Names, characters, places, and events are products of the author's imagination or are used fictitiously. Any resemblance to actual events, locales, or persons, living or dead, is entirely coincidental.

All rights reserved. In accordance with the U.S. Copyright Act of 1976, the scanning, uploading, and/or electronic sharing of any part of this book without the written permission of the publisher is unlawful piracy and theft of the author's intellectual property. Thank you for supporting the author's rights.

Copyright © 2018 Shawn McGuire
Published by Brown Bag Books
ISBN-13: 978-1721863006
ISBN-10: 1721863001

For information visit:
www.Shawn-McGuire.com

Cover Design by Steven Novak
www.novakillustration.com

First Edition/First Printing June 2018

To all those bullied, harassed, or victimized.
Stay strong and keep talking until someone listens.

Chapter 1

TRIPP BENNETT RESTED ONE HAND on the popup camper like a priest administering last rites.

"Why is this such a big deal?" He blew out a long slow breath. "We're only moving it across the yard, not getting rid of it. Winter will be here before we know it, and I won't be able to sleep in it anyway."

The fifteen-foot camper had been sitting in my front yard since the day I hired Tripp to help with the house three months ago. Today it was leaving its post.

Despite Tripp's turmoil, this was an exciting day. After months of backbreaking work renovating and converting my grandparents' seven-bedroom lake house into a bed-and-breakfast, we were done. It was a little bittersweet as well. Opening our doors to guests meant that our time together was about to change in a big way. No more long leisurely nights sitting on the deck watching moonlight ripple off the lake while listening to the goosebump-inducing cries of the loons.

"Take a minute." I placed a comforting hand on his shoulder, doing my best to remain patient with this process.

I really did understand his distress. Tripp had spent five years wandering the country, never staying in one place for long. Making spur-of-the-moment decisions wasn't hard for him. Which paint colors or tiles to use in the nine bathrooms? That took maybe a half hour. Hire a chef or let Tripp do the cooking for Pine Time B&B? That took half a second. Tripp wasn't handing his kitchen over to anyone. Not even me. Of course, I couldn't cook. Deciding what to do with the little camper, however, took weeks.

Finally, we settled on tucking it along the far side of the detached garage where it wouldn't be visible from either the house or by cars approaching on the quarter-mile-long driveway. We started the moving process this morning by hauling all his possessions from the trailer up to the attic. This took approximately fifteen minutes. Tripp didn't own much. For the last twenty minutes he'd been psyching himself up to hitch the thing to the back of his partly red, partly rusty pickup truck.

"Okay." He blew out one more breath. "I'm ready."

"You've got this." Good thing I was standing behind him. The rolling of my eyes was anything but supportive.

He hopped into the driver's seat, put the truck in gear, and backed the camper up like a pro, positioning it next to the garage. Meeka, my West Highland White Terrier, inspected the moving process, barking her approval or giving a scolding *yip* when something wasn't done to her satisfaction.

"I'll get a tarp and cover it—" Tripp paused mid-sentence, squinted, and rushed back to where the camper had been.

"What's wrong?" I jogged behind him, then saw dead spots in the yard from the wheels. A large rectangle of grass had turned yellow-green from being in the shadow of the popup.

Tripp groaned and swore softly, something he never did. "I'll do what I can to patch that up. I'll probably have to fill in the depressions with a little dirt, then throw down some seed."

"Tonight is our grand opening party. You have guests

to attend to. Remember? We hired people to help you with things like the yard."

"You're right." He shook his head in disgust. "I'll call the yard service to come over and take care of this."

"They can do it tomorrow. It's too late to worry about something like this now."

"I knew we shouldn't have waited until the last minute. We should've moved the thing yesterday."

I stood on my tiptoes and placed a kiss on his cheek. "I love how you obsess over every little thing around here. That's why I know this is going to be a great success."

"Speaking of last minute, where are the tables and chairs?"

We'd ordered ten round tables and a hundred and twenty chairs for tonight. They were supposed to be here by ten this morning. It was almost one o'clock.

"I'm sure they're on the way, but I'll call the rental company and find out what's going on."

Taking his hand, I led him further out to the middle of the front yard. There, I turned him to face the house. When I had arrived here a little over three months ago, just before Memorial Day weekend, the house … no, the entire property was a disaster. The outside of the grand, fifty-year-old lake house desperately needed a new coat of paint as well as some minor repairs. The gardens hadn't been tended to properly in years. The inside was the worst, though. Vandals had broken in and trashed the place. My grandparents would have been heartbroken by the damage done to their home.

The now lush gardens were back to their original beauty and perfectly accented the fresh storm-cloud-gray exterior and snow-white trim. My friend Morgan Barlow was the best green witch in Wisconsin, which was Wiccan for she had a way with plants. She had come over and given me her opinion on what to do about the landscaping. Then she recommended a few folks from the village who I could hire to make it happen. I swear, all I really needed to do to revive the failing gardens was to have her walk through them. It was like her aura alone was enough to encourage the tired greenery to come back to life.

"Do you remember what this looked like when we started?" I asked Tripp.

"How could I forget? I still can't believe we got all that done."

It had been an intense three months of renovations, website design, and spreading the word that Pine Time Bed-and-Breakfast would be opening ... sometime in August. We made it, but just barely. Tomorrow was September first. Our first guests were checking in this afternoon for the long Labor Day weekend.

Honestly, if someone would have told me a year ago that I would be leaving my hometown of Madison, Wisconsin, and moving to the tiny Northwoods village of Whispering Pines, I would've laughed in their face. But after less than a week of living next to the pristine lake, among a community of people who cared more about their neighbors than themselves, I knew I was never leaving. The villagers had gathered around Tripp and me during the restoration and offered tons of help getting the place ready. To repay them, we were having a grand opening barbecue celebration for them tonight. Tourists were welcome as well.

As we stood there, beaming at our beautiful house and feeling like proud parents, the distinctive rumble of an expensive automobile sounded through the trees from up the driveway. We turned to find a sleek, shiny black sports car approaching the house.

Tripp's mouth dropped open. "I think I'm in love."

"What is that?" This car was super sexy. Low to the ground, as sports cars tended to be, it had an almost predatory look to it like a wolf or panther on the prowl.

Tripp wiped away a little dribble of drool from the corner of his mouth, "That is an Aston Martin Vanquish."

I looked up at him, amused. "How do you know that?"

He blinked at me, confused by the question. "I'm a guy. Knowing these things is in our DNA."

Since he was in little-boy-on-Christmas-morning mode, I let the somewhat sexist explanation go. "What would something like that cost?"

"A few hundred."

I expected him to laugh and then tell me the real price, but he just kept staring and drooling. Who paid multiple six figures for a car? We watched as the vehicle backed in next to my tired, twenty-year-old Cherokee—which cost multiple three figures—and a man just as long, dark, and sleek as his car, unfolded from the driver's seat.

Six foot one, early-thirties, light-brown skin, pale-blue eyes, wavy black hair to the collarbone, shoulders wide enough to take on the weight of the world.

This guy looked like he'd just stepped out of a *Dresden Files* book. Or maybe he was a dark angel. I half-expected black wings to sprout from his back.

"Who is he?" I asked.

Chapter 2

I SMACKED TRIPP'S ARM WITH the back of my hand to draw his attention away from the Aston Martin cooling down in our driveway.

"Who is he?" I repeated.

"Won't know for sure until we ask him, but I believe he's River Carr, one of our guests this weekend." He glanced down at me. "Now you're drooling."

I ran a hand over my mouth to be sure. "I am not."

Our visitor made his way toward us with long, confident strides, his long black leather duster jacket fanning out around him like a wizard's cape or a bat's wings. He held a hand out to me and then pulled back to remove the black leather driving gloves he still wore.

"Good afternoon." His smooth voice held a faint European accent. "I'm River Carr. I have a reservation to stay with you this weekend."

I froze, staring for what felt like an hour but couldn't have been more than a second or two since Tripp didn't step in to greet our guest in my place. Whispering Pines attracted tourists from all walks of life, but I couldn't remember seeing anyone around the village as suave and sophisticated as the man standing before me.

"Welcome to Pine Time, Mr. Carr. I'm Sheriff Jayne

O'Shea." I smiled and shrugged off the title. "Sorry, I am sheriff of Whispering Pines, but I'm also co-owner of the bed-and-breakfast. This is my partner, Tripp Bennett."

The man inclined his head in a small bow as he shook Tripp's hand. "Mr. Bennett. I believe we spoke on the phone."

"We did. It's a pleasure to meet you in person, Mr. Carr. I'd like to welcome you as our first official guest."

"I'm honored to accept such a designation, and please, call me River. Allow me to collect my luggage and then I'd like to check into my room if I'm not too early. I got here sooner than I had anticipated."

"I'm sure in a car like that the miles must melt away." Tripp gave an admiring nod at the Vanquish.

River grinned, his intense pale eyes gleaming as he did. "Would you like to take a closer look?"

Apparently having forgotten I was there, Tripp dropped my hand and, as though following the Pied Piper out of the village, accompanied our guest to the beautiful vehicle.

"Boys and their toys. What about us, hey, Meeka?" But when I looked down, my traitorous terrier was on her way to join the men in the automotive section of our property.

While they appreciated the vehicle, I rushed inside to call my deputy Martin Reed and make sure all was right with the state of the village. Reed had agreed to hold down the fort for me today while we prepared for the grand opening. Three months ago, when I first arrived here, Reed and I would rather have scratched each other's eyes out than work together in the same building. Fortunately, we both got past that and now, mere weeks after hiring him, I had a deputy that I trusted implicitly.

"A what just pulled up to your place?" Reed asked when I told him our first guest had arrived. "Mind if I close up shop early today, boss? Sounds like a vehicle in need of security."

"That's no joke." I leaned back in the comfortably worn

leather desk chair that used to be my grandfather's. This room used to be his den and now served as the B&B's office. "Maybe one of the witches can cast a protection spell over it."

I was joking; I didn't believe in the witchy woo-woo mindset that hovered over this village. In this instance, however, it would be a good thing if one of them could produce an invisible shield.

"You're coming to the party tonight, right?" I asked.

"Wouldn't miss it. You've been talking about this B&B for so long, I feel like I already know it. Now that there's eye candy in the driveway, I have extra incentive."

The front door opened, and male voices filled the foyer. "I have to check in the dark and mysterious River Carr now. Just wanted to make sure everything is okay in the village."

"It's getting busy, being Labor Day weekend and all, but so far so good. If you don't hear from me, then all is well, and I'll see you tonight."

Since Mr. Carr was the first guest to arrive at Pine Time, we gave him the grand suite. My grandmother and grandfather's bedroom was the biggest in the house. I told him a little of the history of both the house and the room while I processed his paperwork and got his key.

With a little bow of his head, he said, "I'm honored to be staying in your grandparents' bedroom."

"It's a rather large room," I commented. "Will anyone be joining you?" My face burned with embarrassment. "Sorry. I didn't mean to ask such a personal question."

He smiled, his brilliant white teeth glistening in an almost animal way that made me a bit uncomfortable. A sort of dark magnetism emanated from the man, and I had no doubt that if someone wasn't already planning to meet him here, he wouldn't be alone for long. Unless he wanted to be, of course.

"Don't worry, I'm not offended. At this time, I don't have a companion, but one never knows what to expect from a day."

I knew it.

He slid his credit card back into a long slim black wallet and the wallet into an inside breast pocket of his duster. "I'll be honest with you, Ms. O'Shea, I felt summoned to come here this weekend. I've never heard of Whispering Pines before, and I don't know who I am intended to be here for, but I feel strongly that I am meant for someone. All will be clear soon."

He was meant for someone? Interesting and slightly arrogant way to label a hookup.

As he took the key from my hand, he let his long fingers trail across the back of my hand. I shivered but couldn't say why. I didn't feel threatened by him or like he was hitting on me with my boyfriend standing ten feet away. It was more that there was such an intensity coming off him, I couldn't help but react somehow.

"Where is my room?" His eyes smoldered, further luring me into his aura.

"Just to your right at the top of the stairs," Tripp broke the spell. "Would you like me to take you?"

With one last pointed gaze at me, River turned to Tripp with the same air of confidence. "Thank you, Tripp. I appreciate the hospitality, but I'm sure I can find my way."

We watched as the man dressed all in black walked away from us. No, he didn't walk. River Carr glided as though moving required no effort whatsoever.

"Guest number one is a little intense, hey?" Tripp asked when River was far enough away that he wouldn't hear. Unless he had the hearing of a bat as well as the appearance of one.

"That's one word for it. He's like a—"

I almost said vampire. There were things I had come to accept living in this village over the last three months. One, in particular, was that if people here wanted to believe that they were witches, fine, I had no problem with that. As long as they didn't hurt anyone with their "spells." If someone told me they were a vampire, I'd call for an ambulance and have them delivered to the nearest psych ward.

"He's like a warlock or something," I said instead, which was equally dumb as emphasized by Tripp's sudden bark of laughter.

"He's intense, but I don't think he's a warlock." He stared thoughtfully in the direction our guest had just gone and then waggled his eyebrows at me. "Who do you suppose he's here to meet?"

"No clue. But I don't know how comfortable I am with him meeting this mysterious someone in my grandmother's bedroom."

His shoulders dropped a little. "You gotta let that go. It's no longer your grandmother's bedroom. It's Pine Time's grand suite."

For the last two weeks, if I wasn't reminding Tripp that moving the camper wasn't the same as getting rid of it, he was reminding me that the grand suite was no longer Gran's bedroom. He didn't understand. Memories of being here with my grandparents, and my parents before things went bad, lived like ghosts in every room. No matter what we did to this place, this would always be my grandparents' home.

Grunting in acknowledgment of his statement, I clicked a few times on the laptop on the desk and brought up the reservation schedule. "Our next guests should be arriving soon."

This group, I was excited about. I wasn't sure if it had been my sister Rosalyn or my mother who had started talking up Pine Time down in Madison, but one or the other of them had bragged about us. It was probably my mother. She was financially invested in the success or failure of this venture and knew the importance of marketing, word of mouth being some of the best. It could have been Rosalyn, as well, because she liked to claim ownership even if she had nothing to do with a thing. Give her five minutes and she'd have people believing the whole concept for Pine Time was her idea.

However it happened, the three friends I had hung out with most in college heard about the B&B. They had called before I had even made the reservations page on the website live. Kristina, Alicia, and Trevor had been there for me not just for the tests and stresses of college, but also when I decided to change my major from pre-law to criminal justice. A move that my friends wholeheartedly supported but resulted in a ridiculous amount of drama from my mother.

"I can't wait to meet these three," Tripp interrupted my trip to the past. "You've been giddy about them coming for weeks."

"The last time I saw any of them was at Kristina and Kyle's wedding a few years ago. Alicia and Derek eloped right after college; she was pregnant and didn't want to spend the money on a wedding with a baby on the way. Last I heard, Trevor is with someone named Jeremy, but that could have changed already. Trevor is always with someone new."

"There's a Jeremy listed on the registry." Tripp read the screen over my shoulder and placed a finger on the fourth couple that would be joining my friends for the weekend. "Who are these other two? Nick and Constance."

"Constance is Kristina's sister. I met her at graduation. Nick is her husband; never met him."

"It's nearly one o'clock." A tremor of panic laced Tripp's voice. "We need to shift focus to the barbecue tonight."

"No freaking out. We'll have plenty of food, so no worry there."

Maeve and Laurel were bringing a bunch of side dishes, a keg of beer, and a case or two of wine. Honey and Sugar said they were bringing dozens of cookies and fifteen gallons of ice cream. Violet promised coffee and other beverages. Peyton, the owner of Sundry, the village's general store, sent over more than enough plates, bowls, napkins, flatware, and cups to cover this party and possibly another.

"Speaking of food, I need to tend to the ribs."

He placed a quick kiss on my cheek and left, Meeka trotting after him. Lately, anytime Tripp was around food, Meeka was around Tripp, looking for dropped bits.

I slumped back in my chair and closed my eyes. After reading Gran's journals a few weeks ago, I knew her intent was always to have this house full of people. Originally, she wanted to fill it with children of her own, but my dad was the only child they ever had. Instead, she filled the house with friends. After they all moved into homes of their own that were scattered across the two thousand acres that held the village, it was just her and Gramps alone in this big rambling house. Then Gramps died ten years ago, leaving just her.

Now, instead of family or friends, her home would be filled with strangers. Nowhere near her original dream but I hoped she would approve of what Tripp and I had done with their home.

Chapter 3

I WATCHED FROM THE OFFICE window as just before three o'clock three vehicles—a huge old dull-beige SUV; a smaller gleaming-white luxury SUV; and a tiny red convertible—flowed down the driveway and joined the Aston Martin. The squealing that ensued when Kristina, Alicia, and Trevor walked through my front door surprised even me.

Choruses of "oh my God, you look fabulous" and "how long has it been?" echoed off the walls. The looking fabulous comment was mostly true. Beautiful Kristina, who had always reminded me of a perfect porcelain Asian doll, looked the same now as she had in college. *Five foot two, sleek black hair twisted into a bun, small mouth with tiny teeth, finely chiseled features.* The only difference was that her face was a little rounder now, but she seemed just as happy as she did five years ago.

Trevor—*six foot two, coppery-red hair, bright medium-blue eyes, round wire-glasses, dimpled cheeks*—had the look of someone who put in a lot of hours at a job he loved. As always, though, there was a flatness behind his smile like life wasn't quite what he wanted.

Only Alicia looked a little beaten-down. From what I understood, she had five children and homeschooled the oldest. In my opinion, any woman who had five children had the right to look exhausted without comment from another soul.

Five foot two, generous hips and bust but otherwise slender, black circles beneath black-brown eyes, dark-brown skin.

"I nearly cried when Derek's parents walked in this morning." Alicia gripped me in a bear hug that I feared she might not release. "Honestly, if you hadn't opened this bed-and-breakfast, I'm pretty sure I wouldn't have gotten a day off for another ten years."

"How old is your youngest?" I asked.

"Eighteen months." She released a weary sigh and glanced over her shoulder at her husband. "How old do they have to be to become emancipated?"

I laughed and gave her arm a playful slap.

"Fabulous house," Kristina's brother-in-law Nick proclaimed as he took in every corner of the great room Tripp and I had worked so hard to restore. Then he turned to me and held out a hand. "Kyle told me you were a beauty, but he understated that by about a hundred percent."

I immediately regretted taking the man's hand. Instead of shaking it, he took my hand and turned it to place a rather moist kiss on the back. I gave him a tight smile, wishing I was wearing my sheriff's badge, and pulled away. Nick Halpern set off my instincts and not in a good way. There was something a little smarmy about the guy. I couldn't say what it was, but I was going to keep an eye on him. Not something I'd been prepared for with our first group of guests.

"I hate to greet you all and walk away," I said after doing paperwork and handing out room keys, "but we're hosting a party tonight, and I need to make sure we're ready. You are, of course, all welcome to come. This is our grand-opening celebration, and since you all are the first to stay with us, I guess you're like the guests of honor."

Alicia slumped a little. "I didn't bring anything nice. I don't have anything nice. Do I have to dress up?"

"You don't have to, no," I assured, and then looked pointedly at her husband Derek. *Five foot nine, goatee, black hair in long dreadlocks past shoulders, athletic build, dark-brown skin, black-brown eyes.* "If you'd like to get something, Ivy's Boutique over in the village has a great selection of really fun things. I'm sure you'd find something over there."

Alicia looked with pleading eyes up at her husband but didn't even have to ask the question.

"Let's go drop our bags in our room," Derek said, "and go get you an outfit for this evening."

Alicia turned to me with a bewildered look and whispered, "What kind of magic goes on in this place?"

I stopped myself from busting out with a laugh but couldn't disguise the smile on my face. "You have no idea."

After directing the four couples to their rooms, I went out to the back patio where I found Tripp surrounded by four charcoal grills and one very large smoker. Back in his element, cooking, he looked significantly more at ease than he had an hour ago.

"How's it going back here?" I asked and added, "It smells wonderful."

"Going well." He spun his grilling tongs around his finger. "Can we buy this smoker? I never used one before and I really like it."

So cute. "Tell you what, let's see how the ribs turn out then we can talk about buying you a smoker. We are a bed-and-breakfast remember, not a bed-and-dinner."

"No, but we do have to eat dinner." He gave me a big cheesy grin.

"What are you making?"

Tripp pointed at each grill in turn. "Burgers will go on this one. Chicken breasts on this one. Hotdogs over here. And shish kebabs on the last one."

"Shish kebabs? When did those get added to the

menu?"

"A few days ago. Didn't I tell you?"

"Nope, I would have remembered kebabs."

"Did you call about the tables?"

"The delivery truck broke down in Minocqua." Since it was Labor Day weekend, every rental table and chair in a fifty-mile radius had been reserved. We had to rent from a discount party place outside of Wausau.

"That's what we get for waiting until the last minute."

"They promised me they'd be here by four." I checked my watch. "That's in a half-hour."

"We're going to have to scramble to get them set up."

Glancing across the empty backyard, I had to agree. We might still be setting up as our guests arrived. "It'll be fine. We'll make the delivery guys help with setup. If nothing else, we spread blankets out on the grass and go picnic style."

Arden and Holly, our new employees, arrived right on schedule for set up. Arden, a slightly plump, fifty-something, unmarried Wiccan woman with her hair always twisted up in a messy salt-and-pepper bun was our head housekeeper. She had lived in Whispering Pines for over twenty years and was happy to have something other than her gardens and crafts to keep her busy. When Arden wasn't on duty, Holly was. A twenty-two-year-old mother of a demanding toddler, Holly welcomed the escape of dropping her little guy at the daycare and tidying the B&B a few mornings a week.

"Knowing that what I clean," she had said during her interview, "will stay that way for more than thirty seconds sounds incredibly rewarding to me."

"What would you like us to start on, sweetness?" Arden asked when they found me in the backyard.

I held her gaze for a moment, and she placed an apologetic hand over her mouth. I had asked her repeatedly to not call me "sweetness." While I understood the woman was older than my mother, I was not only her boss but also the village sheriff. I had to maintain some level of dignity.

"Sorry," she murmured through her fingers.

"As soon as the tables get here, it'll be all hands on deck to get them up. For now, you two can set up the paper products on one of the two tables we do have. Oh, and tubs of ice for the beverages."

"I brought flowers," Arden said. "We've had so much rain, my garden just won't stop producing this year. I brought enough for a small vase for each table. I thought I'd distribute them throughout the house after."

"I love that." I gave her a grateful grin. "Let me know if you have any questions or if you find we don't have enough of something."

Tripp was on grill duty; Arden and Holly had set up covered. Since I had a minute, I was about to get dressed for the evening when our entertainment arrived.

"Where do you want me to set up?" Lily Grace, the village's youngest fortune teller, was going to do free readings.

"What's wrong?" There was no sparkle in her turquoise eyes. No characteristic snark in her voice. "You seem down."

She shrugged, looking more like a morose teenager than I had ever seen her.

"They won't talk to me," she said.

"About?"

"My parents and that dead girl. They know what happened and won't tell me a thing."

The "dead girl" had to be Priscilla, a teenager who had died in Whispering Pines forty years earlier. After piecing together entries from Gran's journals and interviewing villagers who'd been here at the time, I determined that her death had been an accident, ultimately caused by Lily Grace's mother. It was all very convoluted, as most things were in this village, but since there had never been a formal investigation, there were no records. This meant that even though I was sure of what had happened, without physical evidence, there was nothing I could do about it.

"I assume by 'they' you mean Effie and your grandma Cybil?"

"I don't want to talk about it," Lily Grace cut me off before I could ask any other questions. "I just want to tell fortunes." She laughed. "Funny, the one thing I always said I didn't want, to be a fortune teller, is about the only thing I can escape to right now. I can focus on my customers' lives and forget about my own for a bit." As she spoke, she fingered the cat's eye pendant at her throat, which looked like an actual cat's eye, not the stone. It was kind of creepy. "Oren keeps trying to help, which is nice, but the only thing that will really help is answers, which no one will give me." She tilted her face to the sky and groaned.

Oren had to be the most understanding boyfriend on the planet. Lily Grace, high-strung on a good day, was a complete bundle of emotions right now. And it didn't escape me how ironic it was that a fortune teller had no answers for her own situation.

"I promise, I won't ask any questions." I held up my hands in surrender. "Well, there is one thing you have to tell me. How much room do you think you'll need tonight?"

She rolled her eyes at me. "It's just a portable canopy thing with a little platform, table, and three chairs." She pointed to a spot near the front of the yard. "Over there is good if you don't care. The trees and stuff all around will give us more privacy. People like privacy."

"That's fine with me. Do you need help setting up?"

"Just carrying the stuff over there. And maybe with the awning. I can handle it after that."

As I helped her move everything to the far front corner of my yard, silently in respect of her current mood, a wagon full of carnies showed up. The jugglers and the troop of little people tumblers made Lily Grace smile, but only for a second.

"You're good now?" I asked once we had the canopy up. "I'll stay if you need me."

She dismissed me with a flick of her hand. "I'm good."

I crossed the yard to check on the carnies and was happy to see Dallas Brickman, the knife thrower, and his assistant Abilene in the wagon as well. They'd surely draw a crowd.

"The circus is running without you tonight?" I asked Dallas. He and Abilene were the star act.

"We all have to be back in time for the late show," he informed, "but yes, we were released from duty to help you out for a while."

"What kind of setup do you need?" I asked.

"Only Abilene and I need to set up," he said. "The others will be wandering around and mingling with the crowd."

I pointed to the far corner of the front yard. "Since you'll be throwing sharp objects, how about you and Abilene set up opposite from Lily Grace?"

Just then, the truck of tables and chairs appeared in the driveway.

"The rest of you, follow me."

While Arden, Holly, the delivery guys, and the carnies set up tables and chairs, Tripp and I had to go change out of our jeans and T-shirts and into our party hosts outfits. I found him in the backyard, right where I'd left him, obsessing over charcoal, and told him it was time to go get ready.

He checked each grill once more and asked, "How's it going?"

I waved absently at the backyard. "Arden is supervising everything back here." I gestured toward the front yard. "Our despondent fortune teller is setting up in one corner, the knife thrower in the other."

"Despondent?"

"Tell you later. In the meantime, we have fifteen minutes to get dressed before people start arriving."

"Excellent. One more thing." He took my hand and pulled me into a relatively secluded corner of the patio and kissed me long and well. I grabbed hold of his ponytail as his hands roamed down my back and over my hips.

"What was that for?" I asked, a little breathless and far more relaxed.

"Good luck, of course," he said with a self-satisfied grin and then went inside the house, leaving me trying to remember what it was I'd been about to do.

Chapter 4

ABOUT FORTY-FIVE MINUTES BEFORE THE party was officially set to start our inner circle, so to speak, arrived. Between what Maeve brought from the Grapes, Grains, and Grub pub and Laurel's contributions from The Inn's restaurant, there were enough side dishes to cover an eight-foot table. Violet brought two huge pots of Ye Olde Bean Grinder coffee along with juices and seltzers. Honey and Sugar outdid themselves with not only dozens of cookies, but also five gallons each of Treat Me Sweetly's vanilla, chocolate, and caramel-Oreo ice creams. The showstopper, however, was a cake that was an exact replica of my house.

"You made this?" I asked, walking around the three-foot-wide and two-foot-tall cake for the third time.

"I've been practicing," Honey, the younger of the two sisters explained. "Sugar can do cookies, pastries, and candies with her eyes closed. All I can make is ice cream."

"Don't say 'all' like you're a slacker." Tripp crouched down to examine every inch of the cake. "Your ice cream is the best I've ever had."

Honey blushed. My boyfriend was such a charmer.

"I figured there's a market for cakes here," Honey explained. "Many folks come here to celebrate birthdays and anniversaries, and what goes better with celebrations than cake?"

"Brilliant idea. Thank you for this." I gave her a quick hug and couldn't say which of us was more surprised by it; I wasn't really a hugger.

Morgan arrived then, dressed in a low-cut, black dress that highlighted all her curves and exposed just enough skin to be dangerous. She had to be chilly; it was cool next to the lake tonight.

"Blessed be." Her smile faded when she saw our faces, and she looked down at herself as though checking to be sure nothing had popped free. "What? Ivy said it looked good."

"Ivy was right." Tripp stared long enough that I shielded his eyes with my hand.

"I told her to add a scarf," Morgan's mother Briar quipped as she joined our growing group.

"No, that would've been too much." Tripp pulled my hand out of the way. "And a scarf would cover up her necklaces."

"You look pretty, too," I told Briar as I hip-checked Tripp.

Briar smoothed her hands over her simple black-lace shift dress and gave a little curtsey. "I think Ivy dressed half the village tonight."

Ivy, the former assistant manager of Quin's clothing shop, had gone through the involved process of buying the store after former owner Donovan was arrested for instigating and then covering up my grandmother's death. I wanted to slap a murder charge on him, but he had insisted it was an accident, and I couldn't prove otherwise. I'd been wracking my brain to come up with something, anything to charge him with. The most I could come up with was a Good Samaritan law violation, but that wasn't likely to stick. It was a moot point right now anyway; he had managed to escape police custody and was currently on the run.

"What's in the box?" I asked Morgan.

She held a dark-brown wooden box, intricately carved with Triple Moon Goddess symbols and pentacles. She set it on a nearby table and removed incense, three gold candles, a feather quill pen, and a piece of beautiful, handmade paper that must've come from her store, Shoppe Mystique.

I ran my fingers over the bits of plants and flowers embedded in the paper. "You're going to cast a spell, aren't you?"

"I'm not." Morgan winked. "We are."

She gathered everyone around the table—me, Tripp, Briar, Violet, Honey, Sugar, Laurel, Maeve, and Lily Grace who had wandered over from the front yard. Then Morgan drew a large circle in the center of the paper.

"The circle represents your world." She wrote mine and Tripp's names as well as "Pine Time" in the circle and drew dollar signs around the words. "Everyone, please add a single word signifying your hope for Jayne and Tripp's business."

I went first and wrote "independence." Tripp added "contentment." Once everyone had added their words, Morgan placed the candles in a triangle—one in the center at the top of the paper and one at each bottom corner.

"The more attention you give to something," Morgan explained, "the bigger that thing becomes. Everyone, please join hands and focus your attention on Jayne, Tripp, and the beautiful home they are sharing with the world."

As we joined hands, forming a circle around the table, Morgan lit the candles and then the incense while chanting softly about igniting hopes and dreams. Energy began to pulse from person to person around the group. Tripp squeezed my hand, and Meeka pressed against my leg; they must've felt it, too.

"Beautiful." Morgan murmured, ending the meditation. She extinguished the candles and folded the paper into thirds, enclosing the words inside. "Mama and I will now bury this in the front yard where it will infuse the property with our good intentions."

I smiled as they walked away and suddenly felt very emotional. Despite the woo-woo factor, the people I had come to care about most in this village just blessed me, my boyfriend, and our venture.

"Are you okay?" Violet asked.

I nodded. "Just thinking about how much you all have come to mean to me in such a short time."

"Sappiness!" Sugar called out, making everyone laugh, but I saw her blinking her eyes.

There was just enough time for us to eat together before the rest of the village descended. We loaded plates and gathered around one of the tables. We'd barely finished our meals and cleared away our mess when people started pouring in. Guests parked their cars in the public lot, about a half-mile away, and the carnies carted them to the house in their horse-drawn wagon. Food was consumed with abandon; children and adults alike delighted in the troupe of little people tumblers and a mute clown who made balloon hats and animals. Within fifteen minutes, Dallas and Abilene had drawn a crowd, and Lily Grace had a line for readings that would take her well into the night.

Then our B&B guests arrived. Most of them mingled and ate and generally seemed to have a good time. Nick Halpern, Kristina's brother-in-law, acted like the party was being thrown especially for him. Like a campaigning politician, he went around to every table, thanking the diners for coming and kissing the hand of every woman in sight just like he'd done to me when we met. It was charming for a minute and quickly became uncomfortable. He stood too close to women, stepping forward as they backed away from him. His handshakes transitioned to include touching their shoulders, and then his hand rubbing up and down their arms. When a man tried to step between the woman he was there with and Nick, Nick puffed out his chest like he was ready to fight the guy.

"What are you doing?" I hissed at him when a third woman came up to me to complain. His arm rubbing had progressed to "accidentally" letting his hand brush down the women's rear ends.

"You said we were the guests of honor." His attitude had become cocky, or maybe cockier, after imbibing in far too much free beer in the three-quarters of an hour he'd been there.

"You know I wasn't serious about that." I waited for some kind of indication that he understood but never got one. "This party is not for you, Nick, you know that. No one here even knows you. We're celebrating the opening of Pine Time."

"You said—"

Sheriff Jayne, able to maintain control in any situation, bumped Regular Jayne out of the way. "Mr. Halpern, I need you to cool it or I'm going to have to ask you to go up to your room."

He stared at me for a minute, then stuck out his lower lip. "Have I been a bad boy? Do I need to be punished?"

This man was not unattractive—*five foot seven, neatly trimmed hair that was graying at the temples, drab-brown eyes*—but he was not the dreamy catch he portrayed. My hands involuntarily clenched into fists when he turned, stuck his backside toward me as if for a spank, and then strode away into the crowd.

"Problem?"

Fuming, I turned to see my deputy standing behind me, with the lovely Lupe Gomez at his side. Reed stood in ready position, prepared to take on the world if I asked.

"Potentially," I explained my troublesome guest.

"Should I follow him? Make sure he backs off?"

Grateful for Reed's loyalty to both me and the village, I shook my head. "You're off duty. If you want to stay aware of him, I won't object, but don't let it disrupt your fun."

"Will do."

Lupe gestured at the crowd. "This is great. You really know how to throw a soirée." The French word sounded funny mixed with her Hispanic accent.

"Thanks. I had a lot of help."

She held up her professional, digital camera. "Mind if I take pictures? I need another story and this party is perfect."

Lupe had been hanging around Whispering Pines since June, writing pieces for her online magazine about the village and its villagers. Her assignment was only for the summer, but while Labor Day weekend signaled the season's end for most of the country, it lasted one more month in Whispering Pines. Here, we followed the Wiccan or Witchy or Woo-Woo calendar. Whatever it was called, summer lasted until the Wiccan sabbat of Mabon at the end of September. Lupe had convinced her editor that she should cover the festival and got a one-month extension provided she kept sending in articles. I couldn't tell if she or Reed was happier about that.

"Take all the pictures you want," I encouraged. "Get releases and we'll use a few of the best ones on our website."

She gave me a little salute and the two of them wandered off.

"This has been just lovely." Morgan appeared behind me and linked one arm with mine while fanning herself with her other hand. "Mama's getting tired. I'm going to take her home now."

I frowned. "Are you warm?"

"I am." She twisted her mass of hair up and fanned the back of her neck.

"I was just thinking that it's actually a little cool tonight. Are you okay?"

"I'm sure it's nothing to be concerned about." She looked over my shoulder, toward the house, and her mouth fell open. "Who is that?"

Following her gaze, I turned to see River Carr standing

near Tripp on the patio, staring straight at Morgan while drinking from a goblet I'd never seen before. Just that fast, an electric charge filled the air and made the hair on my arms stand up.

It wasn't Wiccan—that would involve incense, candles, and chanting—but magic of some kind was going on between Morgan and River. His light-gray eyes, already preternaturally penetrating, were practically glowing, and she was clearly spellbound. For a few seconds, things became so intense, I felt like I should leave and give them time alone.

"Summoned," I said softly.

With visible effort, Morgan blinked and turned halfway to me. "What?"

"When he checked in, I asked what brought him to Whispering Pines. He said he wasn't sure but that he felt 'summoned' to come here." I looked at the little drops of sweat literally glistening along her collarbones and grinned. "Did you summon him?"

She didn't respond, just stared at him, and then lifted her chin, baring the long expanse of her throat. I couldn't tell if it was a submissive move on her part, like an animal exposing its belly to another higher-ranking animal, or a bold *come and get me* dare. Since I'd never seen Morgan be submissive for any reason, my bet was on the dare.

"Who is he?" she asked again.

River came our way, closing the distance between us in seconds, and stood in front of her. With all the confidence and poise she possessed, Morgan held up a slender hand for him to take. It was like watching a scene from a Victorian romance. Never taking his eyes from hers, he pressed his lips to her hand. Unlike the kisses Nick Halpern had been distributing throughout the crowd, this one was not only welcome but sexy as hell. I felt the sudden need to either fan myself or go find Tripp.

"River Carr," he announced, his voice almost a purr.

"And you are Morgan Barlow."

She arched an elegant eyebrow. "Blessed be, River Carr. You asked about me?"

"I had to."

Yeah, I should probably leave. But this was a lesson in pick-up artistry I couldn't turn away from.

River swept an arm toward the patio. "I'd love to learn all about you. May I get something for you to drink?"

Morgan patted his hands, which were still clasped around one of hers, and then pulled away. "I was just telling Jayne that I need to take my mother home. Another time, though. You'll be here all weekend?"

"I will." He inclined his head in a half-nod. "I look forward to seeing you again." He took a step back, spun slowly on the heels of his black boots, his duster jacket billowing around him, and walked away.

We both stood there watching him for a moment. When I realized I was staring at River the way Tripp had been staring at Morgan earlier, I held my hands up to my eyes like blinders.

"Seriously, did you summon him?"

Morgan leaned in and gave me a cheek-to-cheek air kiss. "Lovely party, Jayne. I'm so happy to see your hard work come to fruition. I'll see you later."

Honestly, the rest of the night was kind of a blur after that, mostly because my mind spun with questions. Who was River Carr? What was this instantaneous connection between him and Morgan? How much damage had Nick Halpern caused? Would there ever be a normal week in this village? Then again, dark, mysterious, and somewhat aggravating was normal for Whispering Pines.

Chapter 5

TRIPP AND I HAD BEEN anticipating a few minutes alone on the sundeck after all our guests left. That was when we'd expected the party to last until ten thirty or eleven, but it was nearly midnight when we sent the last visitor on their way. Breakfast was promised at seven thirty every morning, which meant Tripp needed to be up no later than six, preferably five thirty. Instead of time together on the deck, we settled for him walking me home like an old-fashioned beau.

"I'd say the inaugural gathering at Pine Time was a success," Tripp said and immediately yawned.

"I agree. Want to know something juicy?"

Despite his exhaustion, Tripp looked at me in a way that made me shiver. "Always."

I took a step away from him, letting a little air circulate before I was as overheated as Morgan had been.

"Easy there, big boy. You have an early morning."

"So do you. Remember, you promised you would help me with the first breakfast. Now, what's this something juicy you wanted to tell me?"

"Remember how Carr said he felt summoned to be here?"

"He's here for Morgan." Tripp raised his arms

triumphantly at stealing my thunder and then kissed the tip of my nose in apology. "He strode out onto the patio looking like the Prince of Darkness himself, drinking something red from that goblet that might've been blood but was probably wine, and asked me who 'the breathtaking beauty' standing next to 'the establishment's proprietress' was."

I couldn't help but laugh at that. "He actually used those words?"

Tripp held a hand in the air like a Boy Scout giving an oath. "I swear. Then he must've seen the look on my face and asked again using modern-day English. I think he was playing around, but I couldn't say for sure."

"He's definitely an interesting one. This should be fun to watch play out."

Tripp opened the door of my boathouse apartment for me, and Meeka raced inside and straight to her cushion in the far corner near my bed. She'd also had an exhausting night, running away from both children and adults determined to pet or hug her. I would have put her in the apartment earlier, but she seemed to be teasing as much as avoiding.

"I was thinking," I began, "since we're not fully booked for the weekend, and no one will be in that bedroom on the main level, I think you should stay there."

Tripp had been prepared to sleep on the lumpy old sofa up in the attic. No reason for that when there was a perfectly good bed available.

"Excellent idea," he said without hesitation. "The only place that sounds more welcoming than a comfortable bed in our bed-and-breakfast would be your bed."

A flush spread over my body as he wiggled his eyebrows at me. "Behave yourself."

"I know I've mentioned it before but thank you for trusting me to be your partner."

"Couldn't ask for anyone better to go into business with."

He gave me a long, deep kiss and then winked and turned away. Over his shoulder, he added, "That too."

~~~

My chirping birds alarm went off at five thirty, far too early. I groaned, Meeka groaned, and we both went back to sleep. Fortunately, I anticipated this last night so had set a secondary alarm for five minutes later. When this one went off, I got out of bed, but Meeka rolled over and faced the wall, not remotely interested in getting up yet.

By the time I was done with my shower, Meeka was sitting by the double doors waiting to go outside. I had already explained to Reed that I would be late coming into the station today. Tripp was nervous about preparing his first breakfast. He'd be fine; he just needed a little moral support.

Tripp had been doing practice runs for weeks. When we had finally declared all renovations complete, he invited the crew back for a celebration breakfast that rivaled even The Inn's restaurant's breakfast buffet. The crew unanimously declared Tripp's banana-pecan stuffed french toast the winner. The runner-up was his omelet with Granny Smith apples, bacon, spinach, mushrooms, and shredded cheddar cheese.

Once Meeka had finished her kibble, I grabbed the present I'd gotten for Tripp, and the two of us crossed the yard. We found him in the kitchen, standing in the middle of what looked like the aftereffects of a small explosion. I stared, stunned to see such a mess.

"What's going on in here?"

"What if they don't like it?" Tripp mumbled, clearly in panic mode. "I can't decide what to make for them. I was thinking the french toast, but you know how people are on such an anti-carb kick lately. So then I thought I'd do the omelet, but what if they don't want all the fat and cholesterol?"

As he babbled, I poured myself a cup of coffee. "When did you go from chef extraordinaire to dietitian?"

"I'm serious, Jayne. What should I make? This is important. Half of the expectation at a bed-and-breakfast is the breakfast."

There was only one thing I knew to do to calm him down. I set my full mug on the counter, stood in front of him, and wrapped my arms around his neck. Then I kissed him just long enough to take his mind off his worries, stopping before any other kind of trouble could start. When I pulled away, Tripp looked a little dazed, and Meeka had turned her back to us. Even after five weeks of us dating, she still wasn't sure how to interpret our public displays of affection.

"I got something for you." I handed him the present.

"For me?" Giving me a suspicious look, he peeled off the wrapping paper covered in tiny kitchen whisks. When he pulled out the white chef's coat with black buttons, his eyes went wide. "You had our logo embroidered on it."

Our logo, designed by the multi-talented Violet, was a cluster of pine trees with "Pine Time" written below them in a rustic font. Squiggly baby-blue lines below the name represented the lake.

Tripp slid it on. "Fits perfectly. Thank you, babe."

Momentarily flustered by the pet name, I cleared my throat. "What did you put on the menu for today?"

"The french toast. But then I started thinking maybe I needed more of a test market than the construction crew. Guys always like carbs."

"First, you're never going to make everyone happy. You know this." He nodded as he buttoned his coat. "Second, this is why I'm here with you today. Why don't you do both the french toast and the omelet this one time? Make enough that everyone can have a little of each and then ask what they think afterward. I'll set the table in the dining room and help with whatever else you need."

He paused to consider this option and nodded again. "I like this plan. Before you set the table, will you slice bananas and chop pecans for me?"

"Sure, but you know I work best with a microwave."

He showed me how thick he wanted the bananas sliced and how fine to chop the pecans, then we worked in an almost meditative silence until I had completed my task. When he declared my work perfect—I'm pretty sure he was just being nice—I moved on to the dining room.

As I set out nine place settings, using my grandmother's purposely mismatched collection of china in shades of blue, I thought of the meals I'd had in this room over the years with my family. Most of them were during the summer, but I was sure I remembered a Thanksgiving here once. That had been before the feud started between my parents and my grandmother. Gramps was innocent, as far as I knew, but Gran had taken it upon herself to reveal a secret that had all but destroyed my parents' marriage. That secret being that my father had sired a third child with Priscilla, the "dead girl" as everyone called her. That had happened well before my parents had even met, but because Dad never told her, Mom couldn't handle the lie. I couldn't blame either of them for being angry at Gran. It hadn't been her secret to tell.

I had pieced all this together a month ago. Not only was there the initial shock of learning I had a half-brother, there was the bigger shock of learning that this brother was Donovan, the man currently on the run from the law for Gran's death.

"You know," I announced after my table-setting assignment was complete, "we only use the dining room for breakfast. Arden and Holly could set the table after they're done with the rooms and that will be one less thing for you to worry about in the mornings."

Tripp looked at me and blinked. "Why didn't we think

of that before? It's brilliant. I'll talk to them about that today. They're both coming to clean up from the party last night."

Tripp seemed to have calmed down and had settled into a rhythm with his breakfast preparations. With ten minutes to go, the french toast was stuffed, grilled, and warming in one of the two wall ovens. All the ingredients for the omelets were chopped and ready, but he said it was best to put that together right before serving it. He indicated a platter loaded with different types of sliced breads and muffins and asked me to put it on the sideboard in the dining room next to the toaster. Breakfast at Pine Time would be buffet style where everything would be laid out on the sideboard and the guests could serve themselves.

With five minutes to go, he wandered into the dining room, inspected everything there, and then back into the kitchen. "I think we're ready."

Chapter 6

THE AROMA OF BREWING COFFEE and sizzling bacon brought Kristina down first.

"I can't believe I'm so hungry after the feast you gave us last night," she said. "Everyone else is up and almost dressed. They'll be down in a minute. Can I eat?"

Tripp told her that he would start the omelets. "Help yourself to some coffee and have a seat in the dining room. I'll bring everything out when they're ready."

I chatted with my old friend while she waited and caught up on the past few years. She claimed to be over-the-moon happy with her life, but there was something underneath that made me wonder if she was telling me the whole truth. I had been a patrol officer for four years and a detective for a year before becoming the village's sheriff. I was used to reading people. I couldn't always decipher what it was that I was reading, but I could tell when something wasn't quite right.

"Okay, I have to tell you," she blurted as though reading my mind. "I do know why I'm so hungry." She got up and peeked around the corner then sat down again. "I'm pregnant! I've been waiting for just the right moment to tell Kyle."

"He doesn't know yet?"

"No. I was going to tell him before we came here, but then I thought up here where it's so beautiful would be more romantic. Last night, he was exhausted after the drive and the party. I'm going to tell him today."

"That's fantastic news."

"You have no idea." She was so excited, I could barely get words in. "We've been trying for two years. All I want in the world is to be a mommy and was starting to think it would never happen. Kyle will be so happy about this."

If I was that excited, I wouldn't be able to keep news like that to myself. Maybe from others but not my husband. Of course, Kristina had always been big on presentations and setting just the right mood.

A voice from down the hall announced, "Seven thirty is a ridiculous time for breakfast." Then Nick Halpern entered the dining room, Constance glowering behind him.

"This is a bed-and-breakfast, Mr. Halpern, not a hotel and diner." I vacated the chair next to Kristina after giving her hand a congratulatory squeeze. "We'll leave coffee, fruit, bread, and muffins on the sideboard until ten o'clock. If you'd like a hot breakfast, however, you need to be down here at seven thirty."

I did my best to not sound like a kindergarten teacher scolding a naughty child but was pretty sure I failed. I had anticipated being more patient with my guests, more understanding to those not used to getting up so early, but I hadn't factored in someone like Nick Halpern. As a cop, I'd dealt with guys like him on a regular basis. I guess I hadn't expected street sludge to come into my B&B.

As the rest of the group filed in, got cups of coffee or tea, and chose seats, Tripp brought out a huge tray filled with hot food. Everyone, except for Nick, complimented the lovely spread.

"What kind of fancy pants food is this?" Nick complained. "What's wrong with scrambled eggs and sausage?"

"What's wrong," Kyle asked, "with being grateful for what you've got?"

"You're one to talk." Nick snickered and then leered at Kristina, his eyes trailing up and down her body. "Got yourself one fine-looking wife and you're never around."

Kristina ignored the comment, focusing instead on selecting her breakfast. When Kyle was about to say more, she put her hand on his arm and shook her head.

Nick sniffed. "Good thing she's got a neighbor nearby who's willing to keep an eye on her when she's home all alone."

"That's enough," Constance hissed.

Nick shot a glare at his wife that she matched for a second before turning away. Once Constance had finished filling her plate, I caught her eye before she took a seat at the table. I jerked my head for her to come over to me.

In the hallway between the dining room and the kitchen, I asked her, "Is everything okay?"

"Everything is what it is," she replied. "Nick feels inadequate around these guys. He lost his job six months ago and I think he lost some of his manhood at the same time."

"I need to ask a question, but before I do, remember that I am the sheriff and public safety is part of my job. He's obviously vulgar. Is he violent as well? Are you in any danger?"

She laughed loudly enough that she covered her mouth and looked over her shoulder to see if any in her party had heard. Her husband sat silently in his chair, ignoring everyone and everyone ignoring him.

"Constance!" Nick hollered when he saw her looking. "Get in here and eat. Your hot food is getting cold."

She closed her eyes, an expression that said *give me strength*. "I'm not in any danger; his bark is far worse than his bite. Someday, though, he's going to get bit."

Constance—*five foot five, late-thirties, straight black hair to her shoulder blades, crinkles around her dark almond-shaped eyes*—struck me as having a cold edge. Maybe that was because she and her little sister were so different. Kristina was bubbly and full of life while Constance was poised and very serious.

She placed a hand on my upper arm, a gesture I'd seen nurses and doctors use to comfort a patient. "Thank you for your concern."

She returned to the dining room, and I went to the kitchen where I found Tripp sitting at a bar stool with a glass of orange juice.

"You didn't spike that with anything did you?" I teased and then added seriously, "Did you?"

"I thought about it. But no, once they're done and the dishes are cleaned up, I'm going to prep for tomorrow. Every little thing I can do beforehand, even measuring out ingredients, will make the mornings smoother."

"First one's out of the way. That's the hardest, right?"

"I sure hope you're right."

"Just don't ever get sick. If breakfast is left to me, it will be cold cereal, bananas, and juice boxes. I'm not even sure I could make coffee to your standards."

He set down his glass, took one of my hands, and pulled me in for a hug. "Maybe I'll have to give you some lessons."

A jolt of heat shot through me at that implication.

"Something occurred to me." I leaned back in his arms so I could see his face. "If I get up early with you every day, we can have some quiet time together before I leave for work."

His eyes lit up. "I'll run over to Sundry this afternoon and buy all their alarm clocks. You sleep through your chirping birds sometimes."

"That happened once. Speaking of work, I need to get going. In case you were wondering, breakfast is a big success."

"Except for our one grumpy guest."

I shrugged. "Like I said, we can't make everyone happy."

I headed for the back doors just as River Carr descended the stairs.

"Good morning, Jayne. Tripp."

"Good morning, Mr. Carr," I returned.

"River, please. No need for formality. Especially because I have a feeling we're going to get to know each other better."

"If you hadn't asked me about Ms. Barlow last night" — Tripp stood to shake his hand — "I'd be a little concerned that you were hitting on my girlfriend."

"I would never infringe on another man's territory," River assured.

"Territory?" I gave them both a raised-eyebrow stare. "This may be a good time for me to leave."

River placed a hand over his heart and bowed his head in apology. "No offense intended, Jayne. Where will I find the food connected to the delicious aromas I've been smelling?"

Despite all the charm, or maybe because of it, my guard stayed up with this man. I led River to the dining room. Nick, of course, had to start in immediately.

"Maybe they didn't tell you, but breakfast is at seven thirty. If we want anything hot, we are to be here by then." He looked pointedly at Kristina. "Of course, there are other hot things I can think of."

"Halpern." Kyle was clearly struggling to hold himself back. "Shut your damn mouth."

River ignored the conversation as he piled his plate high with almost everything that was left on the sideboard, leaving one serving of each item behind.

"I'm just trying to be friendly." Nick's gaze stayed locked on Kristina as he spoke.

If there was something going on between them, and

Nick seemed desperate for everyone to believe that there was, Kristina gave away nothing. She never once looked away or indicated shame of any kind. A small smile and quick shake of her head told Kyle that their brother-in-law was nothing but a bag of hot wind.

"What's with the vampire getup?" Nick pressed on when River took the open chair at the head of the table. "I mean, if I shove you out into the sun, are you going to burst into flames?"

Nick laughed, looking around the table like the lunchroom bully expecting the others to join him in his badgering. The only one to speak up was Constance.

"I knew we shouldn't have come." With a graceful hand over her heart, she gave apologetic glances to me and each of the others around the table. To her husband, she said, "Kyle asked you to be quiet now."

This only succeeded in encouraging Nick. "Think you're something special, don't you, *Connie*?" She cringed at the nickname. "You couldn't survive without me."

Nick continued his tirade, about how she should be by his side supporting him instead of kicking him when he was down. Sheriff Jayne was about to evict him from the dining room, so the other guests could finish their breakfasts in peace, when River made a move. A very subtle move.

River said nothing, just locked his weird gray eyes with Nick's drab-brown ones. As Nick shoved half a blueberry muffin into his own mouth, River slowly and deliberately ran a long finger down his own throat from the tip of his chin, past his Adam's apple, and stopping at the jugular notch. That electrical charge feeling from last night filled the room, and a second later Nick's eyes went wide and he started to choke on the muffin. We all sat there, watching the man convulse, none of us making a move to help him. Of course, medical advice stated that it's best to not touch a choking victim until they indicate they couldn't breathe. In this instance, it's like we were all frozen and couldn't have moved to help him if we wanted to.

"See what happens when you never shut up?" Constance said quietly when he finally recovered. "Now keep your mouth shut and finish eating. You're not only humiliating yourself, you're embarrassing me."

I felt a touch on my shoulder and turned to find Tripp. "I thought you left for work."

"Morbid curiosity got the better of me." I turned back to the group one last time before walking away. "Please tell me we're not going to have guests like him all the time. Honestly, this guy is awful."

"I wish I could, but I told you I'd never lie to you." He guided me out onto the back patio and gave me a playful swat on the butt. "Go be a sheriff."

Chapter 7

AFTER CHANGING INTO MY UNIFORM, loading the pockets of my cargo pants with handcuffs and my other tools, and securing Meeka into her K-9 harness, we were ready to go to work. When we got to the Cherokee, we found that Lupe's old Land Rover had joined the collection of vehicles parked in my driveway, but I didn't see Lupe anywhere.

"Where is she?" I asked Meeka who gave a sharp bark and pointed her nose toward the back patio. There, Lupe was interviewing Kristina and Kyle.

I walked over to say hi when Lupe asked them, "What brought you here this weekend? Why Pine Time?"

Kristina explained how she and I were longtime friends and that she wanted to support my new business. Then she said, "I also thought this would be the perfect place to tell my husband some exciting news."

Kyle looked at his wife, his brow creased with confusion. "Exciting news?"

The question and the tone of his voice were lighthearted, but a shadow behind his eyes and the way he stood back with his arms crossed revealed a man prepared to not be happy.

"I was going to tell you before we left Madison,"

Kristina assured, "but look at this place. It's so peaceful and beautiful here. I thought this would be an even better time to tell you ... I'm pregnant!"

Kristina bounced on the balls of her feet as the color drained from Kyle's face. I'd seen the shock of a father-to-be taken by surprise many times. That's not what Kyle's expression told me.

"You're sure?" he asked. "I mean, you took a test?"

I gave a gentle tug on Meeka's leash. "Let's go. I can't handle anymore Pine Time drama this morning."

We parked in the small lot behind the sheriff's station and checked in with Reed, then Meeka and I went to patrol the village commons. To get there, we had to walk along the Fairy Path, a wood plank walkway that wound through the woods. In the three months that I had been in Whispering Pines, I had walked this path probably a hundred times. I had yet to see a fairy. Violet, the owner of Ye Olde Bean Grinder told me it had earned the name because mushrooms grew in circles at the base of the pine trees in this area. They called them fairy circles. Whatever that meant. I'd seen the mushrooms, they were indeed in circles; I guess the fairies were avoiding me.

It was easy to tell that summer was coming to an end. The plants looked tired and like they were ready for their long winter's nap. This was especially evident when I got to the massive pentacle garden at the center of the commons. Throughout the summer, the plantings within the star portions of the pentacle—dozens of varieties of flowers, a few kinds of vegetables, and enough herbs to supply both The Inn's restaurant and the Grapes, Grains, and Grub pub—were lush and overflowing. Now, they all reminded me of aging starlets fighting to hang on to their fading beauty. Head green witch Morgan had swapped out summer plants for cooler weather ones.

"Sheriff O'Shea," an older man called from within the garden. He shuffled my way along one of the pea-gravel paths that made up the lines of the pentacle. "My wife and I were at your party last night. Your bed-and-breakfast looks very restful."

"Thank you. I hope you had a good time." An all-white cat darted from one garden section to another, and my all-white terrier made a lunge for it. I warned, "No attacking," and let her leash out a little more.

"We did," the man assured. "I'll be calling soon to make a reservation."

"Please do. We'd love to have you."

I got several promises to stay at the B&B as I wandered through the garden and chatted with people while Meeka searched for that cat. Then came the inevitable shadow to balance the brightness.

"Sheriff O'Shea."

This sharp, crisp, and obviously unhappy voice came from one of the women who had complained to me about Nick Halpern last night.

"I hoped I'd be less upset about this by now," she said, "but I feel so violated by that man."

"I assure you, I understand exactly. I'm horrified by his actions."

"I assume you're doing something about him? Someone like that shouldn't be allowed in this village. It only takes one bad grape to sour a whole bunch, you know."

I understood that exactly as well. She was talking about Halpern, but the face that flashed before my eyes was Flavia Reed's. Flavia, self-proclaimed mayor of Whispering Pines and an Original or member of one of the first families to move here, hated me because of things my grandmother had done to her forty years ago. Talk about sour.

"I had a talk with Mr. Halpern," I assured the woman. "I agree, we can't let one person ruin things for so many others. If he does anything else, I'll ask him to leave."

Satisfied with my response, the woman continued her journey around the garden.

The commons area of Whispering Pines looked like a Renaissance faire or medieval English village. A red brick pathway encircled the garden, and next to the pathway were small cottages that had once been the villagers' homes and now served as shops and restaurants. In this area, as well as most of the village, the slightly crooked buildings were all white stucco with black-brown stained trim. If thatched roofs weren't such a fire hazard, they'd all have those as well. Instead, they were topped with realistic-looking cast cement thatch. On the porch of Shoppe Mystique, Morgan Barlow stood in a short black tank dress fanning herself.

"Blessed be," she greeted, miserable.

"Are you kidding me?" I asked. "You're still hot? I was just thinking I wish I would've brought a jacket. At least I wore pants instead of shorts. I'm about to drape Meeka over my shoulders for a little extra warmth."

The little terrier headbutted my leg in annoyance.

"Oh, settle down," I told her. "I was joking." Mostly.

Morgan twisted her hair into a knot to get it off her neck. "I swear, it's getting worse."

"How can you be getting warmer when the temperature seems to be dropping by the hour?" I studied her with narrowed eyes. "Hang on. Are you doing this?"

It sounded ridiculous, and I could hardly believe I'd even asked the question, but Morgan had told me that, as a green witch, she was connected to nature. She and I had hiked through the woods a few weeks ago to visit Blind Willie, one of the more reclusive villagers. While I tripped over practically every root and got stabbed by every other low hanging branch, Morgan glided through the woods as easily as walking through an open field.

"Of course I'm not," Morgan dismissed with an edge in her voice. "That kind of magic, an ability to control the elements, does not exist. It's simply a cold front pushing through. Why my temperature is off, I'm not sure."

"Speaking of magic," I began and proceeded to tell her

about Nick Halpern choking on the muffin this morning and how it seemed that River Carr had somehow influenced that.

"That kind of magic doesn't exist either. There are certain people that can influence others' way of thinking. I can't explain how they do it but think of the great illusionists. David Copperfield, for example, did not really pass through the Great Wall of China or make the Statue of Liberty disappear. But we believe he did because he influenced our minds to make us believe that he did. Perhaps Mr. Carr has this sort of ability."

"You're saying he made Nick believe he was choking on a muffin? That's upsetting."

"Do you have another explanation?" She held her arms out wide and flapped them like a bird, except this bird was trying to cool down not take off. "The shop is packed already. All those bodies in there are raising the temperature. I'll have to open all the windows."

"You do realize you're the only one who's hot, right?"

"You do realize it's my shop?"

"Don't you have an herb in there that could help you?"

She gave me a little finger wave over her shoulder and went inside.

As had become our pattern when patrolling the village, our last stop was Ye Olde Bean Grinder to say hi to Violet and get a beverage and dog biscuits. A really big mocha sounded good today with an extra-espresso shot. I grabbed the metal handle of the shop door, which resembled an arch of coffee beans, and pulled just as someone pushed. Reeva Long and I nearly collided.

"Good morning, Sheriff O'Shea. I was hoping I'd run into you. Just not literally." Reeva's voice had an especially happy lilt to it this morning.

I always found it hard to believe that she and Flavia were sisters. While there was a family resemblance in their bright-blue eyes, it stopped there. Reeva was sleek and confident with her short honey-blonde haircut and classic clothing style. Flavia disguised her looks beneath tent-like dresses and straw-blonde hair pulled into a tight bun. Their dispositions tended to match their external appearances with Reeva being the more approachable sister and Flavia being the one people spoke to only if they had to.

Reeva had returned to the village about two months ago, after twenty years away, to go through her late-husband's estate. Understandably, she'd been a little quiet and kept to herself. Word around the Pines was that Reeva was slowly becoming more of her cheerful old self.

"You seem to be in a good mood today," I commented. "What can I help you with?"

"It's a simple question, really. One I could have asked Violet, I suppose." She indicated she'd just seen her by holding up her coffee cup. "I wanted to verify that there is a village council meeting this week."

"There is. Tomorrow morning at six o'clock."

"My, that's early isn't it?"

"We always plan for about an hour, but they can run long. Those who have businesses that serve the public first thing, such as Violet's, can't wait too long to open. In fact, she usually opens at six during tourist season, so her brother is here alone until she gets back. That's probably more information than you needed."

Reeva laughed, a warm sound on such an unexpectedly chilly day. "Not at all. I'm always eager to know as much as possible about my fellow villagers. Are the meetings usually on Sundays?"

"No, they're usually on a Monday or Tuesday, but with the holiday and some scheduling conflicts ... Any particular reason you're asking?"

"There's something I would like to discuss with the council. Would you make sure I'm on the agenda?"

I was about to ask why she hadn't asked Flavia, since Flavia ran the meetings, or so she thought, but Reeva and

Flavia didn't have the greatest relationship. I'd thought their animosity was a more recent thing; turned out, it had been going on their entire lives.

"I'll do that," I promised. "See you tomorrow morning."

Inside the Bean Grinder, every café table was full and each of the four overstuffed leather chairs surrounding the corner fireplace were occupied, as they had been every day since I'd first come to the village. The difference today was that there was a fire in the fireplace for warmth instead of vanilla candles for ambiance. I dreamed of the day, in about a month after the Mabon harvest festival, when I'd be able to walk in, drop into one of those welcoming leather chairs, and hang out for a while with my coffee and maybe a book. The short ceilings and dark paneled walls made this one of the most inviting, cozy places in the village. The permanent aroma of coffee in the air didn't hurt.

"Morning, Sheriff," the five-foot-tall barista greeted with her usual bubbly attitude. Seriously, Violet was one of the happiest people I knew.

"Morning, Violet." I slid my travel mug across the counter to her. "My standard mocha sounds good today, with an extra espresso shot, please."

"I figured you'd be dragging a little after the party." Violet had started making my beverage before I'd even finished ordering it. "I got to chat with Tripp for a couple minutes last night. Sounds like he was a little nervous about his first breakfast."

I smiled. Dear Violet, so charmingly nosey. "I'm sure you understand how he felt. His first day of deciding what people would eat. He was worried they wouldn't like it or that what he prepared wouldn't fit with their diets."

"I do understand that. For the first few weeks after I took over the business from my dad, I was terrified to change anything from the way he had done it. That meant we served only regular coffee and tea, but no blended drinks."

"No scones?" I asked while taking one from today's countertop container.

Violet smiled as she squirted whipped cream on top of my mocha, added the lid, and slid it back to me. "Oh yes, always scones. My parents started exchanging scones for coffee with Honey and Sugar years ago. There were no blended drinks, though. The day I took the leap and added those, sales doubled. Tripled the next. That's when I learned to read my customers. What did your guests think of Tripp's food this morning?"

"They all seemed happy. Well, all but one."

"I bet I can guess who that would be."

I didn't have to ask to know she meant Nick Halpern. "Was he giving you a hard time, too?"

She pursed her lips, angry—a look I didn't like seeing on her pretty face. "Among other things, he asked me what it was like to be the only beautiful black woman in Whispering Pines."

My mouth dropped open. "He really was making it his mission to offend as many people as possible, wasn't he?"

"No doubt. What's wrong with that guy?"

"I don't know, but there have been a lot of complaints about him. I won't deal with any more." I took a sip of my mocha and exhaled a coffee sigh. "Thanks for the pep talk for Tripp. I'll tell him what you said."

Meeka and I returned to the station, a simple rectangular building that would fit better in a metropolitan industrial park than in our charming village, to find Reed sitting at his desk in the main room. He had a strange look on his face. My eyes darted to the two jail cells to the left of the front door. Both were empty.

I removed Meeka's harness, and she immediately darted to the jail cell in the back corner. Her favorite spot was beneath the cot bolted to the wall in that cell.

"What's wrong?" I asked Reed.

"Someone's waiting in your office."

"Who is it?" Then I noticed a box of scones on Reed's desk. I expected Sugar but walked into my office to find Honey, the younger of the Treat Me Sweetly sisters, sitting in a chair across from my desk. The frown on her normally happy face immediately concerned me.

"Hey, Honey. What's going on?"

Her frown intensified. "We're worried about Whispering Pines."

Chapter 8

BY "WE," HONEY MEANT HERSELF and Sugar. Funny how even when they weren't together, they spoke for each other. If they were twins, the two couldn't be closer.

"What are you so worried about?" I got comfortable in my desk chair, preparing for a long conversation.

"Do I really have to tell you?"

I waited for her to do exactly that, but she didn't. "It would be helpful, Honey."

She perched on the edge of the chair, feet together, hands resting on her knees. "You must feel the tension in the village. There was a little before, but since the truth about what happened to Priscilla came out, it's gotten worse."

She bobbed her head up and down the whole time she spoke, as though trying to subliminally convince me.

"I do feel it," I admitted. I did before the head-bobbing. "Everyone who knew about the Priscilla incident did their best to keep it quiet, but when Donovan was arrested, it was a lost cause."

"You know how word spreads around here." Honey tugged at a string on the hem of her shirt. "We waited until your B&B opened, which is beautiful by the way, you two did a great job, but it's time now. You know Flavia instigated what happened to Priscilla. You have to do something about her."

Nothing would make me happier. Well, except for seeing Donovan rotting behind bars.

"There's not much I can do about a crime that happened forty years ago, especially when there's no physical evidence to back things up. There isn't even a police or medical examiner's report. All I've got are Gran's journals and people's forty-year-old memories."

Honey's mouth hung further open the more I spoke. "You're just going to ignore what she did?"

"I told you—" I stopped myself and instead asked, "What would you like me to do?"

She folded her hands and scooched back in her chair. "Make her leave the village."

Offering an empathetic smile, I said, "Look, there's a small handful of us who know what she did that night. Flavia wants us to stay quiet about it, so I think she'll lie low and behave herself, but rest assured, I am keeping an eye on her."

A close eye. I believed Flavia had instigated other deaths in Whispering Pines, as well, not just Priscilla's. I believed she was responsible for the death of her own daughter, the young woman whose body I found in my backyard the day I got here. I believed that while my grandmother's death had been an accident, caused by my scummy half-brother Donovan, Flavia had been involved with the cover-up of it.

Honey's mouth twitched as she tried to fight off her objection and ultimately failed. "What if she does something else? What if someone else gets hurt?"

"Think about that. Do you really believe she'd do something to endanger more people? Or her own standing within the village?"

"We didn't think she would before." Honey looked pointedly at me. "We can't put anything past her."

Time to wrap this up. "I appreciate your concerns, I

truly do. I heard everything you said, but I have a current problem that I need to deal with now."

"You mean that horrible man who's been terrorizing the village?"

"Terrorizing?" Honey tended toward exaggeration. "Did you have an encounter with him?"

"That's really why I'm here. I brought up the Flavia thing since I had your attention." She gave a little can-you-blame-me shrug. "Anyway, Sugar is very upset about that man. He came into the shop with a group of people yesterday and complained about everything. The line was too long. The decorations on the wall were cheesy. The cookies looked overbaked."

"I'm sure Sugar had a thing or two to say about that."

"Oh, did she." Honey pinched her lips together and then blurted, "He said the ice cream flavors were predictable. Can you believe that?"

Honey took great pride in her ice cream creations. Like Tripp had said, I'd never tasted better. To Honey, criticizing her ice cream was akin to calling someone's baby ugly.

My list of people upset over Nick Halpern's bullying and harassment kept growing. Maybe it was time for me to make him leave the village.

"Not to downplay what you just told me," I said, "but did he actually do anything, or just spout off?"

She exhaled a shaky breath and pulled herself together. "I didn't see the event, but I saw the aftereffect. It seems that man ... *touched* the woman in front of him. I don't know where he touched her, but she was furious. Her boyfriend is a huge man, looks like Arnold Schwarzenegger in his younger days. The boyfriend exploded at the man."

"They got into a physical fight?"

"Not a physical one, no. Well, the girlfriend slapped the man, if that counts. There was a lot of yelling and general chaos between the two men. It got so bad, Sugar finally kicked them all out and gave everyone in line a discount on their orders." She counted on her fingers. "We lost ten sales and probably twenty more dollars because of that man and his groping. Not that that's our biggest concern. The poor woman."

"I'm sorry this happened in your shop. Thank you for telling me about it."

"And the Flavia thing?"

"I promise you, I'm keeping an eye on it." I thanked her again for stopping in and walked her to the front door. Once she was gone, I went straight to Reed. "Did you know she wanted to talk to me about your mother?"

"I knew." Reed avoided making eye contact with me. "Both Honey and Sugar have told me … no, more like warned me that they'd be in to talk to you just as soon as your B&B was open."

"I'm sorry you're being harassed." An angry little fire flared in my chest. "You know what? We're done with this topic. There are, what, a dozen or so people who know the full truth about what happened forty years ago, and they're not talking about it. Honey and Sugar are upset because they were excluded that night."

He finally looked at me. "You're probably right about that. They can't stand not being in on everything."

"This isn't a matter of public safety. If they or anyone else brings it up again, tell them it's a closed case and we will not be doing any more with it. Because honestly, there's nothing we can do."

Reed seemed grateful for this decision. His shoulders dropped and he eased back into his chair, visibly relaxing. I understood. He was embarrassed by the actions of his mother, same as I was embarrassed to find out some of the things my grandmother had done back then.

We spent the rest of the afternoon dealing with unhappy tourists. I could empathize with those who came in to complain about things like loud and obnoxious people or a pickpocket who was allegedly wandering through the crowds. But complaints about the weather? What did they expect us to do about the cold? My deputy fielded the majority of the complaints like a trouper, patiently listening to every disappointed tourist. He never once lost his cool, until they left the building and then he'd stomp around and let loose with all the things I'd been thinking but had kept mum about. Unused to that kind of emotion from Reed, Meeka disappeared beneath the safety of my desk.

At twenty minutes to five, I told him to go home. "You've done enough for today."

"Don't have to tell me twice." He had his desk straightened and lamp off in about five seconds.

"Forgot to tell you, your girlfriend was out at my place this morning."

"She wanted to interview your guests." Reed flipped his keys in his hand as he stood in my office doorway. "She's desperate for any kind of a story that will let her stay here. I swear, she'd interview your dog if she thought she could turn it into a public interest piece."

Knowing we were talking about her, Meeka crawled halfway out from beneath my desk and struck a pose as though ready for questioning.

"You have to admit," I teased, "Meeka would be a very interesting subject."

After Reed left, we hung around for another hour before I decided we'd done enough for today, too. I posted the emergency contact information on the front door, our version of a closed sign, and made sure I had my walkie-talkie so I was reachable should any emergencies occur. Befitting our frustrating day, our drive home topped out at ten miles per hour. Even though there was a bridge, people insisted on darting across the two-lane highway that separated the village commons from the residential area of Whispering Pines. Funny how knowing that, in a few short weeks, there would only be a handful of tourists left in the village made the crowd even harder to deal with.

Pulling up to my house and finding other cars gathered around the garage with Tripp's truck didn't help. After today, all I wanted was a little peace and quiet. As I grumbled to myself about it, Meeka gave me a look that said, *you asked for this, sweetie.*

"I know I did," I called after her as she started her nightly laps around the yard. What was she going to do when there was snow higher than she was tall? We'd have to dig a track around the house for her to run. "Give me time to get used to it."

"Get used to what?"

I jumped and spun to find Tripp standing at the corner of the garage.

"People everywhere." I scowled at him. "Sorry, I'm feeling a little stressed."

"You don't want people around?" He came closer.

I shook my head and pouted.

"Even me?" He closed the gap between us and looked down at me.

"You're not people." I reached up and kissed his mouth, feeling some tension slide away.

"Good, because I've got dinner ready."

"Wonderful. I'm really hungry. Should we eat in the house?"

"Speaking of people, Mr. Halpern is making me a little crazy. I didn't know it was possible to find that many things to complain about or that many ways to offend."

We walked hand in hand over to the boathouse. At the base of the stairway, he said, "Go on up and change. I'll bring everything over."

Dinner was leftovers from the party last night spread out on my coffee table. We'd be eating leftovers for weeks, but that was fine. All I really cared about was my dinner companion. We blew off steam by sharing the frustrations of our day, with the rule that when we were done eating, we were done talking about work things. At that point, we moved out to the couch on the sundeck and sat beneath a blanket together. The unusually chilly night meant the fire in the tabletop fire pit served a practical purpose rather than simply being ambiance.

"I'll just sleep, I promise," Tripp said when I called a halt to our make-out session and told him it was time for him to go to his room.

"You need to be available for the guests."

"Then you join me." He gave me a wicked, sultry grin.

I guided him to the stairway and sent him on his way. The whole "take it slow" thing was my doing, and despite trying for more, Tripp played along well and never seriously pushed. How long would he be patient?

From the deck, I watched him cross the yard, enter the great room, and then lock the back-patio doors. He gave me an enthusiastic two-armed wave before turning down the lights and disappearing into the bedroom off the kitchen. I sighed, already missing him. No matter how often I put on the brakes, I didn't like an empty bed either.

Meeka wasn't quite done securing the perimeter for the night, so I wrapped the blanket tighter around my shoulders and stared out at the lake. The water was dead calm tonight. So were the towering pine trees. That was odd. Even on otherwise calm nights, there was usually at least a ripple across the water. Everything about nature seemed off right now; I understood the tourists' frustration. As much as I was ready for the population around the village to decrease, I wasn't ready for the temperature to do so.

Finally done with patrol and ready for her dog-bone embroidered cushion, Meeka trotted up the stairs and gave a little all clear *ruff* as she passed me. I turned off the gas in the fire pit, blinked a few times for my eyes to adjust to the dark, and took one last glimpse toward the house. Seeing lights burning in the upper floor windows felt strange. There were people sleeping in my house, and not one of them was family.

"I hope you're okay with that, Gran," I whispered softly enough that only I heard.

Out of nowhere, a single gust of wind blew through, twisting the pine branches every which way for a few seconds.

I smiled, my throat suddenly tight with emotion. "I'll take that as a yes."

Just as I turned away from the house, I saw someone enter the great room out of the corner of my eye. Since the only light burning downstairs was the light over the stove in the kitchen, all I saw was a shadowy shape. I could tell that it was a man but not which one since there were six men staying in the house. Thinking it might be Tripp, I watched and waited.

The figure left through the back doors and then headed up the driveway. Seemed that one of our guests was a fan of late-night walks.

Five minutes later, I was tucked into my empty bed, falling quickly toward sleep.

~~~

"Sheriff O'Shea?"

I peeked open one eye and saw only darkness.

"Sheriff?"

I sat up ... in bed ... confused. Was that my walkie-talkie? I grabbed it.

"Hello? This is Sheriff O'Shea."

"Jayne, it's Laurel."

Waking rapidly, I guessed that there was trouble over at The Inn. I twisted side-to-side, stretching and waking further, then asked, "What's wrong? Is there a problem?"

"Not here. We're the only place with lights on this late at night, so they came here. Emery woke me up."

I swung my feet over the side of the bed, ready to act when I knew what was needed of me. "Who came to you? What's going on, Laurel?"

"There's a body in the west side parking lot."

Chapter 9

I CALLED REED ON HIS walkie-talkie and, after getting a firm chewing out from Flavia for waking her at two thirty in the morning, was able to talk to my deputy. I scolded him for leaving his unit charging in the kitchen instead of his bedroom and told him to meet me at the west side parking lot.

"Meeka, let's go." I tried three times to wake the sleepy Westie, but she wasn't interested in nighttime games. "Any other officer would have suffered disciplinary action by now."

With her head still lying on her cushion, she opened one eye but didn't move.

"Meeka, working."

Just once I wished my K-9 would follow my directions without having to resort to commands. It worked, though, like it always did. She eased up from her cushion and shuffled to the door, stopping halfway to stretch. That much I would be patient for; I'd needed to stretch, too.

I debated for two seconds about letting Tripp know where we were going, but he had to get up soon and start making breakfast. No need to wake him. Besides, if this went well, I'd be back before he even realized I'd been gone.

Even though the parking lot was only a half mile away,

I secured Meeka into her crate in the back of the SUV. She was curled into a ball and snoring before I had my seatbelt buckled.

I arrived at the parking lot to find a man in a blue and white Milwaukee Brewers hat standing between the two huge pine logs that marked the entrance. He tried to prevent me from entering until he realized who I was.

"What's going on?" I asked through my open window.

"We were on our way to Rhinelander and decided to stop for a short nap."

That wasn't what I'd meant. I expected he'd say that he found a body. Observing his eye movements and body language, I asked, "Where were you on your way from?"

"Duluth. We've got family in Rhinelander. We left kinda late but figured we could make it tonight. The roads around here are freaky in the dark."

"The roads around here can be freaky in bright sunlight. I understand you found a body? I assume he's dead?"

"He hasn't moved since we got here, so we figure he's dead, too." He pointed toward the edge of the road. "He's over there. My cousin is kind of keeping an eye on him. Not that the guy's going anywhere."

I looked to where he was pointing and saw a man standing almost in the middle of the road. "The body is in the road? I was told he was in the parking lot."

"Nope. He's on the side of the road near the lot. Kinda half on, half off the shoulder. We practically ran over him."

Hang on. That didn't match up with what he had just told me. "You said you were coming from Duluth?"

"Yeah."

"Which means you were heading east. You're telling me the body is on the north side of the road. To have almost run over it, you'd have to be coming from the east."

Which side of the road they were on wasn't important. I was more concerned about this guy being able to give me details that held together.

The man narrowed his eyes, thinking about what I just said, and then nodded. "Right. We were already past the parking lot by the time we realized it was here. It was late, and we were tired. I was driving and turned back so we could get a little sleep. That's when I saw him."

Okay, that made sense.

"Don't know if it's important," the man continued, "but a light of some kind caught my eye when we drove past the first time. I was paying attention to the road so wasn't sure where it was coming from—"

"Thanks," I interrupted him. "Never know what might be important. I need to check on the victim. We'll talk more in a few minutes." I pulled to the far side of the parking lot and saw headlights through the trees coming from the east. That had to be Reed. I debated about letting Meeka out. Considering how dark it was, and that I already knew where the body was, I wouldn't need her help finding it so left her in the Cherokee with the tailgate open.

The man on corpse duty was waving his arms and jumping up and down to get Reed's attention. Reed slowed the station van to a crawl, made a wide arc around the man, and joined me in the parking lot.

"Quick," I said, "before you do anything else, get some flares out there."

Reed didn't hesitate. He grabbed an armful of flares from the back of the van and hurried to set them out along the road. By the time he was done with that, I had joined him with flashlights and the crime scene investigation kit.

"No way," I breathed as I gazed at the body.

"You know this guy?" the man asked me.

"Thanks for protecting him," I said. "Would you mind waiting by the van for me? I'll have questions for you in a minute, so don't go anywhere."

"Yeah, sure. No problem."

The man didn't hesitate to leave his post, and I couldn't blame him. I didn't consider myself to be squeamish, but this was one of those instances where I looked around the body rather than directly at it. The amount of blood was significant. That was one of the benefits to digital cameras. I could remove myself by a degree or two and then zoom in on the necessary areas afterward. We just needed to be sure to take tons of photos from every angle.

"Who is it?" Reed stopped at my side. "Oh."

His reaction confirmed my initial suspicion that it was Nick Halpern.

"Let's get the portable lights set up."

"Sure thing, boss." He took about five steps toward the van and then stopped and turned back. "By the way, I already called Dr. Bundy. Figured you wouldn't want to have to make that call again."

"You'd be right about that," I agreed with a sigh. "Thanks."

While Dr. Bundy, the medical examiner, was never serious when he complained about having to drive the hour from his home office to Whispering Pines, bodies were showing up at the rate of more than one per month. One and two-thirds, to be precise. He spent more time in this part of Wisconsin than anywhere else.

I turned my attention to Halpern. Before beginning the investigation, I gave myself thirty seconds to get the personal stuff out of the way. I thought about all the horrible things this man had done in the twenty-four hours I had known him. Not only had he offended the guests in my home and at my party, he upset a number of tourists in my village. And I couldn't help but wonder if Constance had been honest with me about their relationship. If he was that disrespectful to her in public, what did he do to her in private?

With my thirty seconds over, I dismissed all emotion surrounding this situation and slid into full cop mode. A man had died ... *Another* man had died in my village, and regardless of who he was or what he'd done, I needed to figure out why and how.

The how, in this case, seemed obvious. While he could have been killed in another location and dumped here, my bet was that he'd been hit by a car.

It must have been Halpern I'd seen leaving through the back doors earlier. A thick layer of clouds blocked out all star- and moonlight tonight. Considering Whispering Pines had maybe six streetlights in the entire village, it was nearly black tonight. Halpern was dressed in jeans and a dark-blue button-down shirt. His medium-blond hair might have shown up in a car's headlights, but by the time the driver would have registered the man walking along the side of the road, it would have been too late.

To me, this seemed fairly open and shut. There were a couple of extenuating factors to that theory, however. The biggest being that this man had upset a great many people since arriving here. Kyle, his brother-in-law, seemed irate over the attention Halpern had been giving his wife Kristina. Halpern's wife Constance had been humiliated by his actions. I didn't know yet how the other people staying at my B&B felt about this man. And there were probably at least a dozen additional people throughout the village whom Halpern had bullied or harassed.

Had tiny Kristina exploded at him after all that innuendo at breakfast? Had Kyle or Constance? What about the boyfriend at Treat Me Sweetly Honey had told me about? I'd have to wait, as always, to see what Dr. Bundy's autopsy revealed, but I was sure he'd say blunt force trauma. An automobile being the weapon in this case. Then the question would be, had the driver known they'd hit Halpern or had they continued down the road, clueless as to what they'd just done? Was this voluntary or involuntary manslaughter? Or worse, had his death been deliberate, and we were looking at another murder?

Working quietly and efficiently, Reed set up the lights so we could investigate. Then I remembered we had agreed

Reed would work the next crime scene. He was already enrolled to take criminal justice classes over the winter, but he was also determined to learn as much as he possibly could from me before then.

"I'll leave this one up to you." I had grabbed the camera from the back of the van when I snatched the investigation kit and offered it to him now. "This one is a little—"

"I can do it." Reed took the camera from me, swallowed, and took a deep breath. "Lots of pictures of everything. Right?"

"Lots of pictures." I told him my tip for not looking directly at the body and then assured him I'd be right here if he wanted me to take over. In fact, instead of going over to the man waiting for me by the van, I called him over to me so I could stay close to my deputy. The second man came, too, and I asked him to stay back a few feet. I'd already heard his version of events.

"You can stand with your back to the scene if that's easier," I suggested. He was immediately grateful and turned away from Halpern. "Tell me your name and what happened here tonight."

The man who had been standing alongside the road was Howard. He confirmed that his cousin Lee had been driving and then gave me his version of the timeline. It matched almost exactly with what Lee had said. The only thing he added was that Lee had run into the village to get help.

"Good thing my cell phone was in my back pocket," Lee said with a tight, nervous-sounding laugh when I asked him about that. "I needed my flashlight app to see. Don't you people believe in streetlights around here?"

I gave a sympathetic smile. "Actually, no. The villagers really like being able to see the night sky. And on nights like this, when it's clouded over like it is, well, you see just how dark it can get."

Lee explained that he followed the pathway from the parking lot, through a small cluster of trees, and finally to the pentacle garden. Shifting uncomfortably, foot-to-foot, he added, "The only place with lights on was that hotel. That poor kid at the desk must've thought I was a crazy person."

Had to be Emery. The pock-faced nineteen-year-old was saving to build himself a cottage and took every shift Laurel would give him.

"Did either of you see anyone else around here?" I asked them both in turn.

They each shook their heads, offering nothing more and obviously desperate to be done talking to me. I took their contact information, just in case I came up with any other questions for them, but really there wasn't anything more for me to ask. They could have found the body and kept going, so I gave them points for stopping and watching over him. As unhappy as I had been with Nick Halpern earlier, the last thing I would have wanted was for his body to suffer even more damage from a vehicle or wild animal.

"You two are free to leave," I said. "I'm sorry that your evening turned into this. The sun won't rise for another few hours. If you keep going east, you'll come to a group of hotels on your right just past the 'thanks for visiting the village' sign. Park in one of their lots and get some sleep. If anyone gives you a hard time, tell them Sheriff O'Shea said it was okay."

Half an hour later, Dr. Bundy and an ambulance arrived.

"You know how strange this is becoming, don't you?" Dr. B asked as he pulled on a pair of latex gloves. There was little levity in the usually upbeat man's voice.

I understood what he meant, though. The mystique of Wiccan magic wasn't the only thing that hung over this village. Everyone, villagers and tourists alike, did their best to ignore the death rate, but every now and then as I patrolled the commons, someone would ask about it.

"Are there murderers running around these woods?"

Or, "Am I safe? Should I pack up and leave before

getting too comfortable here?"

Or, "Maybe Whispering Pines should enlist an army."

Yeah, because the best way to get a handle on the death rate was to arm everybody.

"This one seems pretty cut and dry." I matched his somber tone. "I'm thinking hit-and-run."

I led Dr. Bundy over to the body, although the portable lights in the middle of the dark night made it obvious where he needed to go.

"Deputy Reed?" I called out. "Are you almost done?"

"I think so. I took pictures from every angle, two of each." He paused, staring at the body for a long moment despite my tip, head tilted as though wondering about something, then shook it off. "I searched the area, at least as much of it as the lights illuminated." He indicated a few items scattered about the area that he'd tagged with yellow plastic evidence markers. "Could you help me with some measurements?"

"Give us a few minutes?" I asked Dr. Bundy.

"Why not? Got nothing else to do in the middle of the night."

I couldn't tell if Dr. B was more upset by another death—something he was surely used to after all his years on the job—or if he simply wasn't a middle-of-the-night person.

I held one end of a twenty-five-foot measuring tape while Reed recorded distances from the body on his grid map. Five minutes later, we were done, and Reed was placing items in clear plastic evidence bags—a shoe knocked off Halpern's body from the impact, his wallet, an empty fifth of whiskey, and a cell phone.

"Good job," I told him. "We'll scan the rest of the area once Dr. Bundy is done and we've got more light to work with."

Reed gathered the evidence bags and brought them to the van. Once Dr. Bundy had finished with what he needed to do, and Halpern's body was bagged and in the ambulance, he went to his car without a word to me. I followed.

"Dr. Bundy? Is everything okay? I know there's been a lot going on here—"

He held up a hand to silence me. "It's not Whispering Pines, Jayne. There have been an unusual number of deaths here, but that's not it." He stared straight ahead, hands on the steering wheel. "I've been doing this job for over twenty years. It never stops, does it? I understand natural death, especially in someone who's lived a long life. Natural deaths in younger ones are harder to handle, but I guess certain bodies just aren't meant to be healthy. You know?"

I nodded my agreement, even though he wasn't looking at me, and let him talk it out.

"The accidents, especially the stupid ones, I have a hard time with. People have no idea how fragile these containers of ours are." He smacked a hand against his barrel chest and paused, staring into the darkness again. "Here one second and literally gone the next. And once we're gone ..."

I'd learned a few things about Dr. Wolfgang "Wolf" Bundy over the past three months: He liked his meat on the rare side. He liked jazz music, which was almost always playing in the background when he called me. He cheered for the Minnesota Vikings rather than the Packers, which I did my best to forgive. I'd never seen him like this, though. Maybe something was going on in his personal life. Or it could be that this was a middle-of-the-night call; maybe someone he'd cared about had died in a nighttime accident. We all had our demons.

"I'd been having a good evening," he said suddenly, startling me out of my thoughts. "I left the office early, took my wife out for dinner and to a movie. Spent some quality time with her." His voice trailed off. He turned his head toward me, the lights of his dashboard shining off his mostly bald head, and offered a strained smile. "Gets to me every now and then. You know?"

Look around the body, not at it. "I understand exactly. I'm sorry your night was interrupted. Go on back home now."

He nodded then shrugged and drove off without another word.

Reed's footsteps crunched on the gravel surface of the parking lot and stopped next to me. "He seemed a little down."

"Even the best of us break sometimes. Can you finish up here or do you want my help? If you're good, I need to go wake up Nick Halpern's wife."

Chapter 10

I STOOD OUTSIDE THE PINE Time room we had dubbed The Treehouse. It was located at the front corner, farthest away from the garage. The way the house was angled, the only thing that the people staying in this one could see was trees. I preferred lake views, but this was Tripp's favorite room in the house, other than the kitchen, of course. After I'd knocked softly for the third time, Constance opened the door.

It took her a few seconds to figure out who I was, either the early hour or the sheriff's uniform confusing her.

"Jayne? What's going on?"

"I need you to come with me," I whispered.

She squinted at me, trying to understand, and then her shoulders slumped and her expression changed from sleepy to disappointed. "What did he do?"

I held a finger to my lips. "I don't want to wake the others. Would you get dressed, please, and meet me on the front porch? Bring your car keys."

Ten minutes later, she came outside dressed in athletic gear—black capri leggings, red T-shirt, form-fitting black jacket—like she was planning to go for an early morning run. "What did he do this time?" Now, her voice held a good deal of anger.

"The sheriff's station is less than ten minutes away. Follow me and I'll explain everything when we get there."

~~~

As we entered the dark station, Constance watched Meeka slide through the bars of her preferred jail cell. It was quite chilly this morning, so instead of crawling beneath the cot, Meeka jumped on top of it and curled into a tight, furry white ball. Time to get that dog cushion for the station that had been on my to-do list for weeks.

"He's not here," Constance noted with a nod at the other empty cell. "Sheriff O'Shea, what's going on with my husband?"

I plugged a fresh pod into the coffee maker on a table near Reed's desk, started the cup brewing, and led Constance to the small interview room in the back right corner of the building.

When I interviewed someone, I preferred to have no barriers between the person and me. A table could serve as a type of security blanket, and removing it kept the interviewee a little off balance. While there was a simple five-foot wooden table in the room, I had it pushed up against a wall and the chairs positioned to face each other. I indicated that Constance should take the chair that put her back to the wall. I always preferred to sit so there was no way for anyone to sneak up behind me, which meant my chair faced the room's door.

"I promise, I will explain everything in two minutes, but I need a cup of coffee. Would you like one?"

She held my gaze for a moment and then nodded, indicating coffee would be welcome. I gave her the first cup and prepared a second for myself.

Finally, I sat across from her. "There's been an accident, Mrs. Halpern."

Instantly, she stiffened. "Don't do that. Don't turn

formal on me. You wake me up at five o'clock in the morning and ask me to come to the station with you. You tell me it's about my husband, but you won't say anything more. Now you say there was an *accident* and are calling me Mrs. Halpern. If it was an accident, you'd take me to the hospital. Is my husband dead, Jayne?"

With controlled empathy, I replied, "I'm sorry, Constance. He was hit by a car. Two people traveling through the village found him alongside the road around two o'clock."

Constance sat with her hands wrapped around the hot mug and stared into it. After a long moment, she blinked as though she had forgotten and now realized there was coffee in the mug. She took a sip and cleared her throat. "You didn't answer my question. Is he dead, or will we be going to a hospital next?"

"He is deceased, I'm sorry—" I almost added, "for your loss." *I'm sorry for your loss.* One of the coldest, most clichéd phrases a person could ever offer. A simple, heartfelt "I'm sorry" was a hundred times better.

I gave her a minute to let this news sink in. She took another drink of her coffee, paused with the mug near her mouth, and took one more sip. Then she looked up at me and rearranged the expression on her face from a look of shock into a more business-like one. "What do you need from me?"

Everyone reacted to horrible news in different ways. I hated when people said, "I just know I would" and then proceeded to explain how they would react. No one could know how they'd react until they were right there, living in that awful moment. Some people would become hysterical and cry or throw things or physically beat on the closest person or object. Some went straight to the nearest liquor cabinet. Some refused to accept the news, insisting that I was lying to them. Others would go into a catatonic state, unable to process the information at that moment. Occasionally, there were people that took this kind of news matter-of-factly. Even with those people, I would usually see sorrow or emotion of some kind behind the reaction—rapidly blinking eyes, repeated swallowing, hands fidgeting, heavy sighs. Constance Halpern was stone cold. Not that it meant anything. It could simply be her way of reacting.

I moved to the edge of my chair, a few inches closer to her, our knees almost touching. "Late last night, around eleven, I was out on the sundeck of my boathouse waiting for my dog to come in for the night. I saw someone leave through those back doors off the great room and head up the driveway. A late-night walk, I assumed. Because it was so dark, I couldn't tell who it was."

Constance nodded, not waiting for me to ask the question. "It was most likely Nick. He walks at night when he's upset about something." A small, pained smile turned her mouth. "He's been doing a lot of late-night walking lately." Her expression turned blank, coldly reporting the facts. "We had a fight last night. I'm sure you can guess why."

"You told me that your husband lost his job six months ago. Do you feel that was the reason for his temperament?"

"You mean his piggish, bullying behavior?" She nodded. "Yes, he wasn't like that before. I've been trying to get him to go for counseling."

"Counseling for what in particular? His anger problem? Help getting another job?"

She shook her head. "Neither of those. One of his coworkers accused him of sexual harassment eight months ago. He swears to me all he did was compliment her dress." She drank from her cup. "Our anniversary was a few weeks away, and he had wanted to take me out somewhere nice. I made the comment that I had nothing to wear since my wardrobe consists of jeans and sweaters, workout gear, scrubs, and business suits. I have no evening wear. He told me that he thought the dress looked like something I would wear. He wanted to know where the woman got hers so he could take me to buy one for our anniversary."

There were always two sides to every story. It was very possible that Nick was telling her the truth about the dress. It could also be that he complimented this woman in such a way that it appeared to be sexual in nature. Or maybe something had happened in the woman's life and she was looking to make someone pay. He could have flat out lied to Constance and it had been straight up harassment; it seemed to come naturally to him, after all.

"This is why he lost his job? Because of the harassment charges?"

She paused, considering her answer before speaking. "I've gone through a lot to get where I am—eyes rolling after every suggestion I make; being overlooked for promotions that are given to younger, less-experienced males; fighting off inappropriate propositions that would guarantee me a chance at the next promotion." She exhaled a heavy sigh. "It's hard to go through all that and then be upset at my husband's company for taking a harassment charge seriously. Even one against him. I know it's got to be difficult to understand, especially after seeing the man you saw here, but I believed him. He'd been under a tremendous amount of pressure working on a project that just wouldn't conclude. We'd been planning to go on an extended weekend trip, Las Vegas most likely, but he couldn't take even two days away. All we could manage was dinner and maybe a movie."

I empathized with her position, but I couldn't let her know that. "These harassment charges were simply one more frustration for him?"

"Frustration?" She laughed, annoyed. "Those charges pushed him over the edge, one that he'd been standing on for months. It was too much. The proverbial straw, and his was the camel's back it landed on. I swear to you, something snapped in his mind. It became almost a self-fulfilling prophecy."

"You mean he was accused of sexually harassing a woman, so he started sexually harassing women?"

"Exactly. Nick always had a temper, but he never exploded. His was more of a slow burn, and he rarely lost control. This was too much, though." She paused for a moment, thinking. "About nine months ago, I finally got that promotion I deserved. Of course, everything has a payoff and this one was that I had to work even more hours. He'd been killing himself over this project, though, and not getting anywhere near the recognition he deserved. I guess his anger started rising then."

"You mean, because you were rewarded for your hard work and he wasn't, that was one more push toward that edge?"

She barely heard my statement, just continued to vent. "He never saw how hard I worked. Partly because he was so wrapped up in himself, and partly because I've always preferred to keep work at work and did my extra hours in the office whenever possible. As far as he was concerned, I got a promotion and salary increase I hadn't done anything to earn, while he was being ignored. I saw how stressed he was so kept my frustrations over that to myself."

I smiled at her. "Even if we're not literal mothers, women always find someone to mother."

Once again, she turned stone cold. "I find that mindset offensive, Sheriff O'Shea. Just because we have the physical ability to bring a child into the world doesn't mean we are all genetically programmed to *mother* others."

I nodded my apology and redirected the topic. "You said you and your husband had a fight last night. About what exactly?"

"About him being so obnoxious. He didn't want to come this weekend. He wanted to stay in Madison and go sit at the corner bar until they kicked him out like he'd done every weekend for the past six months."

"What made him come?"

Constance pushed her shoulders back, inhaled, and then blew out a slow breath. She'd done that numerous times since sitting down with me. Deep breathing was a self-soothing reaction to stress few people even realized they used.

"Kyle had been giving him a hard time about turning into a recluse," she explained. "He was trying to help because he had actually gone through something similar a year or two ago. Not sexual harassment, but a conflict with a coworker. Kristina told me that Kyle and one of the men in his department got into a fight at a community gathering one time. The man tried to turn it into a work issue, which it wasn't. Getting in a fight outside the office with someone you work with has nothing to do with the company you work for."

"There was obvious tension between Nick and Kyle at breakfast yesterday."

"Like I said, Kyle has been trying to help. I think what you witnessed was embarrassment on Nick's part. Similar to lashing out at someone who cares about you because you know that person is a safe place to express what's bothering you."

"Nick was making some pretty nasty innuendoes about your sister."

"Yes, he was."

Once again, the lack of emotion, first over her husband's death and now her sister's embarrassment, struck me. She acted more like a human resources manager dealing with employee problems than a wife whose life had been turned inside out by her husband's stress and resulting inappropriate behavior.

"This fight we had last night," she began, almost as though returning to a skipped item on a checklist, "I kicked him out. We came here for a nice weekend to try and get away from the stress we had both been feeling. We had agreed we would let it all go, have a good time, and start trying to put things back together."

Again, I envisioned a vacation checklist. Item one: Let it all go. Check. Item two: Have a good time. Check.

"He seemed flirty," I began, "but not offensive when you got here. What set him off?"

"It was Derek taking Alicia shopping for that outfit. Nick ranted for a good twenty minutes about that when we got to our room. We don't know them well but have seen them at a few of Kristina and Kyle's gatherings. We know they've got five children. Alicia claims they spend every penny Derek makes just to live, but when it came time for this weekend, they didn't hesitate." She put her hands in the air palms facing me, stopping any comment I might want to make. "It's none of my business if they're lying and have a stack of gold in their basement that they're not telling us about, if they have nothing but change in a coffee cup, or if they've got so much debt their children will be paying it off. It's none of Nick's either, but Derek buying that outfit for Alicia infuriated him."

"*Schadenfreude.*" At Constance's confused expression, I explained, "It's a German phrase that means taking pleasure from another person's pain. Guess that doesn't fit exactly in this case. It sounds more like Nick wanted everyone else to suffer along with him."

"That's a fair statement. We don't have his income right now, but we're doing fine with mine. That should have given him comfort. Instead, it made him feel unimportant."

From my office, I could hear someone calling me over the walkie-talkie.

"Excuse me, Constance. I'll be right back." I left the interview room, walked ten feet toward the front of the building, and entered my office at the front corner there. Pressing the talk button, I announced, "This is Sheriff O'Shea."

"Jayne, it's Laurel over at The Inn. Are you going to

make it to the council meeting?"

I dropped my head back and sighed. "Sorry, Laurel. I've been tied up with that incident you called me about earlier. I'm just finishing up here. Give me fifteen minutes."

"Where did they take Nick?" Constance asked when I returned to the interview room.

"The medical examiner has his body," I explained. "It's standard procedure to do an autopsy unless, of course, you have any religious reasons for why he shouldn't."

"No, I have no problem with that. Do you know how long it will take to get the results?"

That's something I forgot to ask Dr. Bundy. He was in such a sour mood I just wanted to let him go.

"I need to get to a village council meeting right now, but I will give the ME's office a call as soon as I'm done and get that answer for you. Just so you know, it could take a few days." My instincts were telling me to keep her around. "You were planning to stay the whole weekend, right?"

She stood as though leaving a boardroom at the end of a meeting. She looked around and then not sure where to put the coffee cup, handed it to me.

"Yes. We were going to leave Monday morning. The room is already paid for, so I'll stay until the results come in. That way I can hear them directly from you. I'll need to make arrangements for his funeral. I can do that from here."

Just that fast, she had another checklist. At least I didn't have to ask her to stay in the village, which was what I'd been leading up to.

"Constance? Are you okay? I have to say, your reaction to your husband's death strikes me as a little odd."

She released yet another heavy sigh. "I am sad that this happened to him, if that's what you're wondering. May I be brutally honest with you?"

"Of course."

"I've lived for months with Nick's anger and attitude. I know the shock of his death will hit me, but right now, I've got to say, I'm relieved that I don't have to go through that anymore."

Usually, brutal honesty made my job easier. This time, it left me feeling a little leery.

Chapter 11

AFTER CONSTANCE HAD LEFT, I locked up the station. Reed hadn't come in yet. He'd become so meticulous with checking and rechecking details, I wouldn't be surprised to find he was still at the crime scene looking for anything that might be important. I hoped that he'd just gone home for breakfast before coming to the station. Traffic would be picking up on the highway soon and the last thing I wanted was for my deputy to get hit while investigating a death.

Meeka and I hightailed it through the pre-dawn shadows along the Fairy Path and through the pentacle garden. We entered The Inn and found Reeva Long sitting in the lobby by the fireplace. She looked stylish yet casual in narrow jeans, a crisp white button-up shirt with a plaid wool shawl over her shoulders, and a single large diamond at her throat. My guess, and Morgan agreed, was that the necklace Reeva never took off had been made from the wedding ring she stopped wearing when she left the village twenty years earlier.

Reeva confused me. Any woman who left her husband and lifelong home the way she did, basically forced to raise the baby from an affair between her husband and her sister, had to have some issues. She seemed nice enough, and I believed she'd grown to love baby Yasmine as her own. But I couldn't shake an underlying feeling that she was up to something.

"You're late," she scolded seriously and then gave me a playful wink. "Flavia has been out here three times to see if you'd arrived yet."

"If I had, wouldn't I go straight to the room?"

"You might." She arched her eyebrows wickedly. "Unless, of course you and I had something conspiratorial to discuss."

"You still wanted to talk with the council? Is that why you're out here?" Curiosity was killing me on this one.

"I do. Flavia assured me she'd call me in when she was ready to deal with me. In the meantime, I'm happy to sit here next to this nice warm fire and absorb the atmosphere."

I gestured toward the door behind the reservation desk. "I better get in there. I'm already twenty minutes late. I'll make sure Flavia doesn't forget to call you in."

Inside the meeting room, most of the members were chatting, drinking the coffee Violet brought over from Ye Olde Bean Grinder, and eating scones Sugar brought from the sweet shop. Meeka immediately wove around the chairs, scrounging for scone crumbs. The only person not conversing was Flavia; with Donovan gone, she had no one to play with.

"Finally," Flavia said and clapped her hands like a schoolteacher trying to get her unruly students' attention. "She's here. Let's begin, please."

I stood in the doorway, which was located at the center of the room, and stared at Flavia. It didn't matter what I said or did, she always treated me like I'd been playing computer games or getting my nails done instead of doing my job. Most of the time, I let it go. Today, I couldn't do that.

"Would you like to know why I'm late, Flavia?"

She sniffed. "I actually couldn't care less. Your disregard for everyone else's schedule is so typical of you."

I turned to Laurel in her standard seat at the far end of the table from Flavia, her back to the door. "Laurel? You didn't tell them?"

She bristled and looked over her shoulder at me. My attitude must have been harsher than I realized.

"First," she said in a gentle tone, "I didn't think it was my place. Second, I didn't know exactly what to tell them. I wasn't there."

I placed my hands together and inclined my head in apology, an unconscious habit I'd picked up from Morgan. "Sorry. Didn't mean to snap at you."

"What happened?" This from Morgan, who was in her usual chair in a tank dress, her hair half pulled up and half hanging down, a look that was fabulous on her. She fanned herself with a black paper fan with stars printed all over it. "No problems at Pine Time, I hope."

Flavia sighed like she had no patience for this.

"A man died last night," I explained to a chorus of gasps and even a stunned look from Flavia. "Laurel called me at two thirty this morning to report that a man had come to The Inn to report a body alongside the highway."

"How horrible," one of the fortune tellers, Effie, exclaimed. "Must've been by that curve that's so hard to see around."

Now that I thought about it, it happened along a fairly straight stretch. People would sometimes go too fast through there since there were no curves and visibility wasn't an issue.

"Anyone we know?" Cybil, another fortune teller, asked in her standard looking-for-dirt way.

I glared at her. Always had to make light of things, didn't she? I rubbed my tired eyes. Maybe Cybil didn't mean anything by the comment. Maybe I was just tired. Still, I didn't like her attitude.

"Cybil, a person lost his life. Please tell me you're not looking for something juicy to spread around."

She squared her shoulders and squirmed in her chair, but she didn't reply to my accusation.

"Don't tell me it was *him*," Violet guessed and looked horrified. "It was, wasn't it?" She groaned when I confirmed that it was indeed Nick Halpern. "Holy cats. He was a jerk, but he didn't deserve that. What happened?"

"All I can say is that it seems he was hit by a car. I can't discuss anything else."

"Alongside the highway?" asked Mr. Powell, owner of the village services business, The Busted Knuckle.

"Right." I knew they'd keep digging for more, but simple answers that revealed nothing was all I would give them.

"Putting up fences," Mr. Powell continued, "along the highway, especially by that spot where folks cross to go up to the Meditation Circle, has come up for discussion before."

This I would gladly talk about. Starving, I grabbed two scones from the box in the middle of the table and a cup of coffee. Then I took my seat at the end of the table, opposite Flavia.

"It's a really dangerous area," I acknowledged as I broke a scone into bite-size pieces. "I can't believe there's never been an accident there before. The odds of that astound me."

Maeve pushed a stack of napkins in my direction. "There have been a lot of close calls. I think it's time to finally do something about this."

I popped a piece of scone into my mouth, chewed and swallowed, and popped in another piece before I realized the flavor was blackberry and …

I held the scone up to Sugar. "What is this?"

"Blackberry basil. What do you think?"

"Really good. Never would've put those two ingredients together." Of course, I couldn't bake so that wasn't saying much. I swallowed another bite, washed it down with a swig of coffee, and continued with the fence discussion. "Mr. Powell and I talked once about what it would take to put up permanent fencing."

"I'm worried it would just get ruined in the winter," Mr. Powell added. "When the snowplows go through, all that snow would just tear them right down."

"We could put up sturdy temporary fencing," Creed suggested. "It works for us at the circus. You'll have those who try to hop over, but if we make it high enough, that should eliminate the problem."

"I agree with this idea," our newest board member Jola said. "You all know we're only equipped to deal with minor issues at the healing center. In the event of a car collision, we can reset broken bones and clean up road rash, but that's about it. I vote that we put these fences up now."

I held my hand up, holding off more votes. "Mr. Powell, is this something you could do right away?"

"Supplies for fencing …" Mr. Powell, the world's klutziest man, stared at the ceiling as though doing an inventory count up there, leaned back a little too far, and ended up tipping over backward. He popped up within half a second. "I'm fine. It won't be pretty, but we can get something up today. I'll work on something more visually appealing for a more permanent solution. A peg in a hole type design using pine tree trunks backed with a fine metal mesh. That would be see-through as well as sturdy and tall for tourist season but easy to take down for winter."

"We have to have something aesthetically pleasing," Flavia sniffed. "No one wants to see industrial metal fencing around our village."

"It was just my first thought," Mr. Powell apologized.

"And it's a good start." Violet gave him a thumbs up.

"Look," I told the group, "I can't say for sure that Mr. Halpern was hit, but until I know otherwise, I'm going to proceed like this was a hit-and-run. Tourists are going to care less about aesthetics and more about safety. I think it's important that they see us acting on this right away."

In a rare unanimous vote, the board agreed that Mr. Powell should get a crew installing temporary fences immediately and be ready with his peg-in-a-hole design by spring.

Flavia cleared her throat, taking back control of the meeting. "The only real thing on the agenda today was Jayne's station update. Was there anything else you needed to let us know about?"

I went through the quick rundown of visitors consuming too much alcohol, fighting with each other, domestic disturbances, and the supposed pickpocket which only one man had complained about. From the way the man's son looked anywhere but at me while his dad made his complaint, I was pretty sure the boy had taken the fifty from his wallet.

"There was also a four-year-old boy who had wandered away from his family," I reported. "Deputy Reed found him within an hour by the public swim beach and returned him safe and sound."

"A four-year-old?" Morgan asked, practically in tears. I'd never seen her so emotional. "A little boy wandering the village by himself? The poor baby. Where were his parents?"

"Children wander, Morgan," Effie said. "I'm not defending the parents, but kids are quick. You turn your back for one minute and the next thing you know, she's up a tree with your new tarot cards." She leveled a look on Jola.

Jola shook her head. "You're never going to let me live that down, are you, Grammy?"

"There is one other item for the board," I reminded Flavia and the rest of them. I pointed toward the lobby. "Reeva is waiting for us out there."

Flavia acted as though I hadn't spoken and tried to close the meeting.

"Flavia!" Sugar jumped up and rushed out to the lobby, returning with Reeva in tow.

"We're just about done here," Flavia told Reeva. "What

did you need to speak with us about?"

Reeva nodded at the empty chair next to her sister. "There's an open spot on the board since Donovan left."

"You make it sound like he moved away," I huffed, doing my best to keep the growl out of my voice but not bothering to disguise my feelings regarding that horrible excuse for a human being.

As if reading my mind, Laurel asked, "Any news on him?"

"Nothing," I said. "I check in with the County Sheriff's Department every day, but they haven't caught him yet. There haven't even been any sightings reported. It's like he vanished."

I locked eyes on Flavia as I spoke about the man. If anyone knew where he was, she would. If she did, she was hiding it very well.

Ignoring me and giving her full attention to her sister, Flavia placed a hand on the empty chair. "What about the open spot?"

"You only have twelve members instead of the required thirteen." Reeva walked around the table and sat in the chair, bumping Flavia to the side a little as she did. "I've decided that I'll be staying in Whispering Pines rather than putting Karl's house up for sale. Therefore, I would like this seat."

"The thirteenth seat on the council?" Flavia practically choked as she gaped at her. "We haven't voted on this. You can't just take that seat."

"But I can." Reeva's bright eyes glistened. "Remember the bylaws, sis? An Original may take a board position from a non-Original member at any time. The only time a vote is required is if an Original wants to take a position from another Original. This seat is vacant. I would like it."

Simultaneously amused and horrified, I observed the reactions of the other board members during this exchange. Some sat in wide-eyed shock. Some laughed out loud or chuckled behind their hands. Morgan looked like the only thing she cared about was finding a walk-in freezer to stand in. Flavia, of course, was furious.

"She's right," I said. "It's in the bylaws. Reeva, let me be the first to welcome you as the thirteenth board member."

Tensions had been heating up between Flavia and Reeva since Reeva returned to the village two months ago. As far as I could tell, they had done all they could to avoid each other, but Morgan had warned me on the day Reeva returned, "You've heard the saying 'Hell hath no fury like a woman scorned?' You don't want to be around when the fury of a scorned witch lets loose. Especially fury that's had twenty years to simmer."

That promise I'd made to Honey about keeping an eye on Flavia just jumped up a few notches on my to-do list. And it wouldn't hurt to include Reeva in that watch.

Chapter 12

MEEKA AND I ENTERED THE station to find Reed at his desk downloading pictures from the camera onto his computer. He glanced up from his work, took one look at my face, and knew something was up.

"I was going to ask how the council meeting went, but I'm not sure I want to know."

"I'm not sure you want to know either." I knelt to remove Meeka's harness. "I'll let your mother tell you when you get home tonight. Be warned, she won't be in a good mood. What are you working on?"

"Thanks for the warning. I think." He pointed at his screen. "There's something I'd like to get your opinion on. I'm downloading the pictures I took at the scene this morning. I understand what you mean about looking around the body instead of at it. I might not have taken so many pictures otherwise. Anyway, something didn't seem right to me, so I've been zooming in on a few of these images."

He started with the ones from further back that took in the entire scene. One thing stood out to me immediately.

I pointed at the picture on his computer screen. There was a glow coming from beneath Halpern's cell phone. "Was the phone's flashlight on?"

Reed zoomed in on the cell phone. "It was. I couldn't turn the app off. The screen was locked. Is that important?"

"I feel like it might be." I studied the image for a few seconds. "One of the witnesses told me he saw a light as he drove past. That must've been it."

I stared silently at the image a little longer.

"What?" Reed asked.

"It was dark, and Halpern was using his phone's flashlight app."

"Right."

"A car would've seen a light that bright on a night that dark and driven around Halpern."

"Unless the driver was drunk or otherwise impaired. Could've been falling asleep. You know how hypnotizing it can be driving past all those trees."

"Fair point. Okay, what did you want to show me?"

"I was looking at the details of the victim's body more closely because, like I said, something didn't seem right."

"What do you mean? What doesn't seem right?"

"There's a lot of blood."

"That would be expected. He was hit by a car."

"That's what the first look tells us," Reed agreed, "but are we sure about that? If he was hit, he would've gone flying or at least be in a weird position. His body is too neat, almost like he lay down right there to take a nap. And there's no road rash or visible cuts. No scrapes or bruises. He's covered in blood but look at the blood pattern."

It had already been a long day and it wasn't even lunchtime. I rubbed my eyes and slapped my face to wake myself up a little. Reed said nothing, just waited while I looked closer at the image that had so captivated him. It took a little bit, but suddenly I understood what he meant.

"And the student becomes the teacher," I mumbled. "The entire front of Halpern's face is covered but, more importantly, so is his shirt. At first glance, we could assume that all the blood came from a collision with a vehicle. But in order for his shirt to be covered that way, he would've had to have been upright for a while so gravity could pull it down that far. If he had landed there from a collision, the blood would've run down the side of his head and pooled on the ground, not down the front of his shirt."

"Exactly what I was thinking." Then he added with a smirk, "Don't be too hard on yourself, Sheriff. You would've seen the same thing if you had taken the pictures."

A lesser sheriff might take offense at his ribbing. To me, this was assurance that I'd hired the right guy.

"This is why we take so many pictures," I told my deputy. "So we can continue the investigation later as well as back up the medical examiner's ruling on cause of death." I leaned in closer to the computer screen and squinted. "Can you zoom in on his forehead, please?"

As he did, I saw what appeared to be a gash at the top of the victim's head.

"What does that look like to you?" I asked Reed.

"A nice-size cut. That would explain all the blood. It would also indicate he'd already been bleeding when he got hit. If he got hit."

"Good work, Deputy. We can safely assume that his head was bleeding well before he ended up alongside the road. In that case, what conclusions can we draw from this?"

He considered this for a second and then suggested, "Two possibilities. First, he fell or somehow injured himself, was stumbling along next to the road, and got hit. Although that doesn't correlate with the too-neat position of the body. Therefore, the second option is that someone else injured him and left him there."

A feeling of dread took over me. "We could be looking at another murder. I need to call Dr. Bundy and see if he can at least confirm if Halpern was hit or not."

Two minutes later, Joan, Dr. Bundy's assistant, sounded incredulous. In her nasally northern-Wisconsin accent, she said, "Don't tell me he needs to go back. He just got here with your body. Well, obviously not *your* body."

Dr. Bundy and his staff were an odd lot. "No, he doesn't need to come back. I have a question for him, though."

"Okay, good. You all need to settle down with the stiffs up there." She transferred me over.

"Sorry for my mood this morning," Dr. Bundy said in lieu of a standard greeting. "That doesn't happen often, I promise. Usually only when I get interrupted during a night with my wife." He paused. "Hmm. Maybe I shouldn't go out with my wife. Don't tell her I said that. What's your question?"

Good to hear Dr. B sounding more like his regular self again.

"It's about my supposed hit-and-run this morning. Don't imagine you've started on him?"

"Haven't even unzipped the bag yet. What do you mean *supposed* hit-and-run? What's going on, Sheriff?"

"I don't need specifics, just a direction. Deputy Reed and I think we might have another problem. As in, another murder."

"The words 'murder' and 'problem' are interchangeable in Whispering Pines. What've you got?"

I explained what we saw in the pictures, and knowing how blood worked, Dr. Bundy immediately guessed at what that could mean.

"Okie doke." He groaned and there was a creaking sound like he was getting out of a chair that was in desperate need of a good oiling. "Let's go take a look. I'm going to plug in my earbuds so I can talk hands-free. I tend to hang up on people when I do that. I'll call ya right back if I do."

Despite a great deal of fumbling sounds, he didn't lose me. And instead of dead air or chattering, he whistled a peppy version of a jazz song I didn't recognize as he walked to the morgue ... wherever that was in his building. The sound of a door opening came a minute later followed by the distinctive sound of latex gloves getting snapped on. Then a metallic sliding sound which had to be the tray in the body fridge and finally the zipper of the body bag.

"What have we got here?" he asked himself. More humming followed and then, "Huh."

"What do you see, Doc?"

"I never like to open my mouth until I'm staring at the body. They sometimes tangle together in my mind." He chuckled. "That paints an interesting image, doesn't it?"

"You're an interesting guy, Doc. And an impressive whistler. If you ever want a career change, you could go pro."

"Would you be surprised to hear that I thought about that once?"

"Not even a little bit."

He chuckled again and returned to Halpern. "Okay, I'm looking at the body now, which means I can also picture the scene. When I arrived there this morning, my immediate thought was that it didn't look like a car meets pedestrian."

"Why did you think that?"

"Because everything about Mr. Halpern was too neat. He wasn't in an unnatural position. His arms and legs were perfect, as in no obviously broken bones. If it had been a hit-and-run, I would've expected to find him in more of a pile rather than laid out neatly. To me, it looked like he'd been placed there."

"That's pretty much what Deputy Reed said. So, nothing appears to be broken."

"Not that I can tell just by looking at him."

"Is there a cut on his forehead?"

More humming and shuffling sounds. "His face is a mess ... Yep, I do see a cut of some kind."

"Heads bleed a lot."

"Holy mackerel, do they, and this guy is covered. One time, when my boy was little, he fell and split his forehead on the corner of the coffee table. My wife was sure he'd need not only stitches but a transfusion as well. By the time we had him buckled into his car seat and she found her shoes, it had pretty much stopped bleeding. I told her it would be fine, but would she listen to me? A two-hundred-dollar urgent care bill for a Band-Aid later and she admits that maybe we didn't need to go."

I smiled, glad that Doc's dark moods didn't last long.

"I'll get more specific," he continued, "once we clean him up and I do the official autopsy, so this is just another gut reaction. Understand?"

"I understand."

"A cut from a blade would leave a smooth, more even line. Blunt force trauma would leave more of a jagged wound because the skin would split from the impact. Picture squeezing an overripe tomato and how the insides would burst free."

I grimaced. "Do I have to?"

"Sorry. You've got to admit, though, that's a good visual. Anyway, this appears to be more of a slice than a split, I'll be able to tell a lot more once I wash him off."

"So," I summarized, "no visibly broken bones. A slice on his forehead, not a split. Anything else that might indicate foul play?"

"Not that I can see right now, but I've only got the bag unzipped to his waist."

Once again, I heard a zipping sound followed by the metallic sliding. Presumably, he was putting Halpern away.

"You think you've got another murder on your hands? There isn't much at this point to support that."

"In the interest of erring on the side of public safety, I'm going to start investigating like it's a murder." I'd start with the people at my B&B. Reed could talk to the tourists who had made complaints. "I know you're busy, and I hate to ask, but when do you think you can get to him?"

"Sounds like the clock might be ticking on this one," Dr. Bundy said. "I'll review the cases I've got here and see who I can move around. I'll examine Mr. Halpern ASAP."

"Thanks, Doc." I slumped back in my chair after hanging up with him. Reed appeared in my doorway.

"What did he say?"

"That there's definitely a head wound. A quick glance indicated that it seemed smooth, like a knife slice, not jagged from an impact. He didn't see any obviously broken bones and felt a car would've done a lot more damage to the body. He agreed with your thought that the placement of the body was too neat. Good catch."

Reed stood a little taller but his expression didn't change. "We're looking at another murder, aren't we?"

I rubbed my aching eyes. "It doesn't look like a hit-and-run. What do you suppose the chances are of a man happening to have a fatal accident all on his own so soon after offending that many people?"

"He was out walking in the middle of a very dark night. He could have tripped or run into something."

"There was a lot of blood but not enough for him to have bled to death. No, until we hear differently from Dr. B, we're going to treat this as a murder."

I could always tell when Reed was thinking about challenging me. He'd shove his hands deep into his pockets, gaze down, and alternately kick first the toe of his boot and then his heel on the ground. He did this now for fifteen or twenty seconds then looked up. "How do you want to proceed?"

"We need to divide and conquer. I want us to assume murder and that whoever killed Halpern is still in the village. I'm going to talk to the guests at the bed-and-breakfast. I'd like you to track down the people who made formal complaints about Halpern and talk more with them."

Reed swallowed, a little nervous about this directive. "You know I haven't done much interviewing."

"You haven't, but you have good instincts. Tell them you're following up on their complaint and making sure that everything is okay now. Ask them about Halpern and what exactly he did to them. Watch their body language and facial expressions. Are they looking at you or away from you? Are they fidgeting? Pay attention to the words they use and listen to the tone of their voice. Do they sound natural or like they're covering something up? Trust your gut. If they seem like they're hiding something, keep them on the list and I'll follow up with them later."

"I can do that," he murmured, reassuring himself as much as me.

We took a few minutes to go over those who had made formal complaints about Halpern. Based on things they'd already told him, we eliminated all but half a dozen people. If necessary, we could always go back to those we'd cut.

"Last tip," I told him as I locked the front door and flipped the open sign to the emergency contact side. "Always remember that an innocent person will relax more as you talk to them. The guilty guy will stay nervous."

Reed analyzed that statement for a moment and then gave a nod of understanding.

"Ready?" I asked. "Go team?"

He laughed. "Go team."

Chapter 13

MEEKA WAS CONFUSED THAT WE had returned home in the middle of the day. In fact, when I opened the door of her cage so she could get out, she stood there for a moment as though this had to be a joke. She probably thought we'd lost our jobs again.

"We're not staying long," I told her. "We're interviewing suspects."

To her, this translated to "your services are not needed." She trotted off into the woods, probably to find a squirrel or rabbit to play with. Tripp was sitting in an Adirondack chair on the front porch, taking a little break.

"What are you doing here?" He greeted me with a kiss. "Not that I have any objections to you coming home early."

"Sorry, Charlie, I'm here on official business."

"Uh-oh. I figured something was going on when you didn't come over for breakfast."

"I probably should've called first. Please tell me that our guests are here."

"River Carr took off between eight and eight thirty, and I didn't see him come back. Lupe was here interviewing everyone, and Kristina and Kyle left a few minutes after she was done with them. I saw the other four about ten minutes ago; they were in the great room reading and playing chess."

"Constance didn't leave, did she? She told me she'd be staying."

"Yeah, what's going on with that? She came down for breakfast and asked if she could take a tray up to her room. I told her that was fine, to leave it in the hall when she was done, and asked if something was wrong with Nick. I haven't seen him all day."

"You could definitely say that something is wrong with Nick." I told him the basic information, that Nick was found dead this morning and that there was a possibility that it had been murder. Watching people's reactions to news like that was so ingrained in me that I found myself watching Tripp for signs that he was hiding something. It only took a few seconds for him to realize the same thing.

"There's another checkmark in the sleep in the same bed column," he joked but his smile was tight. "With all the murders going on around here, looks like everyone needs an alibi now."

I took his hand, pulled it to my mouth, and kissed his knuckles. "Are you saying you need an alibi?"

"You don't really want me to answer that, do you?" For the briefest of moments, he looked offended but then acknowledged that he knew I was joking.

"If you were guilty of something like that, I would be the world's worst detective. And I pride myself on being a pretty damn good detective. For the record, I'd be your alibi anytime."

He pulled me into a hug. "That's why you're here? To talk to our guests about Nick?"

"I am. Hopefully, this won't take long."

Releasing me again, he said, "I was about to make myself some lunch. Would you like me to get something ready for you?"

"I'd love that. I'm starving." When had I last eaten? Oh yes, at the council meeting. "As much as I love Sugar's scones, they don't hold me like your breakfasts do."

We went inside, Tripp to the kitchen and me to the great room, where I found Alicia, Derek, Trevor, and Jeremy as Tripp had said. Alicia and Derek had books in their hands. Trevor and Jeremy were indeed playing chess. They all looked up as I walked in and Alicia jumped to her feet.

"What's going on, Jayne? Constance refuses to answer her door. Nick never stops talking, and we haven't heard him all day."

"I have some bad news. Nick's body was found early this morning."

Gasps of surprise sounded in the room, and Trevor jumped up this time. "His body? As in, he's dead?"

"Yes, he's dead. I can't give you any more details, but I would like to talk with each of you to see if you can give me any help in figuring out what might have happened."

"Do you think he was murdered?" Trevor asked.

"I can't make that determination until the autopsy results come in," I explained. "Information about him and what's been going on with him could be helpful. Who would like to start?"

As the rest of them seemed too stunned to speak, Jeremy volunteered to go first.

Five foot six, dark-brown cropped hair worn spiky on top, dark-blue eyes, square black plastic glasses, forty pounds overweight, large gap between front teeth.

We went out onto the back patio where we could talk without being disturbed. I indicated he should sit on the loveseat, which put his back to the great room windows, and I chose a chair next to him that allowed me to see both the house and the lake.

"Please state your full name," I began, placing my voice recorder on the table between us, "and tell me how long you've known the deceased."

"I'm Jeremy Levine. I haven't known Nick very long. Trevor and I met at a New Year's Eve party and started dating shortly after that. What's that? Eight months ago? I didn't meet Nick for a few months after that. I think it was March or April at a birthday party." He narrowed his eyes, recalling the timeline. "Before the party, so March. I don't remember whose birthday it was. Someone in this group. Alicia maybe?"

Jeremy was an extraordinarily nervous guy. He performed a new fidget with every sentence he spoke—eyes darting about, legs bouncing, hands worrying together or tugging at the collar of his wrinkled blue button-down shirt ... He'd struck me as nervous the moment I met him, so it was hard to know if this was a common characteristic for him, or if it was something unique that I should be concerned about. I made a note to ask Trevor about him.

"I believe you're correct," I said of his last statement. *Alicia in April is an easy alliteration.* Trevor created rhymes when the four of us first met so we'd remember each other's birthdays. *Jayne's new year starts in January, too.* "You've known the deceased for about six months, then, and everyone else for eight."

"Sounds right." Jeremy stared out at the lake and then frowned. "No, wait. It was February. Valentine's Day."

"What was February?"

"When I met Nick and Constance. It was just supposed to be the four of us—Kristina, me, Trevor, and Kyle—and then Nick canceled some meeting at work, so they came, too. Kristina prepared dinner for us all and set up a romantic table for each couple in a separate room in their house. I remember her saying that she had to scramble and make two more servings of everything and set up one more table."

That sounded a lot like the Kristina I knew in college. Always doing special things for people.

"You're the newest member of the group," I began, and Jeremy's attention snapped from the lake to me. From the scowl on his face, I guessed that he didn't like my statement, which was simply an observation, not an accusation of any kind. I jotted that down in my little notebook; the voice recorder couldn't capture gestures or facial expressions. "What can you tell me about the group dynamic? There seems to be a lot of tension there."

The furrow in his brow smoothed over. "I couldn't say if anything was wrong before."

"Before?"

"Before I met Nick. He's the one you want to know about, right?"

"You've known him for six months but can't say if there was any tension between him and the others?"

"Well, he lost his job not long after I joined the group. Kristina mentioned that to me. She said he turned into kind of a jerk after that." He pushed the tip of his tongue through the gap in his front teeth while he thought. "I guess I only saw Alicia and Derek one time. You know, all those kids." He paused. "Right, it was Alicia's birthday. That's when I met Alicia and Derek."

"In April, five months ago."

"Yeah. Usually it was just me, Kristina, Kyle, and Trevor. Constance and Nick didn't come around very often. That's when I noticed the tension, at the party in April."

Good thing I was recording this. Jeremy was hard to follow. His statements started out big and required a lot of whittling to get to the facts that mattered.

I stretched my neck to ease some of the tightness forming there. "So, basically you noticed things weren't so good with the group the first time you saw everyone together."

After a moment's consideration, he agreed. "I guess that is how it went."

"Okay, now that we've worked out how and when you met everyone, tell me about this tension. Was it between everyone or just specific people?"

"Everyone. I'm not sure how to explain it exactly. Flirting, I guess, that was disguised as being innocent fun, but nobody took it as being fun."

"Who flirted? Everyone?"

"No. Just Nick." He looked at me like I was the one convoluting this interview.

I was going to need a beer after this. Or a cream puff. Maybe I'd stop by Treat Me Sweetly later to see if Sugar made any today.

"You're saying that Nick flirted with the other guys' wives and acted like it was just fun and games?"

"Right. He flirted with everyone except his own wife. Well, he tried with Alicia, but honestly, she was so exhausted from their five kids, I don't think she noticed anything except the lack of screaming children."

"That leaves Kristina." Whittle, whittle, whittle. "Nick flirted with Kristina."

Jeremy slumped back in his chair, apparently as frustrated with his own statements as I was. Or was he angry? It was hard to distinguish the two sometimes. I noted this in my little book, too.

"I guess." Jeremy's eyes were on my notebook. "He paid a lot of attention to Kristina. It got to the point where Kyle refused to have him around anymore. Which was fine as far as I was concerned."

"All right, let's move on. We've covered Nick and the women. How were things between Nick and the men in the group?"

"We were only with the group at parties, and Nick and Constance didn't come to many of them. Good thing because Trevor can't stand the guy. Never could, far as I know. Neither can I. Any man who treats a woman like that—"

He cut himself off mid-sentence and shook his head. A telling reaction, but a reaction to what? That Jeremy had a father who was abusive to his mother? A perverted neighbor who made inappropriate comments to a female friend? Sadly, the possibilities were endless. This was also the second time Jeremy expressed his dislike for Nick.

"Sorry." Jeremy had pulled himself back together. "The one time I met Derek, he was chasing his kids around the yard, so I never saw him and Nick interact. As for Kyle, things were obviously not good between them because of the Kristina thing."

"You mean him flirting with Kristina."

"Right. I've never seen them like they were yesterday, though."

"How were they before yesterday?"

"You know, kind of cool to each other. Didn't speak unless they had to."

More whittling. "It sounds like the only actual trouble within the group was between Nick, Kyle, and Kristina."

"I guess." He tugged at his collar. "And Constance."

I really wanted that cream puff now. Maybe two. "Anything else you can tell me that might help me understand what happened to Nick last night?"

He thought for a minute, shifting to sit squarely in the chair, hands resting on his thighs. "Don't know if this will help you understand, and I don't want it to come across like some kind of accusation or whatever, but I sincerely believe that Kyle would do anything to protect his wife."

Depending on the inflection, that statement could mean Kyle was the romantic type, ready to swoop in and save the woman he loved from a predator. Jeremy, however, made it sound negative like maybe Kyle was more controlling than caring.

"If Nick Halpern's death comes back as being suspicious," I concluded, "you would consider Kyle Mandel a suspect."

Jeremy shrugged. "I don't have any proof, but I guess that is what I'm saying."

Again with the *I guess*. He'd make a statement and then cover possible errors by negating it with, "I guess." I wasn't sure how to interpret this interview. There were probably some grains of truth in it, but it felt like Jeremy was covering up more than possible inaccuracies.

"One last question. What is your relationship with Kristina?"

"Kristina? I met her soon after Trevor and I started dating. The two of them are real close. I swear, they can't go a week without seeing each other."

"Right, but I'm asking about *you* and Kristina. You've mentioned her a number of times, so I'm wondering about your relationship with her."

This question gave him pause. "We're friends, I guess. Like I told you, she and Trevor are super close. He talks about her a lot, so I guess I know things about her through him." He tugged on his collar. "I'm not sure what more to tell you about that."

He wasn't sure, or did he know something that he didn't want to reveal? Had Kristina done something to Nick in an attempt to help her miserable sister? Or in retaliation for the things he'd said about her? Or to cover up a secret between them?

I thanked Jeremy for his time and cautioned him to not leave the village until I had given him the okay to do so.

"Why not? I didn't do anything to Nick."

I looked pointedly at him. "You were planning to stay for the whole weekend, weren't you? Any reason you suddenly feel the need to leave early?"

He opened his mouth, closed it, and then shook his head.

"Would you tell someone else to come out now, please?"

A minute later, Trevor Dale was sitting in front of me looking ready for a fight.

Chapter 14

IT TOOK ME A FEW seconds to remember that when stressed or concentrating on something, Trevor's default expression made everyone think he was angry. During finals week, he always got a library table to himself because the other students at UW Madison thought he was about to snap.

"What the hell is going on, Jayne?" His heavy sigh told me that right now he was stressed, not angry. It might be because of the Nick situation; Trevor had always been a very empathetic person. Or it could be something personal; there was always drama of some kind in Trevor's world.

"Honestly, I'm not sure. I was hoping you'd be able to tell me something about your group."

"I can't say that I'm surprised Nick is dead. If you would have told me this was going to happen a year ago, I would've said you were crazy. He was always kind of … boisterous might be the right word. He liked to tell jokes and be the center of attention, but I can't say anyone disliked the guy."

I flipped back a page or two in my notebook. "Jeremy seems to feel you can't stand the guy. That you never liked him."

Trevor shook his head, annoyed. "That's not true.

Jeremy only knows my life for the last eight months. I admit, since Nick turned into such a pig, I've had big problems with him. Before he lost his job, he was fine. Stressed, so sometimes edgy, but he seemed like an okay person. If anything, my feelings about him were neutral. I mean, I barely knew the guy."

"But you have known him for a while, right?"

"A few years. He and Constance dated for a long time, and they got married a few months after we graduated."

"The trouble with him started when he lost his job?"

Trevor nodded, pushing his glasses up. I had to laugh. He still wore the same loose glasses that used to slide down his nose in college.

"Losing his job seemed really hard on him," Trevor confirmed. "You know guys, their jobs define them. Well, not all guys." He snorted. "Jeremy would be overjoyed if he lost his. Honestly, I've never heard anyone complain so much. I'd tell him to quit, but then I'd be responsible for him."

And there was the current drama. Would the time ever come when Trevor could just be happy?

"Speaking of jobs, what does everyone do?"

"Kristina and Constance work at the same clinic. Constance is a doctor of nursing, I'm not sure what her actual title is, and Kristina is an RN. Kyle owns his own business, an athletic club or something. Derek teaches high school math and coaches the football team. You know that Alicia is a stay-at-home mom and homeschools a kid or two, so I consider her a teacher as well. I'm a junior attorney in Milwaukee." He paused before saying, "Jeremy does general office stuff at my firm."

"What about Nick?"

"Nick was the CTO at a security company before he lost his job."

"Chief Technology Officer. That's a big job to lose."

"It was," Trevor agreed. "Especially because he hadn't

really done anything."

"Hadn't *really* done anything. Do you feel he had done something though?"

He thought about that before answering. "Don't know. Like I said, I didn't see him all that often. He was impressed with his own success, had a big ego, which was probably justified. Because of his sometimes-cocky attitude, it didn't really surprise me that he had been accused of harassment. But did he do it? I can't say."

We chatted a little more about the other members of his group. He had nothing bad to say about Alicia and Derek. He felt they had the perfect life.

"Everyone has something going on behind the curtain." Was that true or was I cynical?

"As for Kyle and Kristina, they've been having some problems over the last year."

"What do you mean by problems?" I asked.

"Oh, you know, the typical married-couple stuff. They've been trying to get pregnant for a long time. Just never seems to take."

Kristina still hadn't told the group. I bit my tongue, not about to break that news.

"Anything more than that?" I asked.

"She never complained about anything else. All she wants is to be a mom." He smiled, dimples piercing his cheeks. "She'd be a good one."

"She would be." I waited a few seconds before asking, "What about that exchange at breakfast yesterday? Nick said some pretty rude things about her."

Trevor waited, expecting me to say more. "Are you asking if there's any truth to it? Absolutely not. She would never hurt Constance that way."

I waited for him to offer more, which he didn't. "What about Kyle?"

"Do you mean, would she do anything to hurt him?"

For as long as I had known him, when Trevor was

disappointed with you, every molecule of his face showed it—his smile disappeared, his blue eyes turned stormy, he seemed to age twenty-five years into a stern father figure. That was the look I was getting now.

"Jayne. How can you even ask that?"

I shrugged. "On the job training?"

He rolled his eyes and turned back into my twenty-six-year-old friend. "You know Kristina."

"I do, but I also know that people can surprise you. Anything else you feel I should know regarding Nick?"

"Nothing I can think of that would have led to this."

I gave Trevor the same warning I had given his boyfriend about not leaving the village, and he assured me he wasn't ready to leave yet.

"I hope it doesn't sound horrible," he said softly, "but other than this unfortunate situation with Nick, it's so peaceful here. I'm just not ready to go back to Milwaukee."

"That doesn't sound horrible," I assured him. "But I thought you loved your job."

"I do love my job. If that's all I had to deal with when I got back—" He shook his head, a crisp, never-mind movement. "I'll be here."

I asked him to send out Alicia or Derek, and Alicia came next. Like Trevor, Alicia had always been sensitive but also no-nonsense. Good qualities for someone who'd planned on becoming an elementary school teacher. I could only imagine what kind of an amazing mother she must be.

"Can't tell you anything," she informed me as soon as she sat down, and I had restarted my recorder. "I guess I could repeat some things that Kristina has said over the years, but I know nothing about Nick. I know Constance a little better."

"Oh come on, you must know something. Sometimes it's the littlest things that lead to breakthroughs."

She repeated what Trevor had said about Nick's job, that he'd been a CTO. "Other than that, I met him once. That was four years ago. We only had Olivia at the time." She smiled, one of those proud mom smiles. "Livvy was such a good baby. We could take her anywhere. She was fine in her little snuggly on my or Derek's chest. She was snug as a bug sitting in her stroller. Seriously, she never caused a problem. So that was the one time we met Nick. At a gathering that Kristina and Kyle were having. I was pregnant with the boys at the time. Triplets—Rudy, George, and Corbin. Lord, what a handful." She stared blankly at the lake, probably lost in a triplet memory, then came out of it with blinking eyes. "Just as they started walking, I found out I was pregnant again, this time with Michelle. You would not believe what we had to go through to get away this weekend."

"Your oldest is four and you're already homeschooling her?"

Once again, that proud mom smile took over her face. "She is so smart. She already knows all her letters and numbers up to thirty. She can write her name and her brothers' and sister's names. Sometimes the boys sit for lessons. Corbin mostly, but not often."

As much as I'd love to sit and hear about her brilliant kids, and I didn't doubt for one second that they were brilliant, this was not the time for it.

"You first met Nick four years ago. What about at your birthday party? Weren't they there?"

She stared at me like that day only five months ago was so far in the past she couldn't recall it. "Were they? Oh! They were, I remember now."

"Anything significant happen that day? If you can remember that far back."

She pursed her lips and looked sideways at me. A look that had always meant, *hush up your mouth*. She closed her eyes for a minute, trying to bring up that day.

"Oh, yes," she said mostly to herself. Then to me, "He was being a class A jerk, and none of us were as impressed with him as he was with himself."

"Do you remember him harassing any of you? Either that day or any other?"

"You mean sexually?" She closed her eyes again and nodded her head a few seconds later. "There was one incident. On my birthday, in fact. He said something about me being beautiful and kissing my hand. I told him that unless he could offer me free nanny service for a year, I wasn't interested in any of his sweet talk."

I burst out laughing. I could easily imagine her saying exactly that. "What about Kristina? Has she ever told you anything that might be helpful for me?"

"Honestly, no. Kristina and I see each other pretty often, but all we talk about is kids. She snatches Michelle out of my hands the second after she puts her purse down. She wants a baby so badly."

I questioned Alicia for a few more minutes and wrapped up the interview, there really wasn't anything she could tell me that would help with this investigation. When Derek came out next, he wasn't any more helpful.

"Four years? Has it been that long already?" He thought on this. "Yeah, guess that does sound about right. I remember him because he's Kristina's brother-in-law, but I can't say as he stood out otherwise." He shrugged his broad football-player shoulders. "We just had Olivia the first time I met him." He smiled, as proud as his wife had been. "My focus was pretty much on her. At Alicia's party, my job was to watch the kids. I was wiped out after three hours. I don't know how she does it by herself all day."

After a few questions, I ended our short interview. "Thanks for your time. I have to ask that you and Alicia stay in the village until—"

He held up a hand, stopping me. "You remember we got five kids, right? We got two sets of grandparents taking shifts with them for four days. I'm sorry about what happened to Nick, but we're good right here."

For now, I was out of guests to talk to. "Do you have

any idea where Kristina and Kyle went? Or River Carr, by chance?"

"Kristina said something about going hiking. That River dude is one interesting guy." Derek had the same look of awe, envy, and admiration on his face that Tripp had when River pulled up in that car. "Is there someone in the village named Megan?"

I ran through the villager database in my mind. "No Megan. There's a Morgan."

Derek pointed at me. "Morgan. That's it. He was going to find her."

Chapter 15

AS PROMISED, TRIPP HAD LUNCH ready and we brought it up to the boathouse sundeck.

"What is this?" I peered at the items inside the pita pocket he handed me along with a sectioned orange. "Ten points for portability, by the way."

He gave a little bow of thanks. "It's one of the leftover shish kabobs from the party. I just warmed it up, stuffed it in, and drizzled on a little sauce."

"Would that mean it's just a shish now?" I took a big bite, realizing suddenly how hungry I was.

"Did you learn anything valuable during your interviews?"

Poor Tripp. He wanted to help me with investigations. Before I became sheriff, he was right at my side while I tried to figure out the truth surrounding my grandmother's death. The police report my family had received was wrong, she hadn't died from an accidental slip and fall into the bathtub. Numerous people — Donovan, Flavia, Sheriff Brighton, and who knew who else — had conspired to cover up her death to make it look like an accident. I sincerely hoped there weren't any more secrets to uncover about Gran. Or her death.

"I learned some things," I told Tripp, "but nothing that's leading me to a killer. If there is one."

"If?"

Giving him as much information as I could, which wasn't a whole lot, I explained the situation.

"How soon will Dr. Bundy have results for you?" Tripp asked.

"He's bumping it up on the schedule as much as he can. Hopefully, that means soon. I asked everyone to stay in the village, but I can't hold them here."

We finished our lunches and discussed the option of a wine and cheese gathering for the guests.

"If we keep it lowkey," I suggested, "that could be a nice distraction for them."

"I'm going to go study up on wine and cheese pairings." Tripp stood and took my plate and iced tea glass. "If we're going to do this, we should do it right."

"But let's also stick to a budget."

"I know. Profit and loss. We want profit. Will you be home for dinner?"

I watched Meeka, curled up at the end of the sofa, and debated about leaving her home for the rest of the afternoon. "I'd like to say yes, but this could be a long day. If you make something, don't do anything fancy."

Tripp had just gotten to the top of the boathouse stairway when he paused and turned back. "I almost forgot to tell you, your mother called the B&B earlier. She would like you to call back 'as soon as you have a moment.'" He smiled, amused. "You're right, she is a character. But it was a nice conversation."

"Conversation? You had a *conversation* with my mother?"

He was halfway down the stairs at that point, so didn't reply.

I crossed through my apartment's small sitting room, past the kitchenette and the bathroom, and into my bedroom. On the night table next to the bed was my landline phone and answering machine. Looked like she had called the apartment as well since the light on the machine was blinking impatiently for me to retrieve the message.

"Jayne, it's your mother." She paused, probably waiting to see if I was screening calls. "I just got off the phone with your friend, Tripper Bennett. He's quite a pleasant young man."

That sounded vaguely like an approval.

"I've been expecting a call from you," Mom's voice continued, "I realize you're busy up there, but you did promise to let me know about your opening weekend. Call me when you have a moment."

She, of course, meant that I should call her at home. Phone calls to her day spa, Melt Your Cares, were only tolerated in emergency situations. I needed to get back to work. In particular, I needed to find River Carr. Or Morgan since Derek claimed Carr was looking for her. Since I was standing right here by the phone and had no idea if I'd get another chance to call today, I picked up the phone, planning to leave a quick message.

"Jayne? I wasn't expecting to hear from you until this evening."

"What number did I call?"

"Did Tiffany answer?"

Tiffany was Mom's receptionist. "Why are you at home in the middle of the day?"

Mom put in a minimum of twelve hours per day at the day spa. When busy, it wasn't unusual for her to spend eighteen hours there.

"I left the spa at noon today. We're closed tomorrow and Monday for the holiday."

"You left at noon? Are you okay? You're not sick, are you?"

"I don't get sick. Why on earth would you think that? I took the afternoon off to take Rosalyn shopping. She needs a few supplies for school. Her senior year starts on Tuesday, you know. Then we're going out for dinner and to a play."

At the very bottom of my Fun Things To Do list was "go shopping with Mom and Rosalyn." All the same, a jolt of jealousy stabbed at me. They had always been closer to each other than either of them was to me. It hadn't always been that way. It started during Rosalyn's junior year in high school. She'd been kidnapped and when the FBI recovered her a few days later, she and Mom became almost inseparable. I, on the other hand, became even more of an outsider within my own family. Granted, I was already in college at the time, so I didn't see much of them anymore. My trips home became fewer and farther between. Anytime I did visit, I was practically a ghost in my own home.

Still, I choked out, "That sounds like a fun way to spend the day. So, you're looking for an update on the B&B?"

"I am. How has everything gone so far with the grand opening?"

I told her about the party Friday night—the food, the jugglers, Lily Grace's fortune-telling. I left out all details regarding Nick Halpern.

"That sounds very pleasant," she commented. "It's not what I care about, however. How are your bookings? Are you full?"

"We had six of the seven rooms booked but one of those reservations had to cancel. We kept the fifty percent deposit like we warned him would happen upon cancellation. Right now, we've got four couples and one man traveling alone. Do you remember my friend Kristina from college?"

A humming sound came from my mother's end of the line. Not at all like Dr. B's happy humming, Mom's was more of a brain vibrating buzz. "No, I can't say as I remember a Kristina."

"We were really close. She and two more of my friends from college are here along with Kristina's sister. Everyone's significant other is here as well."

"But you're not fully booked."

"It's the opening weekend, Mom. We only opened for

reservations six weeks ago. Five rooms means we're seventy percent booked. I'm happy with that."

"You should never be happy with less than one hundred percent. If you settle for less, that's what you'll get."

She was like a negative-inspiration fortune cookie.

"You'll be happy to hear that we are fully booked for the last two weeks in September as well as the week before Halloween, the week of Halloween, and the week after. Considering the official tourist season is over at the end of September, I think that's pretty good."

All those folks were coming for the Wiccan Mabon and Samhain celebrations. I left out that detail since she was opposed to all things Wiccan.

"And what about November? And December? What are your plans for over the winter?"

Were her expectations too high, or were mine too low? I'd seen her push her employees hard the first year she was in business. A handful were still with her, but many left within the first few months. She was very successful, but at what cost?

I wanted to dismiss her questions, tell her this was my business, thanks very much. My parents were footing the bill at this point, though. They'd given us one year to prove that the B&B could be profitable, or it would all go up for sale; the house and the two thousand acres. This meant that for this first year I had to answer all her questions.

"We've been discussing winter sports activities for our guests. You know how much people in Wisconsin love snowmobiling and ice fishing."

She paused before saying, "That sounds like a viable option. Keep in mind that there will be people, like me for example, who don't care to do any sort of outdoor activity."

"I'm aware. We're planning indoor activities as well." I scrambled through the drawer of my nightstand, pushing aside the charm bags and amulets Morgan had given me, for a pad of paper and pen. Once I found them, I quickly scribbled down INDOOR WINTER ACTIVITIES and underlined it about six times. "Anything else going on? Do you have plans for tomorrow and Monday?"

"I have a small amount of paperwork to take care of. As you are aware, now that you're running a business, you're never really off the clock."

"I do understand that. The sheriff of a small village is never really off the clock either."

There was another pause at her end. This one made me feel a little uneasy.

"Has there been any word on this Donovan person?" Mom asked. "By the way, does he have a last name?"

I'd wondered the same thing. None of the villagers ever called him anything but Donovan. I finally asked Briar, Morgan's mother. She knew everything about the village's past, including family names.

"It's Page. Donovan Page. And no, I haven't heard a word. Don't worry, I'm staying on top of it. I check on the status of his APB every day. He's out there somewhere. We'll find him."

She hummed softly again. This tone was slightly different from her thinking hum, this one indicated she was releasing stress. "I'm sure you will."

"I'm also staying in touch with Captain Grier at Madison PD. He knows that Donovan hasn't been caught yet. You and Rosalyn are perfectly safe."

"Well, as safe as we can be," she said in a way that meant we were done talking about this. "Is there anything else I need to know about?"

"That's an awfully wide-open question."

"Very funny." And there was actually a bit of levity in her voice. "I meant with the B&B. Or you."

"Nothing with the B&B." I closed my eyes and prayed I wouldn't regret my next comment. It was best that she found out from me, however. Not that she would find out from anyone else in the village. "Tripp and I are dating."

"I got that impression during the conversation he and I had." There was a pause, but no humming. "Are you sure that's a good idea? You are business partners after all."

"So far we've been able to keep business and personal separate. We're both determined to make this work. Tripp is convinced that running a B&B is the perfect fit for him. As for me, I like it here and don't want to lose this opportunity. I think we're a pretty good team."

"It's your choice, but I recommend you stay in control of your business. Remember, you are the one who will ultimately be responsible in the end."

"Rest assured, I am handling all the financials."

"Good." She paused. "I hope you're taking things slowly."

I knew what she was referring to. When I broke things off with my ex-fiancé Jonah Price after seven sometimes good, sometimes painful years, my mother had been almost as upset as I was. Since Rosalyn and I were little, Mom talked about her daughters being involved in the political climate in Madison. She was captivated with the prestige and power of that world. To make her happy, I started down that path but found law enforcement far more interesting than politics. Since Jonah aspired to be a senator, Mom was appeased by the promise of me being a politician's wife. Turned out, I didn't have any interest in that either.

"I hate to cut this short," I said. Actually, this was one of the longest conversations Mom and I had had in a long time. "I need to get back to the station, though."

"Very well. I appreciate the update and hope everything is all right up there."

For half a second, I considered sharing a little of my life as sheriff and telling her about Nick Halpern, but I knew nothing good could come from that.

"Everything's fine, Mom. Have fun with Rosalyn this afternoon. Tell her I said hi."

"I will do that." I thought she had signed off without a goodbye, as was standard for her. As I was pulling the phone away from my ear, though, I heard her say, "Thank you for calling me back, Jayne."

Then she hung up.

Chapter 16

SOMETHING HAD CHANGED BETWEEN MY mother and me. It was subtle, and I couldn't quite put my finger on exactly what it was. I think it started when I pleaded my case to turn the house into Pine Time. Maybe I had echoed her strong businesswoman personality, a trait which always made her pay closer attention whether it came from a stranger on the street, a vendor at her day spa, or her own daughter.

It grew deeper when I told her what I had learned about Donovan being Dad's son. I had discovered her biggest secret and hadn't taunted her with it. I could have, that secret affected my life in a huge way as well, but what kind of a person would do that?

I couldn't say that these two events necessarily made things better between us, but they had added a new, more adult dimension to our relationship.

I pulled the Cherokee into my spot behind the station and let Meeka out of her cage. At the top of my priority list was finding River Carr. Since Derek thought Carr had gone in search of Morgan, we'd stop by Shoppe Mystique first.

We had just gotten to the pentacle garden when Meeka spotted that all-white cat jumping from one triangular section to another. She tugged on her leash, whined, and gave me her sad Meeka face.

"Five minutes," I said while letting out her leash.

"Isn't she great?"

I turned to see Emery standing next to me. "I don't think I've ever seen you anywhere but behind the desk at The Inn."

He held up a triple-scoop ice cream cone. "On a break."

"It's a little cool today for a cone, don't you think?"

He made a face that was part confusion, part pure wicked pleasure. "Weather is never a factor when it comes to ice cream."

Couldn't argue with that. I nodded at the cat who currently had Meeka on her back in a patch of chrysanthemums. "You know this cat?"

"Sure do. Everyone knows her."

"I don't."

"You never met Blue?" He seemed genuinely surprised by this. "She's the community cat. I'm not even sure anymore who actually owns her. Maybe no one ever did."

"Community cat?" Considering where we were, that shouldn't surprise me.

"Yep. She wanders house to house and hangs out until she gets bored. She even makes it over to the rental cottages sometimes."

"No one tries to catnap her?" I chuckled at my own lame joke, and Emery gave me a polite smile.

"They try. Blue knows when someone has nefarious intent, though, and will skedaddle before they can touch her."

"Why is she called Blue?" Just then, as though knowing we were talking about her, the cat looked up at me. Her electric-blue eyes practically glowed. "Never mind. I think I know."

"See ya, Sheriff." Emery continued toward The Inn, enjoying every lick of that cone.

"Nice to meet you, Blue." The cat raised her tail and

turned her butt to me. I didn't speak cat so had no idea what that meant. "Come on, Meeka. We have to find Morgan."

On occasion, I'd find a spouse or someone's child sitting in one of the rocking chairs on Shoppe Mystique's front porch, waiting for their shopper inside. Today, eight or ten people were clustered there, waiting to go in.

"What's going on?" I asked.

"It's jam-packed in there," a woman in her mid-fifties stated.

"We're waiting for a few people to leave," agreed the woman next to her, also mid-fifties.

As I reached for the door handle, the first woman issued a warning about me being sorry. Once the door was open, I instantly understood what they meant. The shop was indeed crammed with customers. Meeka huddled against my legs, shivering with fear, so I picked her up. She didn't do well in crowds. No matter how close to me she would stay, someone would either step on her paws or some naughty little kid would pull her tail.

Willow, Morgan's tall and lanky redheaded assistant, was behind the large wood table to my right that served as the checkout station. A horde of customers was gathered there, both those wanting to make a purchase and others who just seemed to have questions. I tried and failed to catch her attention so, like a Ping-Pong ball in a whirlpool, Meeka and I joined in the flow of people and went in search of Morgan.

To the left of the front door, we passed by two huge bookshelves loaded with apothecary bottles of dried herbs and plants. The bottles were usually full to the top, now many were nearly empty. The little Lotions and Potions table, normally loaded with Morgan's homemade bars of soap and pots of cosmetics, was down to half its normal inventory. The Crystals and Stones cabinet was a chaotic mess with items scattered everywhere. The Oils and Incense case desperately needed organizing. Even the hot water carafe on the complimentary tea station in the back right corner was empty, as were the containers of Morgan's signature tea blends on the wall shelf above it.

The chaos and clutter indicated a good sales' day for Shoppe Mystique. Seeing the always-tidy shop in this condition, however, was a little upsetting.

One last scan confirmed that Morgan wasn't anywhere in the main room. A quick peek inside the reading room showed it to be just as full of people, none of them Morgan. Maybe Willow knew where she'd gone. We were almost back to the front door when Willow spotted us from behind the checkout counter.

"Oh, thank the Goddess." She gestured me over with a quick flapping of her hand. "Can you cover for me for five minutes?"

"Cover for you? Where's Morgan?"

"Lunch. She said she might be a little longer today. At the time, there were maybe six people in here, so I told her I'd be fine and that she should take as long as she wanted."

"How long has she been gone?"

Despite Willow's consent, I was a little worried. Maybe Morgan was off by herself on an unrelated errand, but she could also be with Carr. He and Halpern had that little altercation at breakfast. I couldn't dismiss the possibility that Carr was the—?

"Morgan's fine." Almost as though reading my mind, Willow interrupted my thoughts. "I'm not. If I don't get to the bathroom soon, I'm going to wet my pants."

"I don't know how to work your credit card machine or—"

"Customers will wait five minutes to pay. Just stand here and make sure no one steals anything."

I could do that. In fact, as seemed to happen every time I entered one of the retail shops wearing my uniform, a handful of "customers" walked out. Hopefully with empty pockets.

The look on Willow's face, and the fact that she was bouncing up and down, said Morgan's safety was the last thing she was worried about right now.

"Okay, go do what you need to do." The word "okay" had barely left my mouth and she was gone.

I set Meeka down behind the checkout table, and she immediately huddled behind a big cardboard box there. She really didn't like crowds.

"Do you have this in tiger's eye?" A woman held up what looked to me like a purple marble disc with a hole in the center.

"I'm sorry," I said, "I'm just standing guard. I don't work here."

"So you don't know if it comes in tiger's eye?"

"Ma'am, I don't even know what tiger's eye is. Willow will be back in a few minutes. She'll be able to answer all your questions."

When five minutes had turned into ten, a few customers left without purchasing. Understandable. Not sure I'd wait ten minutes to buy a souvenir. One rather privileged-looking and insistent teenage girl wanted to purchase a pentacle on a leather cord.

I gave her my spiel about not working here, but she didn't care in the least.

"The sign over the table says these are twelve dollars," she informed in a bored voice. "So, what, will there be tax or whatever?"

"There will, but I don't know how much that will be." I guess I could have done a little math and figured it out.

"Here's a twenty." She slid a bill across the table at me. "That should cover it so, you know, I'm not stealing or anything."

"Hang on." I pulled my cell phone out of its pocket on my cargo pants. There was absolutely no coverage in the village, so phones were only good for one thing. "Let me take a picture of that so I can show Willow what you paid for."

After the girl left with her pentacle, I stood and scanned the crowd, eventually locking eyes with a mid-thirties woman who had just attached a talisman necklace around her neck and stepped away from the table. She paled, returned the necklace to the table, and made a beeline for the front door, my eyes on her the entire time. Hadn't Morgan worked some kind of an anti-theft spell for the shop? I chuckled to myself. No, Morgan would let karma take care of thieves.

"I knew coming in here today would be a challenge," Reeva Long greeted, emerging from the sea of tourists.

"This is what happens when people can't be on the lake," I said. "They shop."

"Are you able to ring me up for these?" She held out two apothecary bottles from the herb cabinet. The old-fashioned tea-stained labels read *Yarrow* and *Frankincense*. She inspected the bottle of frankincense. "Not much in here. I should probably get some rosemary in case this isn't enough."

Witches and their weird herbs. "What are those for?"

"Since I've decided to stay, I have to restock my cabinets. They're practically bare. Karl was never much of a chef."

I didn't know much about cooking, but yarrow and frankincense sounded more like ingredients for one of Morgan's charm bags than anything culinary. What was Reeva up to?

"That's what Karl told me once." My heart tugged at the memory of the tortured former sheriff. "I seem to remember he ate at The Inn a lot."

"The server's uniforms haven't changed since the last time I lived here. Karl liked to look at the girls in their short skirts." Reeva winked like this was so cute. I stiffened but kept my thoughts on men ogling women to myself. "Anyway, I'm quite excited to get back into the kitchen. I've noticed that there are always waiting lines to get into the restaurants here. Maybe I'll open my own place. A diner, perhaps. I just love diners."

"Or something more high-end," I suggested, caught up in her web of foodie excitement. "As good as the food is at The Inn, it's not fine dining." I pointed at the herb jars in her hands. "I'm just here until Willow gets back. If she ever comes back. I can't ring you up."

"I thought as much." Reeva scanned the shop. "I haven't been inside Shoppe Mystique in ages. I'll wander around until Willow returns. I just remembered, I need a silver candle and a container with a tight lid as well."

I watched her walk away, wondering again what she was up to. Over the next three minutes, six more people came up asking if I had an herb or an oil or an incense or certain kind of talisman. I gave the same answer every time. "I'm sorry, I don't actually work here. Willow will be right back."

Finally, Willow appeared at my side looking relieved and refreshed.

"Thank you so much, Jayne."

"That was thirty minutes. You said five."

"Yes, well, there are labor laws entitling me to a break. Can't be breaking laws, can we, Sheriff?"

"Labor laws aren't my jurisdiction. You going to be okay here?"

"I went to the ladies' room and got something to eat. I should be fine now. Thanks again."

I smiled at the genuine words and then gave her the twenty from the teenager and showed her the picture of what she bought. "When Morgan does come back, would you mention that I was looking for her?"

As the customers who'd been waiting for her to return descended on her like crows on carrion, all Willow could manage was a quick nod that she'd heard me.

I retrieved Meeka from behind the cardboard box and carried her outside.

"Little bit crazy in there, hey?"

Still shivering, she burrowed her face into my neck.

I held her close and scratched her ears. "I know what will make you feel better. Let's go up to Morgan's cottage and see if she's there."

Chapter 17

NORMALLY, I ENJOYED WALKING TO the Barlow property. The cottage Morgan shared with her mother was almost directly north of Shoppe Mystique and only took about twenty minutes to get to. That was time I didn't have to spend today, though, so I drove instead. Unfortunately, with all the people crossing the highway and those walking along the dirt road heading north past the residents' homes, driving took just as long as walking would have.

When we finally made it to the cottage and Meeka was free from her cage once again, she raced to the hedge that surrounded the backyard garden. She was probably looking for Pitch, Morgan's all-black rooster.

Standing by the hedge, I called out, "Briar? Are you in there?"

"I'm assuming because Meeka's here, trampling my asters, you must be Jayne."

Briar made me smile. "It's me. Sorry about your asters. Is Morgan here?"

"The front door is open. Come on around so I can see your pretty face."

I passed through the swinging gate on the fence surrounding the cottage's front yard, followed the short stone pathway to the front door, and let myself in. Every time I came here, I felt like I was coming home. Morgan and Briar had become like a sister and mother to me. They listened when I was down. They fed me when I was hungry, both physically and spiritually. They celebrated when I caught the bad guy. I wandered through the cottage to the kitchen with sage-green cabinets and then to the door that led to the garden. There, Briar was tending her plants with a thick shawl wrapped around her thin shoulders.

"What did I do to be so fortunate to receive a visit from you today?" Briar's hunched back was to me as she pushed pine mulch up around the base of the asters Meeka had squashed.

"You just have to be you to make me want to visit."

She let her head drop forward and chuckled.

"I'm looking for Morgan. Is she here?"

Briar got to her feet and faced me. "Why would she be here in the middle of the day? I assume you checked at the shop?"

"I did. Poor Willow was frantic. She's there all alone and the store is absolutely packed."

"Where is my daughter?" Briar murmured thoughtfully, more quizzical than concerned. She closed her eyes, tipped her face skyward, and held her hands slightly out to the side as though expecting the universe to answer her question.

"Willow told me that Morgan went out to lunch and had been gone for quite a while. One of my guests told me that a man named River Carr was looking for her. Maybe you met him at my party the other night?"

A smile turned Briar's mouth. "The intense one who looks like a warlock?"

"That's him. He seemed very interested in Morgan."

Briar crossed the garden to a patch of daisies and knelt next to them. "She seems equally so, if the fact that she kept talking about him last night means anything."

For as long as I had known Morgan, I had never once heard her talk about a man. It wasn't that she was opposed to dating, it was more that she didn't seem interested in any of the villagers. Or in having a man around all the time.

"I have just enough in my life," she told me once. "I don't need to divide my attention among other things."

An occasional tourist would catch her eye, but she never did anything about it. Maybe Carr was different. Well, clearly he was different, but was he one that Morgan would consider worthy of dividing her attention further for?

"Do you have any idea where she is? Not that it's urgent."

Briar squinted at me. "The fact that you bring up urgency tells me that it might be. What's going on?"

I inhaled, called on Sheriff Jayne to take over because Regular Jayne was starting to babble, and exhaled. "I don't want to worry you, but there was another death."

Briar sat back on her heels and folded her hands in her lap. "Morgan told me. The poor man. Why would this worry me?"

"It may be nothing, but I'm trying to locate all of those who'd had an altercation with the deceased. Mr. Carr had a little run-in with him yesterday. I'd like to speak with him."

"You're concerned that River may be a murderer?" She got up from the ground again and pointed to the nearby patio chairs.

"I'm not sure yet," I explained as I sat. "I can't be certain about method of death until I get the autopsy results." Briar arched a questioning eyebrow at me. "I'm trying to be proactive."

"You're trying to protect my daughter from a possible killer?"

I offered an apologetic smile. "See, now you're worried."

Briar patted my knee. "Allow me to ease your mind, about Morgan, at least. If something had happened to her, I would sense it. You know how connected we are."

I did. Nearly every time I was with the two of them,

they were either finishing each other's sentences or knew what the other was thinking after little more than a shared glance. Plenty of couples could do that. Newly dating ones especially tended to think it was so cute and a sign that they were meant to be together. Jonah used to finish my sentences all the time. Bugged the hell out of me because even though he got it right, it was more his need to be in control than a sweet, *he knows me so well, we must be soulmates* thing. The belief that completing sentences meant something significant held no water for me. Morgan and Briar's connection, however, was different. It was almost like they really could read one another's minds. I wasn't comfortable leaving my friend's safety to the hands of woo-woo, however.

"Morgan may be fine," I told Briar, "I certainly hope she is. I can't determine Carr's innocence until I talk to him."

"That is your job. To find guilty people. I wouldn't expect anything less from you."

"But?"

"But you always seem to be running around the village like a headless chicken."

From the depths of the garden, Pitch the rooster let out a noisy, annoyed squawk.

"Cool your jets," Briar called. "We aren't talking about you."

Oh, lordy, the people in this village. I couldn't help but laugh. It felt good.

"Stay a minute." Briar got up and headed for the house. I tried to tell her I was in a hurry and needed to get back to looking for Carr, but she silenced me with a pointed stare. "I'll be right back."

What was it with the internal timeclocks in this place? Willow's ten minutes was thirty. Briar's minute turned into ten. When she did return, she had a tray with tea and tiny sugar cookies.

"Briar, I really don't have—"

"You do have time."

As I forced my knees to stop bouncing with impatience, Briar poured tea and handed me a cup with a cookie tucked onto the saucer.

She sat in the chair next to me, sipped her tea, and sighed. "Morgan's 'Relax' blend. Isn't it wonderful?"

It was, but I'd need a gallon to settle me down today.

"Jayne, you're 'running on all cylinders' as the saying goes. Not necessarily a bad thing if the clock is ticking and you're heading for a final destination. A man has died and it's possible that his life was ended at the hands of another, but it's also possible that he was an unfortunate victim of a hit-and-run."

"That is possible, but not likely."

"Correct me if I'm wrong," she injected before I could say more, "but it seems you're trying to solve a case that may not even be a case."

My mind spun for an objection, and finally, I said, "I can't correct you."

"You need all the pieces before you can put a puzzle together. Remember?"

She had told me the same thing when I was trying to figure out the truth behind Gran's death. Briar knew what had happened forty years earlier but wouldn't tell me anything until I had gathered all the information I could from the others who had been here at the time.

"That's what I'm doing," I objected. "I'm investigating Halpern's death."

"You don't even know what your puzzle is supposed to look like yet," she countered, clinging to this growing-old analogy. "What if you're including pieces for a different picture?" She stared at me until I relented. "Why don't you wait until your doctor has more information for you?"

I agreed and stood to leave, but Briar stopped me again.

"I'm going to give you some advice as though you were my own daughter. Ready?"

That simple sentence caught me off guard. Was I ready? For Briar to treat me like her daughter? I sank back down onto my chair and swallowed the lump in my suddenly tight throat.

"You just opened a bed-and-breakfast. You and Tripp rushed through those renovations at breakneck speed trying to open before the end of the tourist season. You accomplished that goal, which is wonderful, but what are you focusing on now?"

I shook my head, unsure of what she wanted me to say.

"You're focused on a year into the future. Aren't you?"

"We are."

"If you keep doing that, you're going to miss your first year." She took one of my hands in both of hers. "Think of your B&B as a baby. They grow so fast. In two blinks, they're out on their own."

"Not your baby," I teased. "Yours is still with you."

"But I need her more than she needs me now."

I placed my free hand on top of the pile and squeezed. "Don't be so sure of that."

Briar smiled. She liked that comment. "My point is, you worked so hard for this. Don't miss these first rewarding moments."

That's basically what I'd told Tripp about our relationship. Yes, I wanted us to be together, but I didn't want to rush through anything. I wanted to take things slow, so we could learn everything about each other before moving on to … other things.

"That's some pretty good advice, Briar."

"And," she continued, "quit comparing Tripp to Jonah. You're always in the past or the future, never in the present. That's where life is, you know. The present."

While her words stung a little, she was spot on. I did need to spend more time in the moment. And I would, just as soon as I knew Morgan was okay and that there wasn't a killer wandering the village.

I stood and gave Briar a kiss on the cheek. "Thanks for treating me like your daughter. I may regret saying this, but feel free to do that whenever you want."

She pointed a starting-to-gnarl finger at me. "Careful what you ask for."

"Meeka, come!"

The little terrier, now more dirt colored than white, appeared from down one of the pea-gravel paths. Pitch followed, pecking at Meeka's tail like a naughty schoolboy pulling a girl's braids.

"Will you drop me off near Shoppe Mystique?" Briar asked.

"Sure," I agreed, confused. "Why?"

"You said Willow needs help. It's been a few months, but I think I remember how things run there."

Chapter 18

NOT THAT BRIAR NEEDED MY assistance, she was more physically fit than I was, but Meeka and I walked with her from the station to Shoppe Mystique. Besides, the more time with Briar, the better. She had a way of helping me feel more in control of situations.

"Before you ask me," Briar stated as we approached the shop, "yes, I'm sure I want to do this. I enjoy being around the customers."

Briar used to run the shop, but the stroke she suffered late last year ended that. To her, it had been a blessing in disguise, because now she got to spend her entire day tending the plants and herbs that would fill the shop's apothecary bottles. She also skillfully wove the grapevine wreaths Morgan sold there.

"Would you like me to stop back at the end of the day and see if you need a ride home?"

"That would be wonderful," she agreed. "I could walk, but I'll be tired after all this excitement, and it might be tomorrow before I get there."

She climbed the porch steps, opened the door, and had taken one step inside when I heard Willow's same calm yet frantic war cry from earlier. "Oh, thank the Goddess."

"Good deed done, Deputy Meeka."

She wagged her tail and pranced her paws.

"You're right. We do deserve a treat."

The good thing about the cooler weather was that the line at Treat Me Sweetly was half of what it normally was, not that Honey and Sugar would see that as a positive thing. There were a few people sitting at the pink metal café tables, but it wasn't nearly the crowd I'd become used to. My first impression of the Whispering Pines sweet shop was that it was one-part old-world bakery, one-part vintage ice cream shop, and one-part Willy Wonka candy store. I still thought that every time I walked in.

"Hey there, Sheriff," Honey greeted from behind the ice cream counter. She was making fresh waffle cones, wedging large handmade chocolate chips into the pointy ends to prevent drips. The shop smelled delicious.

"Looks like the weather is keeping customers away," I commented.

"Oh, that's no big thing." She swatted a dismissive hand at me. "Gives Sugar a chance to make more cookies and me a chance to whip up more ice cream. If we didn't have some down times, we wouldn't be ready for the busy times. What can I get for you?"

I stared into the ice cream freezer at the dozen and a half different flavors. Then I looked up at the hand-drawn chalkboard menu sign. Two items stood out to me.

"I think a chilly day like this calls for a hot fudge sundae with nuts and a mug of hot cocoa."

Meeka let out a little *ruff*.

"I would never forget your biscuits, Miss Meeka," Honey assured. "Go on and have a seat, I'll bring it right over to you."

We chose a table in the corner, and thirty seconds later Sugar dropped into the chair across from me.

"Any news on the newest dead guy?" she asked.

"Nothing yet. I'm waiting for a callback from the medical examiner."

"Your deputy was in here earlier." She glanced under the table at Meeka and amended her statement. "The human one. He was asking about a customer of ours who made a complaint about Mr. Halpern. He was really upset."

"The customer who made the complaint was upset or my deputy?"

She made a face at me. "The customer."

"Were you able to help Deputy Reed? Is he tracking the man down?"

"I gave him a description," Sugar said, "but I don't know if the guy is still in the village or even where he was staying. Martin was going to go around and try to track him down. There are only a handful of places to stay in Whispering Pines."

Those would be my B&B, The Inn, the rental cottages, the campground, or with one of the villagers. That last option would make the man harder to find.

"This guy must have been really upset if you were able to give a description. You have so many people come through every day, you can't possibly remember everyone."

Honey set my sundae and mug of cocoa in front of me along with a little paper sack of biscuits for Meeka.

"Enjoy," she chirped like a songbird. "Let me know if you want seconds."

"Seconds on dessert?"

The sisters looked at each other and then at me like I'd slipped a cog.

"That's never up for debate around here," Honey said with a shake of her head and then went back to her waffle cones.

Sugar returned to our prior discussion. "I don't remember everyone. You're right, that would be impossible, but this guy was very memorable. First, you can't miss him. He's huge. Second, he made a bigger commotion than Halpern did."

Folks like Sugar made my job easy. They were always

happy to talk, so I could sit back and take notes. Or eat ice cream in this instance.

"I didn't see the actual event, only the aftermath. There was a woman making a big deal about Halpern touching her. Rightly so. Then the big guy, her boyfriend I guess, went nuts. He started hollering and making a scene. Honestly, he was so loud he was scaring customers away. I finally had to kick them all out." She sat back, crossed her arms, and pursed her lips. She was getting upset about the incident all over again. "Not that I'm trying to tell you how to do your business, Sheriff, but I suggested to your deputy that he take a close look at that guy."

Sugar liked to be in charge. I could have pointed out that taking a closer look was exactly what Reed was doing when he came in to ask about the man, but instead said, "I agree. Thanks for the information."

She stared absently across the shop. "It's starting to wear, you know? All these deaths, I mean."

"I do know. Four murders and a suicide in three months in a village this size? Plus, my grandmother's questionable death in February. Not sure what the statistics are, but I know this is way outside the norm." I took a sip of cocoa. "If I didn't know better, I'd swear I had something to do with them."

I was joking, but Sugar fixed a look on me.

"You mean because the murders started when you arrived? Hate to tell you, but some people around the village have wondered the same thing." She patted my arm, a more condescending than comforting gesture. "Most of us know it's not you."

"We all know it's not her." Honey joined us at the little table.

"Of course, it's not me," I echoed around the spoonful of sundae in my mouth then swallowed. "That first death, Yasmine Long's, had been in the works before I even knew I was coming."

I could hear Morgan in my ear whispering, "But the Universe knew."

"Who's saying such horrible things?" Honey demanded of her sister.

"Don't get yourselves all worked up," Sugar said. "We know you're not responsible for the deaths, Jayne, but you might've woken something up. In that case, you'll be the one to shoo away the dark cloud that's settled over the village."

A little girl with huge hazel eyes was staring at us from the only other occupied table in the shop.

"We shouldn't be talking about such things out in the open," Honey whispered.

I matched her volume. "This sounds suspiciously like Whispering Pines woo-woo. Tell me that's not what you're blaming this on. You don't honestly think bad juju is causing these murders. Do you?"

"I'm not saying anything." Sugar crossed her arms again.

"It would be bad karma," Honey corrected. "Juju is basically luck. Karma is a bounce back for past behavior. In the village's case, the bad things that happened forty years ago are coming back at us."

Was she serious? I stared at her and blinked. She gave me a matter-of-fact nod then got up to wait on some people who'd just come in.

"Isn't it your job," Sugar asked, "to look at all possibilities before coming to a conclusion?"

"You actually want me to consider karma as a murder suspect? Who am I supposed to send to prison?"

Sugar sat straight in her chair, not backing down from this. "You read your grandmother's journals. You know something negative has been slithering through this village since it was founded. And you know who a majority of that negativity is coming from."

"You mean Flavia." She was the most negative Original I knew. While I'd be happy to pin the blame for everything bad on her, I couldn't prove she'd done anything. "Do you honestly think her lifelong bad attitude is the reason for a rash of murders?"

"Maybe not her alone, Goddess knows Donovan did some damage. Sheriff Brighton was also far from innocent. None of us are perfect and all contributed a little. The point is, only so much will fit in a pot before it overflows."

I studied her for a few seconds. She seemed serious about this. "How do you propose I go about fixing this kind of problem?"

"Don't know, that's not what I get paid to do."

Anger flared in the hollow of my chest at the tone in her voice. "Are you saying I'm not doing my job?"

She stood, avoiding my eyes, and gestured at my sundae. "Enjoy your treat."

I never quite knew how to take Sugar. She was very friendly when I first got here. Things had changed, though. Since the day the council had voted me in as sheriff, Sugar, who had voted against me, would make me feel warm and fuzzy one minute, cold and itchy the next. Right now, I was hot and angry. I glanced under the table at Meeka who was licking up the crumbs from her biscuits.

"Are you done?"

She wagged her tail, ears perked.

"Wonderful. Let's go back to the station and call Dr. Bundy. I need to know if we should continue investigating or call it a day."

Chapter 19

"WHEN DID YOU GET BACK?" I asked Reed when we entered the station.

"About an hour ago. Did you have any luck with your B&B folks?"

"More insight into our victim, but nothing suspicious." I watched Meeka jump up on the cot in her cell, spin in three circles, and drop down in a furry heap. "Come into my office and let's talk about what we've got."

While I agreed with Briar's assertion that I needed to be sure I was gathering the right pieces for the puzzle, I couldn't just sit and wait for the autopsy results. I'd continue treating this like a murder.

Reed took a seat in a chair across from my desk as I wheeled over our portable whiteboard.

"Here's our victim." I wrote *Nick Halpern* at the top. "We suspect that he died in one of two ways." I added *Murder / Hit-and-Run* next to his name and *Suspects* below that. "I don't know about you, but I don't have anyone leading the pack right now."

More to fill up space on the whiteboard than anything else, I added the names of the B&B guests I'd spoken with—Jeremy, Trevor, Alicia, Derek, and Constance—and gave Reed a quick rundown on each of them.

"None of those people raised suspicion in you?"

I stood back to take in my list. "You know what, I do have someone to put at the top of the list." I drew a red circle around *Constance Halpern*.

"The wife," Reed said thoughtfully. "It's always the spouse, isn't it?"

"In many cases. I made a note that Constance's reactions didn't feel right to me, but I kind of wrote it off as her being in shock. I have to admit, she struck me as being more relieved over Nick's death than upset by it. In fact, she said as much."

"Her husband was a jerk," Reed said with no compassion. "Don't know how many people would admit it, but I'm sure plenty would feel the same way if they were in her situation. The relief will probably wear off."

"She said that, too, that her emotions will change. We have to put someone at the top of our suspect list, though, so for now, it's her."

"You said Alicia and Derek aren't in the running," Reed noted.

"They're not." I drew red lines through their names. "They're familiar with our victim but didn't know him well. I don't in any way think they were responsible for his murder. If this even was a murder. It's possible that it wasn't."

Briar's voice echoed in my head. *Then why are you going through this exercise?*

"What about the other two?" Reed pointed at the board. "Jeremy and Trevor?"

"Jeremy was kind of odd. He seemed, I don't know, angry maybe?"

"At who?"

"The entire group."

He shoved his hands in his pockets. "So that makes him a murder suspect?"

My deputy challenging me was fine on a normal day,

but it was pushing my boundaries after the encounter with Sugar.

"That's not why," I snapped like a petulant teenager. Reed held up his hands in apology, and I waved it off. We'd both been at this for a long time today. "Jeremy's interview was strange. I had to keep digging to get at the truth for even the simplest of questions. I couldn't tell if he has a memory problem or was trying to cover something up." I shook my head, still confused by him. "He's only been in the picture for eight months but couldn't remember when he'd met anyone. And while I couldn't really find a motive for him to kill Nick, I think it's worth noting that he doesn't seem to be a very emotionally stable person."

"Fair enough. What about Trevor?"

"I don't think Trevor was involved either. The problem is, I might be too close to see signs in him. He was one of my best friends in college."

Reed leaned forward in his chair. "I'm not sure I knew that. Did you tell me that before?"

I scanned back over the last twenty-four to thirty-six hours, trying to remember any conversations my deputy and I may have had about my B&B guests. Then I pushed further back into my memory, to when the group had first made reservations with us. Had I mentioned anything back then?

"Probably not," I finally said.

"Sheriff, I know I'm new to this kind of police work, but if you want to hand off things like this to me, I'll pull out every tip and trick you've taught me to make sure we don't get stuck in a loophole."

Once again, as I had felt many times over the last two months, I realized what a good decision it was to hire this man.

"I appreciate that, Reed. And I have to say, it eases my mind greatly that you are so aware of these potential problems. If we start to reconsider Trevor as a suspect, you can question him to see what you think."

A smile turned his lips for a second and then he returned to his serious self. "Will this be a problem with any of your other guests?"

"I haven't spoken with Kristina Mandel yet. She was also a good friend in college. That interview could get a little tricky."

On the board next to her name, I wrote *sister-in-law of victim*. I stared at her name and those words for a long while, remembering Trevor's reaction when I asked if he thought she could ever be unfaithful to her husband. Trevor was right, I knew Kristina. There was no way she was guilty of Nick's death. I turned to my deputy.

"You know what? I can handle talking to her alone." Then, just to make sure I was being a responsible law enforcement official, I added, "But stay on guard just in case."

"Isn't that likely to put a hiccup in your friendship?"

I smiled. "Look at you, playing both sides of the fence. It might cause a small issue, but Kristina is a smart woman. She'll understand that I'm just doing my job and not attacking her."

"When are you planning to talk to her?"

"As soon as I see her. When I was at Pine Time earlier today, she and Kyle were out hiking. I sure hope they're back by now. They left right after breakfast." My tired brain needed a minute to figure out what to do next. "Let's finish with what we're doing here, and then I'll call Dr. Bundy for an update. I don't know about you, but I'm wiped out. We've been at this for more than twelve hours already. If Kyle and Kristina are back, I'll talk to them tonight. Otherwise, I'd like to be done soon."

Reed had started nodding halfway through that plan. "I like it. That means Kyle and Kristina Mandel are on the list until we can take them off the list."

"Right. That's all I've ... Wait, I've got one more." I

added *River Carr* to the bottom of my suspects list.

"He's the dude with the Aston Martin, isn't he?"

"That's him."

"Why are we adding him?"

"Because he had a minor altercation with Halpern yesterday. I haven't spoken with him yet because no one has seen him since this morning. A little bit of asking around turned up that he was looking for Morgan Barlow. I don't know if he found her, but she went out for lunch and no one has seen her since."

I couldn't let myself think that something had happened to her. Until proof showed me otherwise, I'd assume she was fine.

"What kind of altercation?" Reed asked.

I explained to him about how Halpern immediately went after Carr when he came down for breakfast. It seemed absurd, despite what Morgan said about David Copperfield and the Statue of Liberty, to think Carr could have convinced Halpern that he was choking. Still, I told Reed about the finger down the throat thing anyway.

"Sounds like mind control to me," Reed said with a shrug.

"You really believe in that?"

"Sure I do. It has nothing to do with magic, though." He rubbed his chin. "Basically, what illusionists do is they start talking about something." He made a face and rubbed his chin more vigorously. "I might mention that I have an itch, for example, and the next thing you know, you're scratching your chin."

I froze, my hand to my own face. "Nice trick."

"It's not a trick. It's just influencing someone to do what we want them to. People do it all the time. You want your boyfriend to give you candy for Valentine's Day? Start talking about this new type of chocolate you're dying to try two weeks before. Reverse psychology works the same way. Want your kid to eat better? Tell them how much you hate applesauce."

By the look on his face, that was something his mother had tried on him.

"Apples should be crunchy," he added.

"In your opinion, then," I said, laughing, "that's all that happened when Carr dragged his finger down his throat and Halpern started choking?"

"You've said it yourself a hundred times, Sheriff. There is no such thing as magic."

"Carr probably is innocent, but we're leaving him on the list until I talk to him." I stood back, examined my suspect board, and mentally went through the list of everyone I had spoken to today. "Okay, now that's all I've got. Who do you want to add to the list?"

"Two people. I spoke to a lot more than that but going off your tips to watch body language and all that, there's only two that I would go back and look at again."

"Good." To keep things immediately recognizable, I grabbed a green marker for his notes. "Who are they?"

"First is a woman: Elaine Snow. She was one who had been physically assaulted by Halpern at your party."

I turned away from the board to look over my shoulder at him. "Please tell me that by 'physically assaulted,' you mean he grabbed her butt."

That was bad enough. The thought of anything more serious happening to someone I had invited to my home made my blood boil.

"It was a little more than that. He did grab her backside but also brushed the back of his hand across her breast as he was supposedly about to shake her hand in apology."

I put my hands over my eyes and shook my head, counting to ten in my head before speaking. "I will never understand what makes a person—man, woman, or other—think it's in any way okay to do something like that to another person. The one thing we all have is the unalienable right to our own bodies."

I lowered my hands to see Reed staring at me.

He squirmed a little. "First, let me state for the record that I agree with you one hundred percent. However, I can see you're about to go down a rabbit hole with that topic, and we should probably stay on this one."

I took a moment to pace the length of my office a few times and calm down. Reed was right. I'd been standing with my toes hanging over a very large hole. Glad he pulled me away.

"All right, back to business." I returned to the whiteboard. "This woman you feel we need to keep an eye on, Elaine Snow, what's her story?"

"Like I told you, Halpern physically assaulted her. Ms. Snow struck me as being a woman that will fight for injustices until the very last breath has left her body."

"Do you feel she would have done something to our victim? Or was she justifiably angry, possibly to the extreme, over what he did?"

He considered this. "I'm leaning toward that second option. I think she's more of a vocal protestor than a take physical action type person."

"Let me guess, she talked at you for a while."

"Talked *at* me is exactly right. She went on for probably ten minutes and wouldn't let me say a word. She's a tiny little thing, too, so unless I'm dead wrong about her and Dr. Bundy discovers bullet holes or knife wounds, I don't think Ms. Snow is where we should focus our efforts right now."

"In other words, leave her on the board until we can remove her." I would never accuse anyone without proof, but this guilty until proven innocent method of investigating worked for me. Many times, the guilty party surprised me. "She was your first suspect. Who's your other?"

"Doug Croft. This is the guy who disrupted business over at Treat Me Sweetly."

"I was just over there; sounds like he caused quite a scene. Honey is still upset about it. Do you know what actually happened?"

"First off, Croft is big. We're talking six foot four, a good two hundred fifty pounds of solid muscle. He's a bodybuilder who is obsessively protective of his girlfriend."

"And Halpern accosted Croft's girlfriend."

"Exactly. Sounds like Halpern was a serial groper or whatever. The girlfriend's report was almost identical to Elaine Snow's. She said that Halpern was behind her in line and he brushed his hand across her butt. When she spun around to confront him, same thing; he let his arm brush against her breast as he moved to shake hands in apology. She slapped him, and the boyfriend, Croft, went ballistic."

"Good for her. Honey said other customers were afraid enough of Croft that they left the shop. Anything else about him I need to know?"

"I have no proof, but I'm guessing steroid use." Reed tapped his fingers on his upper chest. "He was wearing a low V-neck T-shirt, and I saw what looked like acne marks. There were some spots on his face, too."

"Steroids would also explain his explosive temper."

"Exactly."

"Might be nothing, but I agree we should look closer. Do you know where he's staying?"

"At The Inn. He told me they had planned to be here all weekend, but that if the weather didn't get better, they might leave early. As I was questioning him about Halpern, the girlfriend alibied him. Claimed he was with her all night."

I thought about how to handle this for a minute. "All right, let's leave him alone until we hear from Dr. Bundy. We have a possible motive, but Nick Halpern died in the middle of the night. If Doug Croft is staying at The Inn, what would he be doing clear over by the west side parking lot at two o'clock in the morning?" Reed blinked but didn't offer an explanation. We were both getting punchy. "We'll keep him near the top of the list, but his motive is thin. I'd like a better connection there before we approach him again. Do we agree that we can put Elaine Snow at the bottom?"

He nodded. "She was angry, but vocal doesn't mean violent."

I chuckled. "That's good. I like that."

"If you talk to Croft, would you like some backup?"

"I might. I'll let you know. For now, I'm going to call Dr. Bundy for an update."

As I waited for someone to pick up the line, I stared at our list on the whiteboard. Honestly, we didn't have much. Constance maybe, Jeremy but not likely, and we'd see about this guy over at The Inn.

"Medical Examiner's office, this is Joan."

"Hey, Joan. This is Sheriff O'Shea in Whispering Pines and before you ask, no, we don't have another body. I'm calling to get an update from Dr. Bundy."

"Hmm." A tapping sound, like Joan was typing on a keyboard, came over the line. "It doesn't look like he's gotten to him yet, but I'll put you through. Hang on."

After nearly three minutes, Dr. Bundy picked up and immediately reported, "I've got nothing for you, Sheriff. I know you're anxious, but I told you I'd give you a call as soon as I knew something."

"I know. And I know how busy you are. I was just hoping maybe you had something for me. Even something little. I'm trying to interview suspects and I'm not even sure which questions to ask them. I feel like this is an exercise in futility. You know what I mean?"

"Look, I know your clock is ticking, but I've got" — more computer keyboard sounds — "two more stiffs ... Sorry. I have two more people to take care of before I can get to your guy. I can't promise it will be today, you woke me up at dawn's butt crack. Which probably explains why I'm talking like a teenager today."

"And acting like one," someone in the background called out.

"He's number three in the lineup, first thing in the morning. Does that work for you?"

"What else can I say but yes?" I rubbed my tired eyes. "I've said it before, but I'll say it one more time, I appreciate you, Doc. And I do know I'm not your only customer."

He snorted at this. "Hard to tell sometimes. I'll let you go so I can get back to my bodies. You've been going since two thirty this morning as well. I know you're trying hard to get on top of this, but we're not even sure what *this* is yet. Go spend a little time with that guy of yours. Get some sleep. Then you'll be ready when I actually have something for you."

If I didn't know better, I'd swear he and Briar were in cahoots. "I've got a couple more things to take care of and then I'll do that. Talk to you tomorrow, Doc."

The station's other line had rung while I was on the phone. Whoever it was, I could hear Reed talking to them. Didn't sound urgent, more conversational.

"Okay … Okay, yes, I understand. I'll be there."

"What's going on?" I asked from my doorway when he hung up. "Anything I need to know about?"

"No, that was just my mother. My aunt Reeva invited us over for dinner tonight." He stared at me with a look that begged me to give him an urgent assignment.

I burst out laughing. "Sorry, Martin. You're on your own with this."

"Are you sure the baseboards don't need scrubbing? Files need alphabetizing?"

"Maybe this is a good thing," I offered. "Try looking on the bright side."

"Bright side?" He stared at me, barely blinking. "I'm exhausted, so maybe I'll fall asleep in the middle of dinner. Then I wouldn't have to listen to the arguments. How's that for bright side?"

"More dim than bright. I can only give you five out of ten points for it."

He rolled his eyes at my lame joke.

"All right, we're both beat. Dr. Bundy doesn't have anything more for us today, says he'll get our results in the morning. Go get ready for your dinner. Do you get to bring Lupe at least?"

"First, I would never subject Lupe to the Flavia and Reeva show. Second, she's so busy with her column, I haven't seen her since the party."

"That explains why she hasn't been over here trying to elbow in on this murder investigation." In this village, only Violet found out about things faster than Lupe Gomez.

"She sequestered herself in her cabin. Said something about having her food delivered. I tried to explain the benefit of a break now and then, but she's obsessed with making sure these last articles are perfect. She says they could help her get her next job."

A yawn snuck up on me. "Sorry. I promise, it's not you. Okay, that's it. Grab your walkie-talkie, flip the sign over, and let's get out of here."

I didn't even have to call for Meeka, she was waiting for me by the back door. My deputy and I weren't the only ones ready to be done with this day.

Chapter 20

IT ALWAYS AMAZED ME THAT when Meeka was the most tired, she seemed to come up with the most energy. Maybe she had self-charging batteries and recharged them by running around. I'd barely gotten the door of her cage open, and she was out of the SUV. The little white blur had made two laps around the yard before I made it from the garage to the back-patio doors of the house.

"You're home early," Tripp said when I walked in. "Guess that's a good thing since you started sometime yesterday."

"No, two thirty was officially today."

He had ingredients spread out all over the kitchen island. Something garlicky was bubbling in a pot on the stove. Or maybe it was coming from the oven. Maybe both. Either way, there was a lot of garlic going on.

"What are you working on? It smells amazing."

"It's been so chilly, I thought something warm and comforting sounded good. How does spaghetti with meatballs and garlic bread sound?"

"It sounds like I love you."

We both froze and stared at each other. His eyebrows were arched in surprise and a little smirk turned his lips. Neither of us had said the L-word yet. We hadn't said anything more than that we really liked each other. I knew it was more than that, but it was too soon for love. Wasn't it? We'd only known each other a little over three months.

"Relax," he said with a naughty little grin. "You're exhausted; I can see it in your eyes. I'm not even sure how you're still upright. I'll give you a pass this time."

If I stood there much longer, a slightly embarrassing situation would turn excruciating. I'd take his pass and treat it as a ticket to rewind the last thirty seconds. "Spaghetti sounds wonderful. When will it be ready?"

"I haven't made the pasta yet, so in as little as fifteen minutes or as many as you need. How many do you need?"

"First tell me, do you know if Kyle and Kristina came back from their hike?"

"They did come back, and I think they're still here. They said they were going out for dinner tonight to celebrate her good news. Their good news. You know what I mean."

Finally, everyone knew. I hated being the only one knowing news like that.

"If I talk with them before they go to dinner, I can hopefully clock out for the rest of the night. I'll go find them and let you know when I'm done. Then you can do the pasta while I take a shower. I didn't get the chance for one this morning."

He gave me a little salute and a nice kiss that helped revive my energy. "Go finish being a sheriff."

Was there a more understanding boyfriend in the world? I didn't think so. How lucky was I?

"Come on, Meeka."

She gave me a look that clearly said, *Tripp is cooking. Crumbs might fall.* So I left her with him.

Alone now, I climbed the staircase to the second floor, took a left to go down the hall, and stopped at the room in the center on the back side of the house. The room that used to be my dad's when he was a little boy. It was the second biggest in the house and had an amazing view of the lake.

My favorite of its features was the alcove. I could picture my dad spending hours on top of hours, especially in the winter, curled up in that window seat reading books about Egypt, the pyramids, and ancient mummy curses.

From out in the hall, I could hear Kyle and Kristina laughing. Something that was understandable in that they were about to become parents. Not quite so understandable in that they'd just had a death in their family. I knocked, took one step back into the hallway, and waited. Two seconds later, Kyle opened the door.

"I'm sorry to interrupt," I began, "sounds like you two are having a good time in there."

Kyle's expression went blank for just a second and then he smiled. "I imagine you heard our news."

"I did. Congratulations." I smiled but kept my voice even. "Again, I'm sorry to interrupt but I've been waiting all day to talk with you two. Tripp told me you're going out to dinner to celebrate. This shouldn't take long. Should I come in or would you prefer to go down to the back patio with me?"

Kyle looked over his shoulder into the room and back to me. "Kristina is still getting ready. She'll need a few more minutes. Why don't I come down with you now and she can come when she's ready?"

I looked around him to my friend. "Kristina? Can you meet me on the back patio as soon as you're done here?"

She came up behind Kyle, wearing a lightweight robe and wrapped her arms around his waist. The smile on her face faded when she saw the look on mine.

"You want to talk about Nick, don't you? Does it have to be tonight? It'll kind of put a damper on things."

Never, in all the years I'd known her, had Kristina been selfish. She always put other people's needs first. That's how we all knew from the day we met her that she'd be a great nurse. I wanted to think that this response was due to her excitement over the baby. Otherwise, the person I remembered from college had changed a lot in five relatively short years.

"This won't take long," I repeated. "Just a few questions and you can be on your way."

"Okay." She frowned. "But it's not like we're going anywhere. We could do this in the morning."

Kyle followed me down the stairs and through the great room. I paused in the kitchen for a glass of water and offered him one, which he declined. He made small talk the entire time, commenting on how tired I must've been after such a long day, complimenting Tripp on the wonderful aromas as we passed him, and almost bragging about the great hike he and Kristina had gone on.

On the patio, I indicated Kyle should take the same seat where I'd positioned everyone else, so his back was to the house. I turned on the electric heater before sitting, then made a display of switching on my voice recorder and flipping through the notes I'd taken while interviewing the others this afternoon.

"You were gone a long time today," I began. "Where did you go?"

"We drove over to the Apostle Islands. A visit to the islands has been on our to-do list for a long time and since we're relatively close here ..."

"Apostle Islands? Must've been freezing by Lake Superior today."

"It was strange, we got maybe twenty miles out of the village, and it warmed significantly. It was a beautiful day up there. We hiked along the shore and found a great little burger place for lunch."

That black cloud Sugar claimed was hovering over the village popped into my mind. His twenty-mile comment made me want to turn on the Weather Channel and see if there was literally something over us.

"Maybe that warmth will find us again soon." Enough chitchat. "You two went by yourselves. I thought this was supposed to be a couples' weekend."

"We're in kind of a strange situation."

His words and tone were excited, but his eyes were flat. No joking wink-wink nudge-nudge comment about all the fun they had trying to get pregnant. The sparkle I saw in most excited expectant fathers wasn't there. Neither was there the panic common in unprepared ones. Of course, everyone reacted differently, but Kyle's attitude was very report-the-facts.

"What do you mean you're in a strange situation?"

"Kristina's on top of the world. We've been trying so hard to get pregnant." He pinched his nose, as though fending off a sneeze. "Turns out, she'd been planning that this would be a celebration weekend. She envisioned lots of excitement surrounding the news, but it's a little hard for us, or the others, to show excitement with Nick dying and all. Then she and Constance had a fight this morning, so we thought it would be best to get a little space for a while."

"They fought? What about?"

"I probably shouldn't call it a fight. It was more a venting of frustrations. The sisters tend to obsess, and they'd both been wrapped up in their own worlds lately. Constance has obviously been upset about Nick and his dramas. All Kristina has been able to think about was getting pregnant." He looked straight at me, his expression blank, and then a hint of a smile played at his mouth. "She was on me all the time, if you know what I mean."

There was the wink-wink comment I'd expected, but it was more of a forced afterthought.

I held his gaze. "I think I do know. Speaking of Nick, what can you tell me about him?"

Kyle didn't answer right away. It was like he was waiting for more guidance on the topic. When I didn't supply any, he said, "I can tell you a number of things. I've known him for, what, almost seven years?"

He knew what I was asking, but I could lead if that's

what he wanted. "I noticed quite a lot of tension between the two of you almost as soon as you got here. Has your relationship always been tense?"

"Always? No. I can't say that we were buddies, we never hung out and watched games together or anything like that, but it's not like there was animosity every time we were together." He paused as though waiting for me to fill in the blanks from there. When I remained quiet, he added, "Just because he was married to my sister-in-law didn't mean we had to be friends. I'm not sure what more I can say about that."

I flipped to the notes from Jeremy's interview. "The consensus is that Nick started harassing women after he lost his job six months ago. Does that sound like an accurate statement?"

"It does."

"Why do you think he reacted to losing his job that way?"

Kyle eased back, rested his arms on the back of the loveseat, and casually propped his right foot on his left knee. "Nick was ridiculously proud of his job. They don't have kids, they don't even have a pet, so that job was all he had. Seems he was pretty good at it. Made a boatload of money. Had a lot of clout. I don't know exactly what was going on in his head, but I can understand the devastation of losing all that. Things fell apart fast for him after that woman accused him."

"Talk to me about breakfast yesterday. Nick was saying some rather rude things to and about your wife."

Kyle's arms came down from the back of the loveseat and rested in his lap. "He could really push buttons, couldn't he? I don't know what that was all about. I think Kristina was the most convenient target. Constance stopped taking his guff months ago. No one could take satisfaction in saying anything to Alicia; the woman is a saint. Besides, Derek would've kicked Nick's ass if he even looked at her wrong."

"You were defending Kristina pretty well, too."

He smiled, but his eyes remained flat. "Thanks."

I'd intended it as an observation rather than a compliment. Either way, not the response I'd anticipated. Kyle seemed to pick up on that.

"Any decent man would, wouldn't he? She's my wife, of course I'm going to come to her defense." His nostrils flared, and he rubbed his nose. And through it all, his expression remained impassive.

"A second ago you said that 'Constance stopped taking his guff months ago'. What exactly did you mean by that? Was he being abusive toward her? What had their relationship been like since he lost his job?"

"If you mean did he hit her, I couldn't say. You'll have to ask Kristina about that. She never indicated anything like that to me." He reconsidered that. "Abuse doesn't just mean physical, though, does it? He obviously was verbally abusive to her, very disrespectful. I don't know for sure, I didn't see them much over the last few months, but I can only assume that things weren't good in their home. I could see, the other guys probably could, too, that Nick had a hard time with Constance being the breadwinner. Especially because she wins a lot of bread."

"The 'guys?' Just curious, do you mean that literally or are you including the entire group, the women, too?"

His eyes narrowed. "I meant that literally. For men ... For *most* men, our careers are everything. We're programmed to be the income generator."

I mentally reminded myself that I wasn't here to make character judgments. My job was to gather information. Now was not the time to debate genetics versus sexism.

Tapping my pen on my notebook like I'd remembered a point I forgot to mention, I said, "Let's go back to the topic of Nick and your wife for a moment."

Kyle immediately shifted positions, lowering his right

foot and propping up the left.

"I couldn't help but notice," I continued, "that Kristina didn't react much to Nick's comments yesterday morning. She didn't seem at all offended by his barrage. In fact, she barely responded; her attention stayed focused on her food."

Kyle's only reaction was to clench his jaw. Then again, I hadn't asked a question.

"You know your wife, what do you think she was feeling?"

He lowered his foot, leaned forward, and rested his elbows on his knees. I made a note of the aggressive pose.

"Kristina embarrasses easily and hates being the center of attention. If I had to guess, I'd say she was simply trying to fade into the background. That's what she does."

"Must be something new," I countered. "I never noticed that about her. Do you think that maybe she was angry over Nick's comments?"

"That would be a safe bet. Wouldn't you be angry if someone accused you of being a slut?"

"Angry enough to retaliate?"

This time he laughed, surprised. "Kristina? Retaliate? She took an oath to heal. Not a real one, of course; that's for doctors. Regardless, my wife is a pacifist. Injuring someone, let alone killing them, is not an action she would take."

"Do you know where your wife was the night Nick Halpern died?"

He folded his hands together and placed them over his abdomen. "What exactly are you asking, Sheriff?"

"It's a simple question. Do I need to ask it again?"

He paused and narrowed his eyes at me before answering. "She was in bed with me."

"All night?"

"I can't know what she does while I'm sleeping, can I? As far as I know, my wife was in bed all night?"

"And what about you? Where—?"

Before I could finish my question, the patio door flew open.

Chapter 21

KRISTINA WAS DRESSED TO IMPRESS in a berry-colored sequin-encrusted knee-length halter dress and silver stilettoes.

"Sorry. I took a little longer than I'd planned." She set a glass of water on the table in front of us, dropped onto the loveseat next to her husband, and smiled over at him. "I wanted to look especially nice tonight."

"I assume you're done with me now?" Kyle gestured to the upper floor of the house and then rubbed his nose again. "Is it okay if I go and get ready for my date with my wife now?"

"Do you have allergies, Kyle?" I tapped my nose, and he echoed the motion. Just like Reed's chin trick. How fun. "I noticed that you've been rubbing your nose a lot."

He furrowed his brow, confused at my observation. "Sometimes in the spring. Maybe something on our hike irritated me."

Or he'd been lying through his teeth. There was a reason Pinocchio's nose grew instead of his lies manifesting in some other way.

"You should stop in at the healing center or Shoppe Mystique. I'm sure one or the other would have something to help with that."

He pointed upstairs again. "Are we done?"

"Of course," I said. "I know where you are if I have any more questions."

He disappeared into the house before I could say another word.

I stopped the voice recorder to save Kyle's file, then started it again and turned my attention to Kristina. "Sounds like you had a nice day."

She told me basically the same thing Kyle had, except Kristina added many more details–the heat of the sun on her face, the beauty of the Apostle Islands, the smell of Lake Superior, the salty juiciness of her burger.

"I think the pregnancy hormones are enhancing my senses." She rubbed her belly, even though she didn't even have a baby bump yet.

"A day on the islands seemed like a good thing to do right after finding out that your brother-in-law had died?"

The smile on her pretty face froze. "Constance didn't want me around. We had a fight, and I decided to leave her alone."

"Kristina, I have to say, you don't seem as upset over Nick's death as I would expect."

Her shoulders dropped, and her demeanor changed. She gave the appearance of taking off giddiness and putting on sorrow. She seemed to become visibly smaller almost like, as Kyle had said, she was trying to disappear.

"Of course Nick's death is an awful thing. You don't understand, though. Constance has been going through hell with him for the last six months." She stared down at her delicate hands folded in her lap. "I did my best to help her by being there for Nick."

"What do you mean 'being there' for him?"

"I guess because we're nurses, we treated him almost like a patient getting in-home care. We took shifts, for lack of a better term. When she needed a break, I took over."

"Sounds very clinical. What exactly would you do for

him?"

"He didn't need physical or medical help, so I offered an empathetic ear mostly. He didn't say much, guys usually don't, but when he wanted to talk, I listened. There were times when he'd rant and rage."

"What would he get angry about? Other than the obvious accusation against him."

"Oh, there was more than just the one."

"You mean there were more harassment allegations?"

"Right. He swore he didn't do anything, and I believed him. He said it was a 'join the bandwagon' thing. Women at work looking to get ahead by tearing down a good man."

Possibly. Or maybe Kristina had jumped on the Nick bandwagon. There were always at least two sides to every situation.

"What else angered him?"

"Things like the fact that he couldn't even get an interview much less a new job. Constance being at work so much was a big thing." She pursed her lips and stared out at the lake. "He just wanted attention. Not like a little kid wanting mommy but like someone who simply wanted some of their spouse's time."

She grew quiet and seemed to disappear a little.

"Do you think he was jealous of Constance's promotion?"

She nodded like she'd been expecting this question. "His career meant everything to him. You must understand how much the loss of a job could devastate a man like Nick. He was all but running that place. I imagine it was a sort of power rush for him." She smiled. "That's kind of what Kyle's job is for him, only on a smaller level."

"Kyle runs an athletic club?"

"Not quite. He manages the finances for a chain of martial arts gyms. He loves his job. Too much sometimes."

We were getting off track, and I was getting more tired by the second. "Kristina, was Nick ever violent with

Constance? Or you? I asked her that earlier, and she insisted he never was."

Kristina looked at me as though I had insinuated the earth was flat. For the first time since we'd started talking, she became emotional over something other than her pregnancy. "You think Nick was murdered and that Constance killed him?"

I did my best to remain as calm as she was becoming worked up. "I didn't say that."

"But that's what you implied. No, Jayne ... Or should I say, Sheriff O'Shea?" She glared at me. "I can assure you with absolute certainty that my sister did not kill her husband."

Maybe I should have let Reed handle this one. Taking these questions from him would've been difficult for her. Taking them from me seemed to be insulting.

"Believe it or not, Kristina, I do understand how hard these questions must be."

She continued glaring, then exhaled, blowing away some of her anger. "Look, honestly, I have been worried a little about my sister's safety, but I never once got the impression she was thinking about ending his life."

Her words trailed off, and she paled.

"Something just occurred to you. What?"

"Constance joined a gun club."

This woke me up a little. "She what? When?"

"Last year, way before Nick's problems started. There was a group, six or eight nurses that went together. Constance said she just did it to socialize, but for most of the group, it was a safety thing. Lots of them didn't feel safe walking to their cars or to the city bus stop late at night."

"Does Constance carry?"

"I remember her saying something about getting a concealed carry license one time. Said she didn't like the idea of open carry. That it went against her ethics as a nurse. I have no idea if she got it or not."

I gave this a moment to sink in for her. "Now that you remember this, has your feeling about Constance being responsible for Nick's death changed?"

She pushed her shoulders back. "No. Unless the autopsy comes back stating that Nick was shot and Constance's gun matches the ballistic test, I do not believe she had anything to do with it."

"Now that is a very clear statement." I smiled, trying to break a little of the tension between us. "Kristina, I need to ask you something that might be a bit uncomfortable."

"More uncomfortable than you implying that my sister is a murderer and that I don't care about a man's death?" She arched her eyebrows and gave me a pointed look before easing off. "Okay. What's the question?"

"Yesterday morning, Nick was making some innuendos about you and him. I would have dismissed it as him just being vulgar, especially since everyone claims this is how he's been for months. Kyle seemed to get especially upset about it, though." I paused, steeling myself to ask the question. "Is there any validity to what Nick said?"

Kristina stared, slowly putting together the meaning behind my admittedly vague question. Then she shot to her feet. "You think that I had an aff—"

"Kristina, please sit down. We just covered this. This is a potential murder investigation, and I have to ask these questions. I'm not making any accusations."

Anger seethed as she sank back down onto her chair. "You know me; you did not have to ask that." She took a long drink from her glass of water. Whether stalling for a response or calming herself down, I couldn't say. "I can assure you, there was absolutely nothing, ever, between Nick Halpern and me. He was my sister's husband. The mere thought of it— Oh, god." She put a hand to her mouth as though she was about to be sick.

"Are you okay? You're looking a little green."

She sat back with her eyes closed and blew out a few

slow breaths. "It must be some nighttime version of morning sickness." She opened one eye and looked at me. "Do you suppose a sudden rush of anger can bring on nausea?"

"Wouldn't know. You're the nurse." I gave her a minute for her stomach to settle. "I still need to ask a few more questions, then we can wrap this up. Are you going to be okay, or are you going to puke in one of my potted plants?"

She took one more long breath and shook her head as she exhaled. "It's passing. I'll be okay. Ask what you need to ask so I can go to dinner with my husband."

"Do you know where Kyle was on the night Nick died?"

Her head dropped back. "Oh geez. I knew this one was coming. He was with me. He was as shocked and surprised over me being pregnant as I was. We'd been trying for so long. We talked about almost nothing else all night." An amused smile crossed her face. "He asked a million questions, it was so cute. How far along was I? When was my due date? When did that mean I'd gotten pregnant? How was I feeling? All the standard questions any expecting parent wonders about. Anyway, we told everyone else this morning right before we left. They're super happy for us. We had plans to go up to your circus today. That's what you've got here, right?"

"Right."

"I guess you can understand why no one wanted to follow through with that. What do they call a circus? The happiest place on earth? Or is that Disney World?"

"You said Kyle was with you all night and that you're sure Constance was not responsible. Do you think anyone else in your group could have harmed Nick?"

"No. None of them were around Nick all that much. I can't imagine anyone killing a guy over a bad attitude and some nasty words when they only saw him a couple times a year at best. That would require a hair-trigger temper, and I've never seen that in anyone in the group."

I flipped through my notes, making sure there was nothing else I wanted to ask. "I think that's it. Thank you for talking with me. I'm sorry if any of my questions upset you."

Kristina stood and opened her arms wide for a hug. "I know you're just doing your job. You're one heck of a sheriff."

"Thanks. And if I didn't say it already, congratulations on your pregnancy."

She bounced up and down with me in her arms and let out a little squeal. "Isn't it amazing? Honestly, I didn't think it would ever happen. It's like a genuine miracle."

Chapter 22

KRISTINA PRACTICALLY SKIPPED THROUGH THE house and up the stairs to let Kyle know they could go on their date now. I wondered what everyone else would be doing. Had they even thought about inviting the rest of the group to go with them? Or were they so wrapped up in their own happiness that nothing else mattered?

I stepped just inside the french doors into the great room to find Tripp putting together salads to go with our spaghetti dinner.

"I am officially off the clock," I announced. "Unless, of course, another emergency happens."

"Don't even joke about that," Tripp scolded. "Even if there was another emergency tonight, it wouldn't be safe for you to try and handle it."

"You can start the pasta." I gestured toward the boathouse. "I'm going to go take a shower and put on something baggy and comfortable."

Tripp growled at me. "Sexy. If you're lucky, I'll actually let you eat."

Heat rose from somewhere in my belly. I opened my mouth to make an equally saucy reply but thought better of it and headed for my shower.

Meeka trotted after me, the bounce all but gone from

her steps. She climbed the boathouse stairs like she was making the final push for the summit of Mount Everest. I filled her food dish and gave her fresh water then slipped beneath the heat of my massaging shower head.

Try as I might, and I really did try, I couldn't stop thinking about this case. Kyle and Kristina alibied each other for the night in question. Kristina was absolutely certain that Constance had not killed her harassing husband. As for the others in the party who knew Nick, I had no reason to believe that any of them had done anything.

With my hands braced against the shower wall, I closed my eyes and let the water pound on my tight and aching upper back. It didn't make any sense to me that a random villager or a tourist would have killed Nick. Yes, he was abrasive and insulting, even infuriating to some, but there were people like him everywhere. They didn't get picked off by strangers on the street.

It was a remote possibility that Nick had been the last straw for someone. Maybe that person had been bullied or abused on social media, where people said horrible things from behind the supposed cloak of anonymity and distance that cyberspace afforded. Maybe they'd been bullied in real life. Maybe it was pure and simple bad luck—or bad karma according to the Wiccans—and Nick picked on exactly the wrong person. Perhaps that person came to safe and accepting Whispering Pines hoping for a reprieve from the garbage in their life. Instead, there was this stranger, this otherwise ordinary man who had decided he had the right to do and say whatever he wanted to women. Or maybe it wasn't a woman. He had been picking fights with men as well.

It was more likely that the killer was someone who knew him than a random stranger. Either way, "Served him right."

I slapped a hand over my mouth. As much as Kristina insisted that a nurse taking a life went against everything nursing stood for, a law enforcement officer wishing vigilante justice on someone was equally upsetting. I needed to get some sleep.

The water was starting to cool, so I turned it off and toweled myself dry. Knowing that Tripp would be waiting for me outside when I was done, I took a few extra minutes to dry my hair rather than leaving it wet. I was noticing how desperately I needed a haircut when Jayne in the mirror — the biggest pain in my life, next to Flavia — spoke up.

You know, it's entirely possible that Nick was simply hit by a car. Why do you have this need to be the hero of a scenario that you don't even fully understand yet? Listen to Briar and Dr. B and turn this off for the night.

"I call it preventative investigating. What if he was murdered and that person is still in the village? If I don't start asking questions, how will I catch them?"

As I said the words, I realized even more how unlikely it would be that a stranger had been involved. If it was murder, it had to be someone he knew.

"What am I missing?"

Besides your mind? All the facts, for one. Turn it off and wait for the autopsy report. Go enjoy dinner with your man. And put on something sexy, dammit. The last thing he wants is to see you in a baggy T-shirt and saggy sweatpants.

Jayne in the mirror had no idea what she was talking about when it came to law enforcement. I had to admit, she was pretty smart on the topic of dating, however.

I stepped out of the bathroom and heard Meeka snoring on her doggie cushion. Poor girl. She wasn't any more used to two-thirty wake-up calls than I was.

Instead of the comfortable, two sizes too big outfit I had threatened, I pulled on a pair of leggings and a tank top instead. Then I added an off-the-shoulder slouchy sweater and a pair of ragg-wool socks from my dresser drawer.

Outside, Tripp had turned the sundeck into a romantic bistro. He had strung lights all around the railings, and a fire was crackling in the little gas fire pit in the middle of the big square coffee table.

"When did you have time to do all this?" I asked then

added, "How long was I in the shower?"

Tripp laughed and pulled me in close, running his hands up and down my back beneath my sweater. "I put them up this afternoon and took a chance that you wouldn't notice until I turned them on."

He led me to the sofa that faced the lake. There, a spaghetti dinner complete with garlic bread and a salad was waiting. He directed me to sit, covered me with a cozy blanket, and handed me a glass of wine.

"Wine?" I asked. "We never have wine."

"I told you I was going to start learning about it. I went over to Sundry this afternoon. Turns out, they've got a wine guy there. Who knew?"

I didn't want to tell him, because he was so proud of himself, but I really didn't care for wine. I took a sip, mentally prepared a compliment, and found I didn't have to pretend.

"This is pretty good."

"You sound surprised."

"Well, to be honest, I've never really liked any wine that I've tried."

"That's what the wine guy said. He suggested we start with something a little sweeter. That's a Zinfandel. It's not normally paired with pasta, but it goes well with red meat, which is in the sauce."

I was so impressed with this mini-lesson, I couldn't respond. Instead, I sat back to enjoy my glass of Zinfandel and watch my boyfriend uncovering the dinner dishes, pampering me yet again.

Tripp had been ready for us to have a relationship after knowing each other for a week. No way was I ready that fast, but why I waited so long, I couldn't say. Actually, I could say. Fear of rejection. Fear of someone I cared about trying to control me. Fear of someday losing him. No matter how well things were going, and all seemed well at this point, I would rather remain friends with him and never know him romantically than to lose him from my life.

Briar's words screamed in my head. *Quit comparing Tripp to Jonah. You're always in the past or the future, never in the present.*

With both dinner plates prepared, Tripp joined me beneath the blanket. Between the little fire in the pit, the surprisingly decent wine, and our combined body heat, I was perfectly content.

"Oh my god." I covered my mouth with my hand and swallowed the bite of meatball. "This is really good. Is there anything you can't make?"

"Oatmeal cookies," he said immediately with total seriousness and remorse. "I've tried dozens of times, and they turn out flat like a crêpe and crispy every time."

While we ate, we chatted about the successes of his day. Breakfast had gone well, again, despite the more subdued mood of his guests. Having Arden or Holly set up the dining room the day before was a "stroke of genius." The only thing negative on his list was that he wasn't as crazy busy as he had anticipated.

"That's a bad thing?" I asked. "After a day like today, I'd give anything for a non-crazy-busy day."

"You know what I mean. We were prepared for the place to be packed and buzzing."

"Tripp, it's the opening weekend. Considering the time crunch we were under to get the place ready, I'm thrilled that we have five of the seven rooms booked." I had to push Mom's seventy percent success means thirty percent failure comment from my brain. We'd get to "no vacancy" soon. "I can't tell you how many people came up to me while I was patrolling the commons and said they want to stay with us. Don't worry, in no time, we're going to have a waiting list six-months long and you'll be begging for downtime."

He kissed me on the forehead. "You're right. I know you are. It's just, I feel like all the odd-jobs I did while wandering the country have prepared me for this. Running a B&B is what I want to do, and you are the exact person I want to do it with."

He set our dinner plates and wine glasses on the table,

pulled me onto his lap, and kissed me well and thoroughly. Things got quite heated, as they tended to do, and I pulled away.

"I told you," he said with a husky, sultry voice, "I wasn't going to make this easy on you."

"Are you saying this is easy for you?"

I laughed at the look on his face and snuggled into his arms, enjoying the cool night air, strange as that temperature was for late August. As we used to do earlier in the summer, before I became sheriff and house renovations took over our world, we just sat and enjoyed the fragrance of the lake and the pine trees. A gentle breeze blew the boughs around, causing them to make the whispery *whooshing* and *shushing* sounds I had come to love. From somewhere deep in the woods, a wolf howled.

A tickling sensation down the bridge of my nose startled me.

I blinked and looked up at Tripp. "What happened?"

"You fell asleep. I knew you were going to. You settled in against my chest and your breathing got deeper and steadier."

"How long have I been out?" I yawned.

"About fifteen minutes. I would love nothing more than to sit right here and hold you all night, but it's probably better for you to get into bed."

I yawned again. "Between the wine and the food and the sound of your heartbeat, I'm not at all surprised that I fell asleep."

He scooped me into his arms and carried me through my apartment to my bed. Standing there, still holding me, he said, "I'd volunteer to undress you but then you'd never get any sleep."

Instead, he kissed me again, set me down on the bed, and left.

Chapter 23

I SLEPT DEEP AND HEAVY, straight through the night. I don't think I even moved. What finally woke me was something rubbing against my cheek. I expected to find Meeka pawing at me to wake up and let her out, but I opened my eyes to find Tripp sitting on the side of my bed. When he leaned in to give me a kiss, I covered my mouth.

"Morning breath. It is morning, isn't it? I thought you left."

"Yes, it's morning. Yes, I left. I came back to wake you up. Figured you'd want to go into work at some point today."

I sat bolt upright, nearly bumping heads with him. "What time is it? Did I sleep through my alarm?"

"You must have. It's ten to eight."

"Crap. Now I'm going to be late."

He propped an arm over me, trapping me under the covers. "That's why you have a walkie-talkie. The villagers will contact you if they need to. You worked almost eighteen hours yesterday; no one is going to blame you for sleeping in a little bit."

"Okay." I dropped down onto the mattress and sprang right back up. "I have to let Meeka out."

"Already taken care of. She was sitting by the door and

burst through when I opened it. I gave her some food, too. The furry one is fine. Even she knew you needed sleep."

I lay down again and snuggled in with the blankets pulled up to my chin. "How come you're so good to me?"

"Because I care so much about you. I've got to get back over to the house, though. Our guests were just starting breakfast when I came over, and I need to make sure they have everything. I saved a little for you. Get up, get dressed."

"What's on the menu today?" I asked as he walked away.

"Frittatas with green onion, red pepper, diced ham, a little bit of Parmesan, and a good deal of swiss."

The frittata—accompanied by a small cluster of green grapes, some orange wedges, and a nice thick slice of his signature rustic oatmeal bread—was the perfect way to start a day. Also, the cold snap had finally broken. The sky over Whispering Pines was a bright, beautiful blue without a cloud in sight, and the temperature was easily twenty degrees warmer than it had been yesterday. The first two days of this holiday weekend had been fabulous for the retail and restaurant owners. Today would likely be the last of the ultra-busy days for the marina.

Fully rested from her early bedtime, Meeka decided to explore the station when we got there instead of scurrying to her spot beneath the cot. Reed still wasn't in, so while my K-9 ensured that there were no intruders hidden in the corners or behind the filing cabinets, I settled into my office and stared at the list of names on my suspect board, hoping an answer might be glaringly obvious after getting some sleep.

Since Kristina and Kyle had alibied each other, I drew lines through their names. I had just settled in to evaluate my remaining contenders—Constance Halpern, Jeremy Levine, Doug Croft, Elaine Snow, and River Carr—when Dr. Bundy called.

"Have you got results for me?" I asked.

"I do have results. Want to take a guess?"

"No, because I'm never even close."

"I don't believe he was hit by a car. If it had been a hit-and-run, I would expect significant injuries. He has no broken bones or bruising indicative of that kind of impact."

"You're ruling out death by car. Was he murdered some other way?"

"Mr. Halpern had a heart attack."

"He what? You're saying he was walking alongside the highway in the middle of the night and dropped dead from a heart attack?"

"That's what I'm saying. I can't rule out murder, though. That's your job."

"You're talking in circles. What did the autopsy tell you? What are you putting on the death certificate?"

"I am ruling it death via *commotio cordis*."

"And now, you're speaking in Latin. Help me out, Doc."

"Commotio cordis is a somewhat rare condition that results in sudden cardiac arrest. It occurs most commonly in younger people. You know how every now and then you'll hear of an otherwise healthy teenager who drops dead at sports practice or during a game?"

"Yeah, that's so sad. What does it have to do with Nick Halpern?"

"Commotio cordis is caused from an impact to the chest. Oftentimes it's because the victim gets hit by something—a baseball, lacrosse ball, or a hockey puck, for example. The condition can also occur during sports such as rugby, soccer, karate, or boxing, where body pads are not worn."

"What exactly is this *condition*? Seems like a lot of things cause it, so why is it rare?"

"It's rare because the impact has to happen at exactly the right moment. Or wrong moment depending on your perspective. The impact, from a ball or kick or punch for example, causes an arrhythmia, or a change in the rhythm of a heartbeat, which then causes cardiac arrest."

"Are you saying that Nick Halpern was struck in the chest?"

"He was. While I didn't find any broken bones, I did find a large bruise on his chest over his heart. This led me to the commotio cordis diagnosis."

This wasn't quite making sense to me. "An impact strong enough to stop his heart but not break his ribs?"

"The impact doesn't have to be strong to cause an arrhythmia. It just needs to happen at the exact right moment to disrupt the heart's rhythm. There are cases of athletes dying after a blow while wearing a chest protector. An ill-timed snowball could have the same result. Like I said, it's a rare event, but because it happens most often in healthy young people, the cases tend to make the news."

My brain had zeroed in on one distinct possibility. "We can't rule out murder, then. If someone struck him, causing his heart to stop, at minimum, that would be involuntary manslaughter."

Dr. Bundy paused before saying, "I guess a hit-and-run of sorts isn't out of the question. It's possible that someone threw something from a car as they were passing Mr. Halpern and the object struck him."

"Good point. I was thinking more of someone hitting him in anger, he upset a lot of people around here in a very short time, but a flying object is possible."

And if the blow didn't need to be hard, "tiny" Elaine Snow could still be a suspect.

"What about that head wound?" I asked. "What did you find there?"

"Ah, yes. As we discussed before, a slice from a knife or some other sharp object would create a smooth line. And impact would create a jagged mark."

"Let me guess on this one. The mark on Halpern was neither smooth nor jagged."

"Right you are. What made you guess that?"

"Because nothing is ever easy in this village. What did you find?"

He chuckled softly at my comment. "I found what I'd call a jagged slice. The line wasn't smooth but didn't have the burst tomato quality either."

"What would cause that?" I asked myself more than him.

"I'd say something such as a knife with teeth, like a hunting knife."

My mind started to spin. Which of my suspects would possess something like that?

"I'll email you the preliminary report," Dr. Bundy said. "I don't expect anything to change, however. The ball is now in your court. Don't let it hit you in the chest." He paused for a short beat. "Sorry, that was in very poor taste."

"You're a sick man, Doc."

"A helpful quality in this profession. Talk to you later, Sheriff. Hopefully much, much later."

I leaned back in my chair with my hands clasped behind my head and stared at my suspect board. A knife with teeth would be harder to track down. I'd focus on the other injury first. A blow to the chest that did not necessarily have to be strong. Well, I did have a bodybuilder over at The Inn who'd disrupted Treat Me Sweetly. Even though being strong wasn't a crucial item on the checklist, it seemed best to start with him.

"Let's go, Deputy Meeka," I called out. The little Westie emerged from beneath Deputy Reed's desk and looked at me with a questioning tilt of her head. "We need to go interview another suspect."

~~~

As Meeka and I wandered through the pentacle garden on the way to The Inn, it seemed that every visitor to the village was outside. Unlike the past two days, the sky was cloud free, and the breeze off the lake was like a warm hug. Gone were the sad faces that the cold weather had caused, replaced with plenty of smiles and the kind of happiness we liked to see from our tourists. We were almost to The Inn when I spotted Laurel standing outside. As in, she was literally just standing in front of the building.

"What's going on?" I asked.

Laurel's eyes were closed, her face pointed at the sun. "Isn't it beautiful? Winter seems to last forever this far north, so getting cheated out of even one nice summer day seems cruel. Thought I'd come outside and soak in some rays for a few minutes."

Copying her stance, I stood next to Laurel. She was right, the warmth soaking in felt good. Since I'd never experienced a Northwoods winter, the locals had been trying to prepare me even though I'd lived in Wisconsin my entire life. Some gave little comments like Laurel just had about winter lasting so long. Others gave stronger warnings, like the fact that nothing could prepare me for those days when the wind would bite right through no matter how many layers I put on. Taking care of the new girl. It was sweet.

"Did you come over just to absorb some vitamin D with me?" Laurel asked. "Or is there another reason you're here? The first option is fine, by the way."

"Actually, I'm looking for one of your guests. I imagine you'd know him just from the description. Reed tells me he's a bodybuilder—"

"Doug Croft," Laurel supplied before I could finish. "I know him. I won't ask why you're looking for him, but he's not here right now. I believe he and his girlfriend went down to the public beach."

We stood together for another minute until Laurel said she had to get back to work. Meeka and I started the half-mile walk to the beach. Along the way, we chatted with tourists, many of them saying that they had been at the party Friday night and wanted to make reservations to stay at Pine Time. I assured them that we would be happy to have them, gave them the website address, and explained that they could make reservations there. I needed to get business cards printed and carry some with me.

The public beach area was as crowded as the commons. Screaming children ran into and out of the water while exhausted-looking parents seemed overjoyed by a day of being able to just lay in the sun or under an umbrella while their kids played outside. At the far end of the beach, away from the families, a cluster of millennials had gathered. Instinct told me that was where we'd find Doug Croft.

We were maybe twenty-five yards away when we heard cheers rise from the cluster. A few yards closer, and I saw a very large man posing for the crowd.

"Is he Doug Croft?" I asked a young woman with heavy black-framed glasses at the edge of the crowd.

"That's him." She appeared awestruck.

"Looks like he's putting on quite a show."

"It didn't start that way," she explained.

Her friend, a young woman who made every sentence sound like a question, took over. "I guess they were down here to go for a run on the beach. When they were done, she was just sitting here meditating or reading a book or something, but he was working out. You know, doing pushups and handstands and stuff. Then someone asked him to pose."

The first woman agreed. "Hard to keep walking past when you see someone like him."

I cut my way through the crowd and, as usually happened when people saw the uniform, a bunch of them scattered, cutting the cluster down by almost half.

"Doug Croft?" I called out.

A petite woman, also with a fair amount of muscles, dressed in a bubblegum-pink sports bra and tiny running shorts tapped his arm. The huge man—six foot four, two hundred fifty pounds of solid muscle as Reed had said—turned, and the smile on his face fell when he saw I was the sheriff and not an adoring fan.

"Now what? I already talked to the other guy. What do you want?"

I understood why the customers at Treat Me Sweetly were afraid. Mr. Croft had a loud voice and immediately came across as combative. All I'd done was ask his name. Perfect way to put me on guard.

"Mr. Croft, I'm Sheriff O'Shea. I'm sorry to disturb your workout, but I need to speak with you for a few minutes."

He waved off the crowd then took his girlfriend's tiny hand in both of his large ones. "I'd like Casey to stay if you don't mind."

The way he stood there, clutching her hand, reminded me of a little boy clutching a security blanket. Just that fast, my initial impression was turned upside down.

"For now," I agreed. "She might be able to answer a few questions, too. I understand that you spoke with Deputy Reed yesterday."

Croft leaned in and never took his eyes off me as I spoke. "Yeah, he was asking about that jerk from the ice cream shop. Said he died."

"He did. What did you tell him about that?"

He looked down at his girlfriend. "I told him the guy was disrespecting Casey. I got in his face and told him to stop being such a jerk." He shrugged his massive shoulders. "That's about it."

"The owner of Treat Me Sweetly feels you did more than just tell him to stop being a jerk. She said you were hollering loud enough to scare some of her customers away."

"What did she say?" Croft asked his girlfriend.

Casey turned to me with a smile. "Doug has hearing loss. He can't hear much out of his left ear. So especially in small places where there are a lot of people, like that ice cream shop, everything becomes a hum. No matter how many times I tell him"—she glanced up at him and raised her own voice—"he doesn't seem to understand that he's got a really loud voice."

That explained a lot. I spoke louder and slower, and because he seemed to be trying to read my lips, facing him. "Your statement is that after the victim assaulted your girlfriend—"

"Sorry," Croft interrupted, "but wouldn't Casey be the victim?"

The look of caring for his girlfriend, one I'd seen on Tripp's face plenty of times, made me smile.

"You know what? You're absolutely right. Let me rephrase that. After the deceased assaulted Casey, you claim that you told him to back off. Because it was so loud in the shop, you hollered which in turn scared some of the other customers away."

After a short pause, he nodded. "That's what I'm saying."

"You weren't enraged by the fact that this man had touched your girlfriend?"

"Of course I was, but look at me." He held one arm out to the side, various muscles rippling as he did. "It's taken me years to develop this body. I know I'm big and strong, and I know that if I ever took a swing at someone when I was that angry, I'd probably end up killing them. I might have a problem with volume control, but unless my voice could be considered a lethal weapon, I didn't hurt that guy."

Everyone should be that self-aware. "I need to ask one more question. Where were you on the night that Nick Halpern died?"

He looked at Casey and gave a wicked grin. "I was in bed with my girlfriend. Want to know what we were doing?"

"No, I really don't." I turned to Casey. "Do you agree

with that statement? Were you and Doug together that night?"

"Oh, sure. That was a marathon night."

I held up a hand. "Please, I don't need details."

Casey looked at me, eyes narrowed in confusion, then the lightbulb turned on. "Oh, no, not that. It was a marathon chick flick night."

She proceeded to list all the movies they had watched. Since they had charged all of them to the room, I'd be able to verify their claim with Laurel.

I raised my voice again. "I imagine you can understand why you might be considered a suspect."

"Oh, I totally get it," Croft said. "People make assumptions about me all the time. Blame the big guy, he must be responsible for everything that gets broken and everyone who gets beat up."

"It's very unfair," Casey said, more sad than mad. "Doug is a big marshmallow. Well, if the marshmallows are rock hard. He wouldn't hurt a fly."

"Thank you for chatting with me." I reeled in Meeka's leash and prepared to head back to the station. Then I turned back to Casey. "I'm sorry for what happened to you. Are you all right?"

She looked at me with gratitude in her eyes. "You're the first one to ask. Other than Doug. Yes, I'm okay. Thanks for asking."

I made a mental note to discuss interview techniques with Reed. If he would've dug for more details initially, we could have eliminated Mr. Croft from our suspect list right away. Although, I might not have met this couple and gotten a reminder about discriminating based on appearance. Always valuable but especially so in Whispering Pines.

Chapter 24

ALONG THE LAKESHORE BETWEEN THE public beach and the marina beach was a two-acre plot that had been left natural. Other than a couple dozen picnic tables and some outdoor grills, the only things on this unlandscaped stretch were scrubby bushes and large rocks. It was popular for picnics and cookouts, but plenty of "No Swimming – No Lifeguard on Duty" signs kept bathers away. I took off my hiking shoes and walked along the waterline with Meeka instead of going directly back to the station. It was amazing what sunny skies and warm breezes could do for the spirit after only two days of unexpected cold and clouds.

"Stay out of the water," I warned the furry one. "You get wet, you're going to get a bath."

As much as Meeka loved playing in the water, she hated baths. I kept her on the leash but let it extend as far as it would go. She used this real estate to chase the waves out and scramble back as they chased her inland.

Halfway to the marina, I spotted a girl sitting next to one of the scrubby bushes about fifteen feet from the water.

"Lily Grace? What are you doing here?"

She had her knees pulled up to her chest and her head resting on her knees. She glanced up.

"Hey, Sheriff. I was looking for a little seclusion."

"Oh, sorry, I'll—"

She lifted her head fully. "No, it's fine. You don't have to go. It might be nice to talk to someone normal."

Since Lily Grace wasn't one to ask for things, I took that to mean *please, sit and talk to me* and plopped down next to her. "What's going on?"

She let out a despondent sigh. "Everything is such a mess."

Uh-oh. That could mean anything from one of her customers chewed her out after a reading to she and her boyfriend Oren broke up.

"What in particular is a mess?" I asked with caution. I knew, from experience, that a question asked the wrong way would earn me an evil eye from the teenage fortune teller.

"This whole thing with my parents. Why was everyone hiding this from me?"

"Not everyone was hiding it." And there was the eye. "Sorry. I know you don't mean literally everyone."

"Just when I think I have my life figured out, something new comes up. I knew there was a problem of some kind with my parents. I've lived with my Grandma Cybil since I was really little, not even two years old. I'd see my father sometimes but not very often. I don't remember ever being with my mom. If I ask what happened to her, Grandma says she doesn't know anything, and Dad changes the subject. I think I asked once why I couldn't live with him. He said something about working all the time, and I just accepted it. Whatever. I was fine with Grandma. But now there's this."

Almost afraid to, I asked, "There's what?"

"You know. This whole dead girl debacle gets revealed, and I find out that my parents were kicked out of the village. Now, after all these years—"

Her voice broke, and she couldn't continue.

I gave her a few seconds to collect herself and then prodded with, "All these years what?"

"I was in bed last night trying to fall asleep. That's near impossible lately because all I do is lay there thinking about all this. It's super hard to turn something like that off once you know it. So I'm lying there thinking about things and I remember, after the Priscilla stuff was uncovered, that someone said Rae and Gabe had two babies."

"Right. Rae got pregnant shortly after they left the village. I'm not sure I heard about a second baby."

"Everyone has always known that Effie is Jola's grandmother. A lot know Rae is her mother but never talk about it. They all know that Gabe is my dad." Lily Grace stared at me, waiting for me to connect the dots. "Rae and Gabe were together ..." She gave me a second or so and then slapped her hands down on the sand. "For god's sake, Jayne, Gabe and Rae are my parents. That means Effie is my grandmother and Jola is my sister." She clenched her jaw and breathed hard. "I've lived with Cybil and Effie for over fifteen years and never knew Effie was my grandmother. I've had a sister kept from me my entire life. I'll be eighteen soon. That's almost two decades of time she and I lost out on."

Holy cats, as Violet would say, she was right. Jola had to know. She would've been six when their dad brought Lily Grace here to live with Cybil. That was old enough to remember a sister, wasn't it? Or was this another of those forbidden, never to be told Whispering Pines secrets?

"I've got a brother I never knew about," I offered, trying to ease her suffering. "At least you've got a cool secret sibling. I don't want mine. Wanna switch?"

There was the evil eye again.

I gave her a cheesy smile of apology. "How can these things be right here in front of our faces and we don't see them?"

"I don't know." She stretched her legs out in front of her, flexed her feet, and then pulled them back into crisscross. "Maybe we're not looking or we can't see it until we're ready to deal with it."

"You know, that last option is very often the case. Right now, I've got a whole lineup of suspects for this murder. One of them is the guilty one, but I can't identify them until I have all the information I need." She gave me a bored stare. "Okay, that might not fit exactly in your situation. As far as Jola being your sister, none of us knew any of this until six weeks ago."

"That's not true. Not at all. There are people living here who were here when Rae and Gabe were forced to leave the village."

"But my grandmother swore them to silence on this topic. The only people who knew the full truth were my grandmother, both of your grandmothers, and maybe my dad. Possibly Flavia. Regardless, those who knew were sworn to secrecy under threat of also being kicked out of the village."

A true black mark on Gran's record.

"That may be, but plenty of people who weren't sworn to silence knew that Gabe came back with a baby and gave it to Cybil to raise." Lily Grace put her hands over her face and screamed. "Jola was here so many times. She came to visit Effie every summer. She was right here playing with me and they never said anything."

"Maybe they were trying to protect you from something."

"From my own family? My mother and sister?"

I was struggling here. I didn't know how to help her with this one.

"No one ever told me anything about my mother, like how she struggled with wanting to be a fortune teller just like I do. Cybil and Effie love being tellers, so they don't get it. My mom might've been someone who understood what's going on with me." Seconds ago, her voice shook with emotion, and now it was filling with anger. "And Jola, she's mixed race just like me with skin too white to be brown and too brown to be white. Hair that can't decide if it wants to be straight or curly. I'm completely stuck between staying here with Oren in this god-awful little village or leaving and becoming my own woman and exploring the world."

I jumped in when she paused for a breath. "Being with Oren and being your own woman aren't two exclusive things. At least they sure shouldn't be. Oren should enhance every aspect of your life, not define or dictate it. I know they aren't the ones you'd prefer, but you do have childhood memories with your sister."

She didn't respond, which assured me that she had heard and was processing my words.

"Beyond the obvious," I said after a minute, "what are you thinking?"

"That's the thing, I can't think of anything but being lied to." She had turned from angry to sad again. "I need some space to clear my head. I'm supposed to be at The Triangle doing readings today. There's no way I could concentrate on other people's futures when mine just turned into absolute mud."

We sat and watched Meeka chase the water. The furry one discovered that as the water receded, bubbles rose up through the sand. She started pouncing on them with her front paws and became so engrossed in bubble popping, she forgot the water would come back. When it touched her paws, she let out a yelp and raced over to me. This made Lily Grace laugh.

She pulled a confused Meeka in for a hug. The little Westie struggled at first, but then seemed to understand the girl needed comfort and connection with a living being. Me hugging her would've been weird.

Lily Grace released Meeka and looked over at me. "My other problem is that since you turned on my *gift*"—she gave me another evil eye, determined to make me take responsibility for her becoming a talented and in-demand fortune teller—"I'm becoming more and more empathetic to people."

This she said as though she had contracted the black plague.

"Isn't empathy a good quality in a fortune teller?"

"Whatever. The problem is, I can't turn it off." She rubbed her hands up and down her arms as though suddenly chilled. "Don't you feel what's going on around here? Something is wrong in this village."

At that, I burst out laughing.

"It's not funny, Jayne. I'm not talking about the villagers being outcasts or that we believe in and do things differently from the rest of society. I mean something is wrong with the village." She formed her arms into a circle, fingertips touching, as though encompassing all of Whispering Pines. "Until six months or so ago, people were happy here. Now, not so much."

I shifted, uncomfortable with this observation. I'd only been here since Memorial Day, so I couldn't know for sure. Was she right? "I haven't gotten the sense that people are unhappy. From what I see, everyone feels safe and secure tucked away up here in the Northwoods."

"This location is magical for us, yes, but if we were to pick up the village and put it somewhere else, we should still have each other. That's the part that feels like it's changing. The community or whatever. I don't know how to explain it." She released a heavy sigh. "It's like a thinning of the gene pool or something. Lucy figured out a long time ago that with every outsider that comes and stays, the village becomes less and less of what it was supposed to be."

The village council hadn't let anyone move here recently. Donovan had moved into his grandmother's house eight months ago, but he'd come here throughout his childhood to visit her. The only new people I knew of were … hang on.

"You aren't talking about me and Tripp, are you?"

"I don't want that to sound all negative, but you know

you've changed the village. You opened up what happened forty years ago."

"But that already happened. Tripp and I didn't change the past." The anger I'd felt toward Sugar earlier flared again. This was way too close to her accusation that I had released darkness into the village.

"But you've got to admit, by bringing it into the open, you caused a ripple effect through the community."

Like with Halpern's body, I needed to look around what was in front of me to get at the truth. This wasn't about the village changing. It was about me uncovering something that upset Lily Grace's world. This was bigger than a seventeen-year-old, though.

"Lily Grace, do you understand that if I hadn't taken over my grandparents' home and turned it into a B&B, not only the house but the two thousand acres that my family owns would be up for sale? I can't fathom the price tag that would be attached to all this, but it would be massive. Do you understand what could happen if the potential buyer didn't want a village on their property?"

This was the pressure I felt, the reason I lived in the future, as Briar accused. If I couldn't make the B&B a success, my parents would sell it all. Whispering Pines' future, and mine, was either shiny and bright or apocalyptic and dusty based entirely on my actions.

I could tell by the look on her face that Lily Grace wanted to be angry at me for not just accepting her scolding. At the same time, she looked like a little girl who had just been sent to her room for being naughty.

"I know I haven't been here very long, and I don't know how to make you believe this, but I care just as much about this village as you do. Am I doing all the right things? No, but I'm doing all I can, so don't sit there and lecture me—"

"I'm not lecturing you. And I didn't mean to make you mad." Her voice was shaking, and she was fighting off tears. "It's just that everything is changing."

I wanted to yell at her to quit being a child. But she was a child.

"Lily Grace, sweetie, in two days, you're going to be a senior in high school. You know that your life is going to change when you graduate in about nine months, but you don't quite understand how much yet. You can't because you haven't been there. I know that's scary, and I'm not saying this as a know-it-all adult, I'm saying it as someone who was in your shoes not too long ago. I'm only twenty-six. That may seem old to you, but honestly, I feel like I just graduated from high school. On top of all that, you find out your family isn't what and who you believed it to be."

"You don't understand me—"

"Actually, I do. I just want you to understand that, as upsetting as it can be, your life will be a series of changes. Some will happen slowly while others seem to happen on a daily basis. I do understand what you're saying—"

"I had a vision about the village," she blurted and then cowered as though ducking from blowback.

Time seemed to freeze for a few seconds. Lily Grace's visions always made me pause. I didn't believe in the mystical forces Morgan and the other Wiccans touted, so I knew it was hypocritical, but I also didn't believe in coincidences. Her visions weren't always one hundred percent, but they were uncannily accurate. To me, that made them something to at least consider.

Softly, not quite a whisper, I asked, "What did you see?"

"Things are going to get worse before they get better. The villagers are going to turn on each other." She pulled her knees to her chest and rested her head on them again. She looked over at me and blinked, waiting for me, the big know-it-all twenty-six-year-old, to respond.

"I'll be honest, I don't know what to do with that. Other than stay on the lookout for trouble. Which is my job."

She nodded. "I know how I made it sound, but I am

glad you're here. Sometimes I feel like you're the only one who listens to me. If I would've tried to say all of that to my grandmother ... grand*mothers*, they would've shut me down after one sentence. Thanks for letting me get all that out."

"You're welcome. I'd hug you, but I don't want to spark a vision."

"Thanks. Don't think I could handle one right now. A vision, I mean."

I stared at her while going back through our sometimes-heated discussion. "You know that Tripp and I are trying to make positive changes here."

"I know you're trying."

I expected she'd say more, but she let the unspoken words hang there. "Are you feeling any better?"

"A little. I'm not quite as angry anymore. I was serious about needing some space, though. I've got some big decisions to make about my life. I've been debating for a year between staying here and going to veterinary school. Hanging around Effie and Cybil and all the other fortune tellers isn't giving me the space I need to make it. They just see me as an income generator."

"I don't think that's true." She really was down. "Have you talked to Jola? I don't know if she has teller abilities, but she sure understands being mixed race. Maybe she can help you with the other things, too."

Lily Grace perked up. "I like that idea. Now I'm really glad you're here."

"I'm heading back to the station." The healing center, where Jola worked, was just north of it. "Would you like to walk with me? You could pop over and see her."

"Not yet. I need to stay here for a little longer. You filled my head with a bunch of new thoughts."

I nodded, whistled for Meeka, and stood. "You know, sometimes when we vent, the truth comes out. I know you didn't mean anything nasty about me or Tripp, at least I hope you didn't, but you helped me open my eyes a little.

My focus as sheriff has been on the village as a whole. I need to pay attention to the individuals, too."

"If anyone can fix what's wrong in Whispering Pines, it's you, Sheriff Jayne."

Once again, Lily Grace's words were uncomfortably close to Sugar's. *You'll be the one to shoo away this dark cloud that's settled over the village.*

Chapter 25

ONCE MEEKA AND I WERE out of the sand, I paused to put my shoes back on. What a frustrating morning. A completely worthless trip to talk to a suspect who should have been ruled out from the start. Then again, if I hadn't gone to interview Doug Croft, I never would have crossed paths with Lily Grace. Hopefully, I was able to offer her some help. She certainly opened my eyes to things I hadn't been seeing. That concerned me.

"I need coffee," I told my K-9 deputy.

Meeka's tail started wagging double time. She knew "coffee" meant Ye Olde Bean Grinder and in Meeka speak, that meant dog biscuits. As much as I wanted a caffeine fix, I took my time to chat with people while walking past the marina, The Inn, and through the pentacle garden. The handful of villagers I came across had all darted outside for a few minutes. Almost all of them said pretty much the same thing. First, this was the busiest summer season they could remember. Second, they were ready for the season to be done and hoped there would be more warm days before fall hit the Northwoods.

We were heading toward Ye Olde Bean Grinder when I spotted a small cluster of women gathered near the negativity well at the center of the pentacle garden. Unlike a wishing well, where the hope was to manifest something positive, this well was a place to release something negative. The person would whisper bad feelings or emotions into their hands and throw them into the water below, moving forward afterward, free from what had been dragging them down.

A petite woman, maybe five foot one, with short reddish-brown hair was saying, "Now that we've all thrown our self-doubt into the well, we need to join forces and stand together in this fight."

"What do you want to bet," I asked Meeka, "that's Elaine Snow?"

She gave a little bark that sounded like *yep*.

The woman's speech seemed to be coming to a crescendo, so I waited. When she had finished, the women in the group clapped and walked away, chatting excitedly about what they'd just heard.

"Excuse me," I said to the redheaded woman, "are you Elaine Snow?"

"I am." She glanced at the badge on my shirt. "And you are the sheriff of this fine village."

"I have a few questions I'd like to ask you."

"About the dead groper." Her lip curled into a sneer of disgust.

"You know that he died."

"We all know. What do your witches call it? Karma? Sounds like he got his. And before you ask, no, I didn't kill him. I wouldn't risk my own freedom over a slimeball like that guy."

She spoke clearly and passionately and looked me square in the eye the whole time.

"Where were you the night the victim died?" I recognized my mistake, the same one I'd made earlier, the moment it had left my mouth.

"Victim?" The word seemed to enrage her. "What was he a victim of? You think all those women threw their boobs and backsides into his sweaty hands? He is not a victim, Sheriff."

"I'm not analyzing his personality, Ms. Snow. It's possible he died due to a physical assault, which would put him in the victim category." She backed down, holding her hands up to me in surrender. "I'll rephrase, though. Where were you on the night Mr. Halpern died?"

She pointed east. "I'm staying at one of the rental cottages this weekend. There was a group of us gathered around a campfire last night discussing how messed up humanity is."

"At two in the morning?"

"I'm happy to point you to the people I was with if you want to verify my claim."

I took her information in case I decided to check her out further, but at this point, I stuck with our initial conclusion that Elaine Snow was simply angry about being accosted by Halpern and not homicidal toward him.

After Elaine walked away to rejoin her friends, Meeka looked up at me with her tail wagging at half-speed. "Okay, girl. Let's go get your biscuits."

I was prepared for the coffee shop to be full, it always was, and was surprised to see only a couple people inside.

"Hey there, Sheriff," Violet greeted me. "Your regular today?"

"There's no one in here," I noted dumbly.

"Sure there is." Violet pointed to two villagers: a woman in a tinfoil hat and Agnes, the nun who I usually saw riding her bicycle, sitting quietly drinking their beverages. "You'll see in a day or so, this is what it's normally like. Well, there will be a few more villagers, the more reclusive ones come out once the tourists leave, but we're never as busy as we are during the summer season. It's nice to be able to enjoy life a little more and recharge." She looked at me, her head tilted to the side in question. "What's the matter, Jayne?"

That she knew to call me by my first name rather than my title said she was tuned into my emotions.

"I just got chewed out by a teenage fortune teller."

Violet gasped. "Lily Grace chewed you out? Why?" She held up a hand in stop position and then pointed to the two overstuffed leather chairs in the corner by the unlit fireplace. "Go sit. I'll bring your drink in a sec. Basil? Can you watch the counter for a while?"

Basil, Violet's significantly taller twin brother, appeared from the back room. "No problem. Hey, Sheriff."

I gave him a wave and accepted a little parchment sack of biscuits from Violet for Meeka. I crossed the little shop and dropped into a chair, my back to the wall. This was the first time I got to sit in one of these chairs. It was just as comfortable as I imagined it would be. Maybe "in a few days," as everyone kept saying, I'd come here with a book and spend a few hours reading. Or painting. I still hadn't cracked open the watercolors I'd brought with me from Madison.

A couple of minutes later, Violet appeared with a huge ceramic mug of coffee. Something else I hadn't been able to take advantage of. Whenever I came here, I left with either a paper cup or my travel mug full of one of Violet's magical brews. For those villagers who hung out instead of passing through, she had a rack of personalized mugs in back. Mine was labeled "Sheriff Jayne" and had a little gold star.

"This doesn't look like my usual mocha," I observed.

"It's not. I figured you could use something else today."

I held the mug to my nose and sniffed. The aroma of cream and pumpkin and spice filled my nose. I raised my eyes to her. "Pumpkin spice? Already?"

Violet held a finger to her lips. "Only for you. You look like you need some soothing, and few things are more soothing than pumpkin pie with lots of whipped cream."

I took a sip and instantly felt my entire body sag. "That's exactly what it tastes like. You are magical with your coffee beans, aren't you, Miss Violet?"

She pinched the hem of her pine-green thigh-length apron between two fingers, gave a little curtsy of thanks, then pulled the other chair closer to me and sat. "Now, tell me what's going on. I've seen you stressed, but never like this."

"Funny thing is, I wasn't stressed when I woke up this morning. In fact, I wasn't stressed until I talked to Lily Grace."

"Good Goddess, what did that girl say to you?"

I didn't tell her anything about Lily Grace's personal revelations regarding the grandmother and sister she hadn't realized she had. That wasn't my story to tell. I did tell her about Lily Grace's vision of the villagers turning on each other.

"Is she right about something being wrong?" I asked. "Obviously, some things have changed in the few months I've been here, but enough that we could be heading toward a crisis?"

"A mass, village-wide crisis? I doubt it. You know teenagers; everything is huge, and change is traumatic. I've been here for a while. Nowhere near as long as some folks, but twenty years is significant. I was two years old when my mama and daddy bought the coffee shop. Talk about a change to this village. For outsiders to move in and take over an existing business? The council debated good and long about that."

"But you got in without question, right? I mean your family is Wiccan, and Wiccans pretty much have free access."

"That's true, but by that time, 1998 to be exact, the village had been incorporated for almost twenty years. It was filling up, and your grandma Lucy was becoming very choosy about the wannabe villagers she presented to the board. The fact that my mom and dad wanted to take over the coffee shop and the current owners wanted to sell to them, made it easier. They didn't have to look for jobs or propose a new business."

"How long have you been running the shop?"

The tiny woman who was usually a bundle of energy frowned. "Mama died when Basil and I were seventeen. We helped Daddy around the shop every day, but two days after our eighteenth birthday, he handed us the keys and said he was moving to Florida near his brother. It was just too hard for him to stay here. Everything reminded him of Mama. And the winters made his bones ache."

"You've been living here for twenty years and running the coffee shop for more than four. You must have a pretty good insight into both sides, business and residential."

"I like to think so."

"Lily Grace seems to think that Tripp and I encouraging guests to come year-round might not be good for the village. What do you think she means by that?"

"Year-round?" Violet gave me a sad smile. "First thing I can tell you is that the shops around the pentacle garden don't stay open all year. During the worst of winter, we usually only open two or three days a week. Unless there's a blizzard blowing, we always open on Sunday. That's partly so we can get our shopping done, but mostly that's gathering time. Winters get long up here, so getting together with other people helps a lot."

"You agree with Lily Grace, then? You don't think we should be open in the winter?" This would put a serious damper on us becoming profitable by the end of the next summer season.

"I'm not saying that, but if you're going to have guests up here all winter long, you're going to have to restructure the way you run your business. You give your guests breakfast. Where will they eat lunch and dinner if Triple G and The Inn are closed? Treat Me Sweetly hardly ever opens during the week. Honey and Sugar let us in on Sundays, so we can get bread and treats for the week, but your guests won't even be able to get scones if they're here Monday through Saturday."

I pulled my notebook out of the cargo pocket on my right thigh and wrote these things down. Tripp could cook any meal, not just breakfast, so that wouldn't be a problem.

"What if we were to offer things like ice fishing, snowmobiling, and cross-country skiing. Do you think the villagers would have an issue with that?"

"Maybe not snowmobiles," Violet said honestly. "It's so peaceful up here in the winter, and we really do like the quiet. The other things are fine." She sat back with her arms crossed and tapped her fingers on her rather-impressive biceps. Seemed hoisting those massive bags of coffee beans was a good workout. "There's something else you don't quite understand yet and probably won't until you've been here for a year. The summer season is intense. You've seen that. After going at full speed seven days a week for four months, you'll be ready for a little R&R."

Our goal to break even in a year was looking more remote by the minute. "What do you recommend?"

"At minimum, shutting down for all of February. We get a handful of Wiccans who like to come up and celebrate the Imbolc sabbat with us on February first, but after that, we pretty much close the gates to the village. Like I said, unless there's a blizzard blowing out there, we always open on Sunday, and usually a few hours on Tuesday and Thursday, as well, because people do stop on their way to someplace else. Those three hotels over by the swimming beach found out real fast that they were not going to fill up year-round."

"That's why only one of them stays open after the summer season?"

"That's why. All of the rental cottages close up. Since Laurel lives in The Inn, she'll let people stay there. Something you and Tripp have going for you is that you serve food like The Inn does. The one hotel that stays open has a hard time because they don't serve meals. They'll shut down after New Year's and won't reopen until the end of March."

"This is all really good information to have. Wish I would have chatted with you before I put together numbers for my parents."

Lesson learned. Market analysis was important.

"There's one other benefit to closing down in February," Violet added as she got to her feet and pushed her chair back into its original spot. "You and that man of yours can have some alone time."

She gave me a wink, said, "I best let you get on your way," and headed into the back.

I'd have to talk with Tripp about this new information. He wouldn't have a problem serving three meals a day, but would that be enough to get people to come all the way up here in the winter? Where were the nearest snowmobile trails? Not having that option could make a huge difference. I sat there for a few more minutes contemplating this problem. After all our hard work, had we bitten off more than we could chew?

Meeka stood with her front paws on my knees and looked at me as though to say, *can we worry about this later? It's nice outside.*

I grabbed her little face and ruffled her ears. "You're absolutely right. Let's go."

We'd barely gone five feet when I spotted Morgan on Shoppe Mystique's front porch watering the flowers. I practically ran over to her.

"You're back."

"I am."

"Not to sound like I'm mothering you, because I know you've already got an awesome mother, but where have you been?"

Morgan stiffened. "I was with River."

"This whole time? Willow told me you left for lunch on

Saturday."

She laughed at my distress. "It's not like I just now left him. I slept in my own bed last night."

"I stopped in to look for you yesterday, and Willow was frantic. The shop was absolutely packed. She seemed angry."

"Not at all." She leaned in and whispered, "Willow can be a little dramatic. And she has a tiny bladder. I explained that I might be gone for a while, and she was fine with that. I understand things got a little crazy for a while, but she said you stood guard so she was able to get lunch. As they always do, things quieted down later in the afternoon."

"But she couldn't make witch balls or charm bags."

Morgan's mouth twitched like a mother trying not to laugh at her insistent child. "And you're very concerned about our customers getting charm bags?"

"No," I admitted, "that's not what I was concerned about. Nobody knew where you were; that worried me. It also seemed odd that you'd take off for so long in the middle of a busy day."

"This was the only time I can recall that I was away from the shop so I could tend to something personal. Unfortunately, the shop got busy while I was away. Everything turned out fine, though. Willow is not angry with me."

"What did you need to tend to?"

This question resulted in an arched eyebrow. Morgan placed her hand on my shoulder and gave it a little pat, silently letting me know she wasn't going to explain herself. "Your concern is very sweet, but I assure you, nothing is wrong. What did you think? That River had kidnapped me?"

I guess she didn't realize her date was high on my suspect list. Then again, why would she? She disappeared before I could share that with her.

"Actually, River doing something to you is exactly what

I was worried about. There was another death in the village. Remember? Turns out, there's a high probability it was another murder. And you vanished without letting anyone know where you'd be."

"Oh my Goddess." She placed both hands over her heart. "I wasn't aware the man's death was a murder. Last we spoke, it was accidental."

I gave her the quick-and-dirty version of Dr. Bundy's commotio cordis explanation.

"Dr. Bundy found a large bruise on Halpern's chest over his heart, and while it's possible the blow came from something other than someone hitting him, a random strike seems unlikely."

"That is concerning," Morgan agreed.

I relaxed more knowing she was all right but couldn't stop myself from scolding her. "I'm trying to find out who the killer is, and Carr is on my list. How would you have felt if you were me and your friend had gone off somewhere with him?"

She gave me an understanding smile. "Again, your concern is appreciated but not necessary. River and I had lunch together at Grapes, Grains, and Grub. Plenty of people saw us together and can verify that if you'd like to check. He took me for a drive in that sexy car of his, and time flew. When we got back to the village, it was nearly dinnertime. Since there's only one place for a nice, proper dinner, I took him over to The Inn. Laurel saw us, she can also verify for you."

I blinked at her. "You're humoring me, aren't you?"

"Yes, I am. Seriously, Jayne, I'm a grown woman. I know what I'm doing and am cautious about who I do it with."

"What did you do?"

She narrowed her eyes at me, growing annoyed with my badgering. "One thing you can always trust is that I would never leave Mama—"

"I forgot to bring her home," I blurted. I told her I'd come back for her."

"No need to worry. Willow gave her a ride on her bicycle. Mama loved it." She smiled, amused, and turned serious again. "As I was saying, I would never leave her home alone all night. Ninety-nine percent of the time, she's fine, but that one percent means I will always be there with her. She knows this and would sound the alarm if I didn't come home."

True. Briar hadn't been at all worried about her daughter.

"I'm sorry, Morgan. Forget everything I said about this. I'm obviously concerned that there's been another murder, but there's some personal stuff, too. It looks like we'll have to reevaluate keeping the B&B open year-round. And I had a run-in with Lily Grace earlier and I'm still a little upset."

"With Lily Grace? That's surprising."

"It really was. She—"

Morgan silenced me by placing a hand on my arm. "I'd love to have you come in for some tea and tell me all about it, but since I was gone all yesterday afternoon, I have a bit of work to catch up on."

This day was completely catawampus, and I didn't like it anymore. Lily Grace yelled at me. Violet counseled me. Morgan was sending me away. And one of my strongest suspects in what was now a full-on murder investigation was no longer a viable suspect. Meaning Doug Croft. I still didn't know where River Carr had been the night Halpern died.

"Can I at least see you later? Or do you have plans with River again?"

Geez, that was snippy. If I got on my knees and begged her to please, please, please still be my friend, I wouldn't sound more pathetic.

"River will be coming over to meet Mama this evening," Morgan explained, "but you and I could meet for a quick dinner. Would that work?"

"He's meeting your mother?" Suddenly, I was concerned again. Considering his supposed mind-control skill, was he trying to get something from her? Smooth talkers conned highly intelligent women out of millions all the time. Not that Morgan had millions, as far as I knew, but she might have something he wanted. I laughed, trying to make my words seem lighter than the worry behind them. "That's quick. Don't tell me you're serious about a guy you just met thirty-six hours ago."

She gave me a look that said, *stop questioning the witch.* "Dinner?"

"Dinner sounds good." Then, in a rare move, insecure Regular Jayne pushed Sheriff Jayne out of the way, which couldn't lead to anything good. "Just curious, will he be hanging around all the time now? Am I going to have to pick a number to schedule time with you?"

Morgan laughed, thinking I was joking. "Not at all. Let's call this a whirlwind weekend romance. Pure innocent fun, something I haven't had in a very long time."

This time, the look on her beautiful face said, *just be happy for me, okay?* Of course I was happy for her.

Looking around to make sure no one was watching us, I gave her a quick hug. The sheriff embracing one of the villagers might come across as odd to some people.

"I'm sorry to give you a hard time," I said as I pulled away. "I was worried about you."

"And that is very much appreciated. I'll see you after work."

For the first time since I'd met her, I walked away from Morgan feeling rather unsatisfied. Like her mother, Morgan always made me feel more in control of situations. Looked like I was on my own with this one. Meeka headbutted me.

"I know, I'm being very self-centered. I am happy for her. I just don't want her to get hurt."

A cluster of tourists walking by stared at me and then

sped along around the pentacle garden when I looked up. The sheriff hugging a villager would've been fine. The sheriff having a conversation with her K-9? Not so much.

Chapter 26

JUST WHEN I WAS SURE this day couldn't get any stranger, I walked into the station to find Reed and Reeva Long sitting at his desk studying something on his computer.

"What's going on here?" I asked when neither of them looked up.

"Hello, Jayne," Reeva greeted.

"Hey, Sheriff," Reed said. "Aunt Reeva is helping me with—" Reeva touched his arm lightly. "She's helping me with a project."

Reeva gave a proud aunty smile and placed her hand to Reed's cheek. He looked at me, eyes wide with mortification.

"Actually, I'm teaching my nephew a bit of kitchen witchery. Flavia never did get the hang of cooking."

Reed made a face and shook his head, indicating the quality of meals in their home were far from fine dining.

"She hasn't taught him much," Reeva concluded.

"You're stepping in, then?" I asked. "Does Flavia know?"

"The walls are still standing." Reeva grinned like she was joking then turned serious. "No, she doesn't know, but I've tried to help her with some tips and tricks as well."

Tips were fine. It was the tricks part, especially from one

angry sister witch to the other, that made me nervous.

"Aunt Reeva let Mother make the salad dressing last night."

He seemed pleased with this, but Reeva's too-innocent expression said there was more to that than domestic instruction.

Meeka stood with her front paws on one of my feet. I'd forgotten to take her out of her harness. I knelt to do so. "That's right, you all had dinner together last night. How did it go?"

Reeva sighed. "Flavia stayed for the minimally acceptable length of time for a proper house guest and then shot into the woods like a fairy in search of a frolic."

She seemed amused with her own analogy. I had no idea what she was talking about.

"What it comes down to," Reeva continued, fully serious now," is that I've lost far too much time with my family. Twenty years to be precise. My nephew was just an adorable three-year-old when I moved to Milwaukee."

This time, Reed squirmed uncomfortably and shot a *help me* look my way. I laughed and went to my office. He was on his own.

While Reed and Reeva discussed pastry recipes, or whatever they were doing at his computer, I sat at my desk trying to avoid the fact that my suspect board was looming large over me. I stared at all the names I had written there, knowing that one of them was responsible for Nick Halpern's death, and wished the guilty party would step forward.

Voices from the main room caught my attention.

One was Reed. "Did you finally finish? I wasn't sure when I'd see you again."

"I did finish." The accent identified the new voice as Lupe's. "Then I got involved with that novel I told you I wanted to write while I was waiting for my editor's response."

"Lupe, this is my aunt Reeva."

The voices grew softer as Reed most likely led Lupe away from the door and over to his desk. After another minute, the front door opened again, this time slamming open hard enough to knock against the bench sitting next to it.

"You!" This screeching voice could only belong to Flavia. "You did this!"

I jumped up from my desk and rushed out to the main room in time to see Flavia removing a thin scarf from around her face. She was covered everywhere — her face, arms, what I could see of her legs — in tiny red dots.

"I knew there was something suspicious about that salad oil. You hexed me."

Discretely, Lupe slipped into my office, leaving me to deal with the family.

"It wasn't a hex," Reeva insisted, as calm as Flavia was furious.

"Then why am I full of pox marks?"

Reeva appeared to be running through something in her mind, and a few seconds later, her face brightened with understanding. "It was probably the cactus." She placed her hands palms together and bowed her head. "My mistake. I apologize."

Flavia glared and ignored the apology. "And what was in that salad? My tongue puffed up, and my eyes nearly swelled shut."

Reeva ticked off lettuces on her fingers. "Red leaf, arugula, baby kale, dandelion, escarole—"

"Dandelion?" Flavia demanded. "You know I'm allergic. What was the cactus for?"

"All right," I interrupted. "Flavia, you really should calm down. Reeva, what did you do?"

Holding her head high and not showing an ounce of guilt, she said, "I was trying to clear her karma."

"With Four Thieves Vinegar?" Flavia took on a

confrontational pose. "Didn't think I'd figure that out, did you?"

"Reeva, come with me please." I led her into my office, found Lupe hiding there, and took Reeva out the back door instead. "What's going on?"

"You know as well as I do that Flavia has always been trouble. It's only getting worse. Believe it or not, I love my sister and was trying to help."

"By cleansing her karma with vinegar?" There's a sentence I never thought I'd say.

"By allowing her to prepare it, her intent was infused into the vinegar. Before I went to bed, I wrote her name on a strip of paper, soaked the paper in the vinegar, and poked it into my cactus pot. I intended that the cactus spines, being sharp, would keep bad karma away from her." She blushed. "It's been a long time since I've done that spell. It seems the cactus attacked her instead, which honestly was not my intent."

Morgan had warned me Reeva's return to the village could lead to problems.

"Was there yarrow and frankincense involved as well?" I knew she was doing more than stocking her cupboards when she stopped in at Shoppe Mystique. "Look, I know you've both got a lot of anger and resentment for each other. Duke it out all you want but keep it away from everyone else." Reeva reached for the door handle. Before she could, I added, "The dandelion thing better have been a mistake, too. If you knowingly gave your sister something she's allergic to, and her allergy is severe enough, I could charge you with attempted murder."

She nodded her understanding. If she had done it on purpose, she gave nothing away. Back inside, I went right to my office and found Lupe still hiding out there.

"I overheard you say that you finished your last article."

"Not my last," she insisted. "I've got one more month. If I can come up with more articles about the village before my time here is up, maybe I can stay even longer." She pointed at the suspect board. "What is that?"

"Remember the man from my party who was causing such trouble?"

"Yes, what a horrible person. What else did he do?"

"When you seclude yourself to write a story, you really seclude yourself. You didn't hear that he died?"

By the look on her face, the answer was obvious. "The only time I opened my door for the last day and a half was to receive a food delivery. I didn't step outside even once. He's dead? How did he die? Is it safe for me to assume that all those names on the board mean it's another murder?"

Lupe and I had made an agreement with each other when she first arrived in the village. I hadn't hired Reed yet and needed help with the investigations of two deaths up at the circus. In exchange for her helping me by interviewing possible suspects, under the guise of doing mini-biographies on the carnies, I would give her the scoop on breaking events. Now, while she stared at the names on the board, it was clear another article had already started forming in her mind. I gave her a quick rundown of what had happened and explained Dr. Bundy's finding of commotio cordis.

She stared at the board as I spoke. "I recognize some of these names. They're staying at your bed-and-breakfast."

I sat forward on my chair. "That's right, the article you just wrote was about Pine Time. You interviewed my guests for it."

She frowned a little as she nodded. "My editor was only okay with this one. He says it's not as exciting as those I did on the villagers. No offense to your B&B." She returned her attention to Halpern's death by standing and stepping closer to the board. "You suspect that the killer is one of your guests?"

"There were a few tourists." I pointed out Doug Croft's and Elaine Snow's names. "We've cleared them."

"I assume the crossed-out names mean these people are

also no longer suspects?"

"Right."

She tapped the board next to the names Alicia, Derek, and Trevor. "I agree with these. After speaking with them, I don't think any of them would be capable of harming another person."

Lupe turned her chair to face the board and sat again.

"I know one of them did it but can't come up with a solid motive," I explained. "My top suspects are Constance Halpern, Jeremy Levine, and River Carr. They all had opportunity since they're all staying at the B&B. Motive is obvious with the wife, but I can't prove she did anything. Levine is squirrely and has my instincts on edge. Carr had a run-in with him, but that feels weak to me. He's still on the list because I haven't been able to track him down to interview him."

"What about Kristina and Kyle Mandel? Why have you crossed them off?"

After explaining the nasty things Halpern had said about Kristina, and Kyle's reaction to that, I said, "I've got nothing on either of them. I just talked with them last night, and they alibied each other. Kyle seemed lukewarm about Halpern altogether. Kristina obviously didn't like that her brother-in-law was such a jerk, but she seemed more concerned about him than murderous toward him. Besides, Kristina is so wrapped up in herself and this baby, I don't think she's given Nick Halpern two thoughts since they got here. I believe them."

Lupe sat with her lips pursed and a leg bouncing, clearly disagreeing with me.

"You don't seem convinced," I said. "Did they reveal anything noteworthy to you?"

She considered the question. "No. The only strange thing was how shocked Kyle seemed by his wife's pregnancy."

"I think most people, no matter how excited they are to

become parents, are a little bit shocked when they learn the truth."

"True," she agreed. "That's nothing that would put him on a suspect board for murder. Unless ..."

"Unless what?"

"They were in on it together."

I paused, let the possibility run through my mind, and then picked up my marker and added an X by each of their names. "I hadn't considered it and doubt that's the case, but it's not out of the realm of possibility. I guess we need to leave them on the list. At the bottom, though."

"Is 'at the bottom' a Sheriff O'Shea decision or one from Kristina's friend?"

Honestly, I wondered the same thing myself. "What do you know about these other people? Let's start with Jeremy Levine."

"I remember him. I got the impression he feels like the outsider of the group."

"He's only been with them since New Year's. While eight months is a long time for one of Trevor's relationships, it's a drop in the bucket for a group that's been together for so many years."

"That must be it. He didn't strike me as a very happy person. He hates his job."

I flipped through the notes in my little notebook. "He's an administrative assistant. Probably doesn't have much chance of moving up. I suppose, if he's any good, he could become an office manager."

"Not at all what his original goals were. He was pre-law in college but wasn't able to finish."

"That could lead to some bitterness. Possibly some feelings of inadequacy in relation to his boyfriend. Trevor has always been a go-getter and it sounds like he's moving up the ranks quickly at his law firm."

"But we're talking about a murder," Lupe reminded me. "How does that make him a suspect?"

"That alone doesn't," I agreed, "but anger can manifest in strange ways. We're looking for something that might have set him up to explode. If he's not happy with his professional life and feels inadequate in his personal life, he might take that out on someone else." I crossed my arms and stared at Jeremy's name on the board. "Why Halpern? If he was angry about his life, why take it out on a guy who feels exactly the same way?"

"Transference?" Lupe offered. "Maybe he took his anger out on a guy who reminds him of himself?"

"Could be, but it's not as strong a motive as I'd like. Jeremy attacking Halpern is too random. That moves us to Constance."

"Isn't the spouse always the prime suspect?" Lupe asked.

"Many times. I spoke with Constance for quite a while immediately after we found her husband. Her reactions struck me as odd, but she was in shock. She told me about how her husband had lost his job and then spiraled into a deep depression."

"I spoke with her as well," Lupe said, "but very briefly. I asked why she was visiting Whispering Pines this weekend, and she said she was hoping to reset her life."

"Her life? Is that exactly what she said? Her life and not *their* life?"

Lupe flipped through the pages of her own little notebook. "That's what I wrote down. A reset for her life. Why does this concern you?"

"The words we choose when emotional can be very telling. The fact that she referred only to herself and not her husband, as well, could mean something. Or perhaps she was just angry at him and fantasizing about starting over."

"You're thinking pre-meditation?"

"Possibly. Starting over doesn't have to mean murdering him. Maybe she was planning to tell him she was done with the drama and wanted a divorce."

"What about your tall, dark stranger?" Lupe waggled her eyebrows.

"You mean River Carr?"

"Yes, him. He looks like the angel of darkness or death or whatever. Does he have an alibi for the night Mr. Halpern was killed?"

"I haven't spoken with him yet. He was out with Morgan yesterday, and she vouches for his character. Not that her word clears him for the death. She wasn't with him at the time."

"Carr is not a suspect, then?"

"I still want to talk to him, but all I have on him is a mild confrontation with the victim. No motive for murder."

Was that my real reason, or was I protecting Morgan from possible heartbreak? But if he was a murderer, protecting her heart was the last thing I was worried about. The more likely reason was that I was trying to prevent a rift from forming between me and the best friend I'd ever had. Either way, not good police work.

"And then there were two," Lupe intoned. "Constance Halpern and Jeremy Levine."

"Unless Halpern was hit in the chest with something that came flying out of a passing car while walking along the highway in the middle of the night, it seems those two are the most likely suspects."

"Talk about fate being out of our hands."

"I think I need to get back over to Pine Time and talk with them a little more."

"Anything I can do to help?"

I smiled. "No, I think I've got this."

Lupe angled her chair so she could see out into the main room. Specifically, she was looking at Reed.

"You really like him, don't you?" I asked.

"I've been traveling so much for my job over the last couple of years, I haven't had time for serious relationships. I didn't expect to like him. I never thought our first dinner would lead to anything, but yes, I really do like him." She looked at me with pleading eyes. "How can I stay in this village?"

"That's the million-dollar question, isn't it? There are rules to staying here."

She swatted a hand at me. "Martin told me about the rules. Aren't you the head honcho around here? Can't you change the rules?"

"Me, head honcho?" I laughed. "Why? Because my family owns the land? That's why there's a village council in place, so no one person has too much power. The rules are clear, Lupe. The only way for you to stay in the village permanently is to have a job here. If you can convince one of the shop owners to hire you, the council would likely let you stay."

She stared blankly into the far corner of my office. Something was twirling around in her mind. There wasn't much I could do to help, but I certainly wouldn't try and stop her from staying.

A new commotion in the main room caught my attention.

"Help us, please. Dustin is gone again."

Chapter 27

I RUSHED OUT INTO THE station's main room to find a teenage girl with tears pooled in her round brown eyes.

Five foot four, straight dark-blonde hair to her shoulder blades, athletic build, approximately fourteen years of age.

I put my hands on her shoulders and stared into her eyes, helping her calm down and get her breathing under control. The girl was close to hyperventilating, and I didn't want her passing out on me. She nodded in unison with me as she took gradually slower and deeper breaths.

"Good. I'm Sheriff O'Shea. Tell me what happened. Who's Dustin?"

She kept nodding as she spoke, a sort of self-soothing motion. "Dustin is my brother. He's four." She pointed at Reed. "He found him at the beach the other day."

"I remember Dustin." Reed's voice was light with no hint of worry. "He wandered off again?"

"Yeah. We were walking in the woods over by that circle?"

"The Meditation Circle?" I confirmed.

"I think that's it. It's got that fire pit in the middle and a bunch of benches all around it."

"That's the place. Okay, so you were there with your family?"

"Yeah, a whole bunch of us came up here for the weekend. There's like" — she looked up, as though into her own brain, as she listed people — "my mom and dad, me and my little brother, my aunt and uncle and three cousins, and my grandma. Is that ten? There's ten of us."

"That's ten," I confirmed. "You were all hiking together?"

"Well, not hiking, really. There's that path that leads up there, so, you know, we were just walking on the path. Anyway, my three cousins were fighting. My grandma was trying to calm them down, and my aunt was all upset because her kids are little demons and never listen to anyone." The girl shook her head in that disgusted teenager way. "No one was paying any attention to Dustin. Everyone was walking and arguing and the next thing I knew, my dad is like, 'Where's Dustin?'"

"Okay, you're getting upset again. Calm down."

She took a breath with me and blew it out slowly.

"Is everyone still at the Meditation Circle?"

"Kind of. My mom and dad and my aunt and uncle are out looking for Dustin. We decided one person should come and get you. Grandma's watching the three demons. That left me. Will you come?"

"Of course I will." I turned to Reed. "I'll go with Meeka. Contact the County Sheriff's Department to be on alert. If we don't find Dustin quickly, I want them to send a search and rescue team." I patted my hip and then ran into my office to get my walkie-talkie. "Let's stay in constant contact. As soon as I'm up there and searching, I'll check in with you every ten minutes with an update."

"Got it." Reed was already reaching for the phone. "Do you want me to come up there and help?"

"Not yet. Stay here until we decide if we need to activate search and rescue." I whistled for Meeka who appeared from beneath her cot. "Meeka, come."

This time, she could tell by the tone of my voice that it

was serious; she didn't hesitate and came right over to me. I strapped on her harness and attached the leash. Before we left, I went back into my office and grabbed a small backpack that I had preloaded with what the Boy Scouts referred to as the ten essentials: a multi-tool pocket knife, first-aid kit, rain gear, water bottles, flashlight, non-perishable food, an emergency thermal blanket, sun protection, compass, and waterproof matches.

I stood in my office with Meeka at my feet, closed my eyes, and took in some deep breaths of my own.

"No panicking," I told myself softly. Missing kid cases always freaked me out. "Pull yourself together. This family needs you."

Meeka leaned against my leg almost as though preparing herself along with me. I blew out one final breath, reached down to pet my dog, and then returned to the main room.

"You never told me who you are, sweetheart," I told the girl.

"I'm Lindy."

I put an arm around her. "Lindy, I'm Jayne. Let's go find Dustin."

~~~

With Lindy in the passenger seat, I laid on the horn as we raced down the two-lane highway and up the dirt road to the bridge that crossed the creek. From the creek, it was a short distance, maybe a quarter mile, to the Meditation Circle. As soon as Meeka was out of the vehicle and her leash was hooked on, Lindy took my hand and ran with me down the path.

"Grandma," she called out. "Grandma, I've got the sheriff."

Once through the trees and into the clearing that made up the Circle area, I froze for what felt like minutes but was probably only a second or two. The last time I was here, Sheriff Karl Brighton took his own life in front of me. I glanced at the bench on the far west side closest to the tree line. That's where he'd been sitting, facing the trees.

I forced my eyes from that spot, and they immediately went to a crescent of bare earth next to the fire pit. That had to be the spot where Priscilla Page died forty years earlier. There, in that crescent, Flavia would've been at the center, Rae to her right, and Priscilla on Flavia's left. Where had my dad been standing? Near Rae, if Gran's journal was accurate.

How many more deaths would happen in this village? What was my role? Was I a part of the problem, or was I here to chase off that black cloud? A quick, warm breeze blew through the area, making the canopy of tree branches above rub together. *O'Shea* they seemed to say and brought me back to the present.

I blinked and noticed a woman who I guessed to be in her early sixties. She looked absolutely worn down, but whether from the stress of little missing Dustin or the stress of dealing with the three "demons" left in her care, I couldn't tell.

Two little boys and one girl, all who looked to be within a year of each other, which meant in the four- to five-year range, were racing around the Meditation Circle chasing each other. They were laughing and having a good time. No one was bleeding, but it was absolute chaos and constant motion, so I wouldn't be surprised if someone was soon.

"You left her alone with them?" I asked Lindy softly.

"She's got a bad knee," Lindy said as though that explained it all, which it did. Of the two, Lindy would get to me faster.

"Oh, thank God." The grandma looked at Lindy and pointed to the trio of terror. With Lindy taking over babysitting duty, Grandma came over to me. "Lindy told you the others are searching for him? They're in pairs so no one else will get lost. Or if they do, at least no one is alone. I wish they could call. There's no cell service in this village, are you aware of that?"

"Painfully aware, ma'am. I'm Sheriff O'Shea. What can you tell me?"

It turned out, Lindy had covered everything perfectly. Grandma, whose first name was Eloise, didn't give me any new information but did confirm what I'd been told.

"Where was the last place either of you saw Dustin?" I asked loudly so Lindy could also hear me over the squealing preschoolers.

"Here," Eloise said.

"Aunt Helen," Lindy looked pointedly at the little ones, indicating she was their mother, "is obsessed with that religion you all do up here."

"She's a practicing Wiccan?" I asked.

"Not yet, but she's working toward it," Eloise said. "We stopped here so she could 'guide us in a meditation.' With those three little rascals, I'm sure you can imagine how successful that was."

"The meditation didn't go so well," Lindy supplied, "and Auntie got upset. A big argument started, and she stomped out of here."

"We all followed," Eloise said. "It's not good when Helen gets upset. It ruins everyone's day. Since our focus was on her, none of us noticed that Dustin wasn't following."

Lindy's face pinched like she was trying not to cry. A second later, the attempt failed, and she burst into tears. "It's my fault. It's my job to watch him."

"He's not your responsibility, sweetie," Eloise assured in a very caring, grandmotherly way. How nice. My mom's mom would've rolled her eyes and told me to snap out of it. "You're the sister, not the mother."

"You're both saying," I confirmed, bringing us back to the present problem, "that this was the last place you saw Dustin?"

They both agreed.

"I'd like for you five to wait over on the footpath by my car. I need to investigate the area while it's empty. Lindy, will you show them where?"

The girl nodded and then herded the little ones out of the Meditation Circle, her grandmother following. Not thirty seconds later, Lindy returned.

"I thought this might help." She handed me a small royal-blue sweatshirt. "This is Dustin's. Grandma thought maybe your dog could smell him on it or whatever."

"Meeka isn't trained in search and rescue, but it sure can't hurt." I held the sweatshirt down to Meeka and she sniffed it eagerly. "I'm going to hang on to this for a little while, okay?"

With eyes locked on the sweatshirt, Lindy sniffed. "My mom's gonna want it back."

"No worries. I'll return it once I have Dustin."

My walkie-talkie squawked. "Sheriff? I contacted County. How's it going? Over."

I pulled my unit off my hip and responded, "Just got done talking with the grandma. Meeka and I are going to start searching in the woods now." I pulled my cell phone out of its cargo pocket and set a timer. "I'll check back in ten minutes." I turned to Lindy. "Don't let your grandma or any of the kids wander off. Stay right here. The last thing we need is more people to search for."

Lindy promised and upped the ante to also keep her mom, dad, aunt, and uncle by the car when they returned as well.

I stood at the entrance of the Meditation Circle and took in the area, trying to envision it as a four-year-old little boy. Too tall. I got down on my knees. Better.

I don't like it when everybody yells. It scares me. They're all going away, so I'm going to stay right here. Tired of all the yelling.

I blinked that vision away, making it vanish like a pixelating video. I was forcing it. That's not what a four-year-old would've been thinking. I took a deep breath, held it, and let it out slowly.

Chipmunk! I'm going to catch him. If I sneak real slow and don't make any noise, he won't know I'm here. Oh, shoot, too loud; he ran away. There he is! I need to be super-quiet. One step. Another step. Darn it! I stepped on a stick and scared him away again. Where is he? Maybe he went this way ...

Among the four or five other varying width groomed hiking paths that led out of the area like spokes on a wheel, I noticed one spot without a path where the weeds looked like they'd been pushed aside. I stood and moved closer. Some of the weeds looked like they'd been trampled. One pencil-thick branch had a fresh break and was flipped over into the bush. I dropped down to one knee again and held the branch out to its normal position. If I was four years old, it would hang right in my face.

Stupid branch is in my way ... There. Now, I gotta stand here like a statue and wait for the little guy to scamper out of his hiding place.

We had to start somewhere, and this seemed the most logical path to follow. "Let's go this way, Meeka."

I offered her the sweatshirt again. After sniffing it, she trotted ahead of me. Whether she was really scenting Dustin or not, I couldn't tell. We'd gone maybe twenty yards when the timer on my phone went off. I pulled the walkie-talkie off my belt.

"Deputy Reed. Ten-minute check-in."

"Go, Sheriff. Over."

"We found what looks to be trampled weeds going into the woods as well as a few small footprints in mud. We're going to follow the trail for a while. Over and out."

Walking slowly, despite Meeka trying to pull me forward, I kept my eyes to the ground and focused on the flattened weeds. Every now and then, the trail would lead us to a bush. Sometimes, the squashed weed footprints went around the bush, sometimes they seemed to go directly into it and I'd find another broken branch or two. At these spots, we'd have to pause, much to Meeka's displeasure, and find the trail again. My timer went off once more.

"Deputy Reed. Ten-minute check-in."

"Go, Sheriff. Over."

"Still following what appears to be a trail through the woods. My guess is that the parents chose one of the already-worn pathways rather than looking for something fresh. We're staying on this and heading north. Over and out."

We did this for two more cycles of my timer. I considered going back, but every time I did, I found another little footprint or trail of squashed weeds so stayed the course. After another five minutes, Meeka halted in her pursuit. She lifted her head, stretched her neck forward, and sniffed. Without warning, she pulled back, darted behind my legs, and hid. Whatever she smelled, she didn't like it. A skunk? A fox?

Thirty seconds later, I had my answer.

"Well, if it isn't Sheriff Jayne O'Shea."

There was only one person in the village I knew who was that big and smelled that bad. Six foot four with long white matted hair and beard to match, this man looked like he'd lived his whole life in the forest.

"Willie? What are you doing out here?"

Blind Willie, one of the most reclusive villagers, stepped aside to reveal a little boy standing behind him. "You wouldn't happen to be looking for Dustin here, would you?"

I said a silent prayer of thanks to the Universe as stress drained from my body. For numerous reasons, I needed this one to end in a win.

"I sure would be. His mom, dad, aunt, and uncle are looking for him, too." I walked over to the little boy and bent over at the waist. "My name is Sheriff Jayne. Your family is very worried about you. What happened?"

"There was a kitty," Dustin said. "I was following a little green snake, but it got lost."

I waited for more, but Dustin seemed happy with this explanation. "I'm confused. What got lost? The cat or the snake?"

He rolled his eyes and started again like I was dense. "I followed the snake, but he slithered into a bush and got lost. Then the kitty came. I tried to catch her, but she was sneaky."

"You've probably seen this cat," Willie said.

"White cat, blue eyes?" I asked. "People call her Blue?"

"Yep. Did you know that the majority of white cats with two blue eyes are deaf?"

"That's specific."

"It's a genetic thing," Dustin explained seriously, like it was a fatal disease, and dropped down to all fours to pet Meeka.

I bit back a smile. He was clearly repeating what Willie had told him. "I didn't know that. Meeka spotted Blue in the pentacle garden yesterday. They became fast friends."

"She's a smart one, our Blue," Willie said. "Led little Dustin right to my cabin. I figured that unless little boys had started sprouting up like weeds in our woods, someone down in the village must be looking for him."

Dustin giggled. "Boy weeds."

"Can't thank you enough, Willie. Any chance you've seen his parents or aunt and uncle?"

"They missing, too?"

"Not missing, as far as I know, but they were out looking for him. If you happen to come across them, will you let them know I've got him?"

Willie gave me a salute, promised he would keep an eye out for Dustin's people, and disappeared into the woods.

"Willie?" I called out.

Like some sort of overgrown forest sprite, he reappeared as quickly as he'd vanished. "Sheriff?"

"Is there an easier way back to the Meditation Circle from here?"

He pointed west and instructed us to go about a hundred yards where we'd meet up with a wide pathway. "Head south on the path and you'll end up at the Circle in about ten minutes, give or take."

"Thank you, Willie."

"My pleasure." He looked down at Dustin and pointed a big beefy finger at him. "Don't go chasing any more snakes, little man."

Dustin giggled again and wrapped his arms around one of Willie's legs in a hug. "I won't."

I let Reed know that I'd found the boy and was on the way back to the Meditation Circle with him. Just as Willie had promised, we found the path and after walking for almost twenty minutes, Dustin had shorter legs than Willie, after all, we saw my SUV in the distance. There were more than just Lindy and Eloise there now. I assumed this meant the other grown-ups had returned.

The trio of preschoolers came running up to him, pushing each other out of the way to get to him first.

"Dustin!"

"Where did you go?"

"You left without us."

After plenty of hugs and lots of tears, Dustin's parents calmed down enough for me to explain what had happened. They were grateful beyond belief and promised they would not take their eyes off him again. Sadly, I was pretty sure that's what they'd told Reed after he found Dustin by the lake.

"I'm going to make sure he doesn't wander off again," Lindy told me quietly and off to the side. "I know I'm not the parent, but sometimes they make me feel like I am."

I returned the hug she had locked on me and realized how much alike the girl and I were. My mother used to put me in charge of Rosalyn all the time. It was too much responsibility, and Lindy, like I had, seemed to be caving under it. On the night I finally said no to being my mother's little assistant, Rosalyn was kidnapped. Logically, I knew it wasn't my fault, but to this day, my heart didn't quite believe my head.

"Don't be afraid to tell them how you feel. You've got enough going on just being a teenager."

Chapter 28

ON THE WAY FROM THE Meditation Circle to the station, the benefit of living in the present hit me. From the moment I got down on my knees, looking at the area as a four-year-old, to the minute I handed him over to his family, I had focused on nothing but Dustin. In a way, the world became smaller because all I saw was what was right in front of me. At the same time, it became bigger because instead of the forest as a whole, I noticed details that I never normally would — the different colors, the smells, and the sounds. It was invigorating.

"Anything you need me to do?" Reed asked toward the end of the afternoon. "Help you with that paperwork?"

"Nope, I'm just about done." I clicked save on Dustin's report and would go through it one last time before closing the file.

"Congratulations on finding that kid."

"Thanks. And thanks for waiting in the wings as my backup."

He gave me a little salute. "That's my job. If it's okay, Lupe is dying for company after nearly two days alone."

"Have a good time. Or at least try to. She's really upset about having to leave, isn't she?"

"She is. If I had my own place, she could come visit me

without having to pay for a rental."

"Careful. That could turn into moving into your place."

He shivered, grinned, and left the building. When I'd completed Dustin's paperwork, I thought about my plan to meet Morgan for dinner. As much as I wanted to spend time with her, I really needed to talk to Carr and either move forward with him as a suspect or cross him off the list. I needed to postpone dinner with Morgan.

As Meeka and I arrived at Shoppe Mystique, we found Willow sweeping the front porch. She saw us coming and held the door open. The nice gesture took me off guard. Willow was never nice to me.

"Morgan told me you'd be stopping by," she said and followed us inside. "I think she's in the reading room."

As we walked through the store, the old wood floors creaking and popping, I noticed that the half-empty shelves from yesterday were almost completely empty now.

"Looks like you had a good weekend here," I told Morgan who was right where Willow thought she'd be.

"The timing is perfect." She was straightening the bookshelves along the wall that hid the altar room. "Whatever seasonal things we don't sell will have to be packed up until spring. It's time to bring out all the autumn items. Mabon is less than a month away, and everything harvest now reigns."

Her eyes sparkled at the mention of autumn, the Wiccans' favorite time of year. The Wiccan new year started with Halloween, or Samhain, as they called it.

"I know we planned to have dinner at Triple G," I began, "but I'm going to have to postpone. I need to get over to the B&B."

"That's fine. I was going to tell you the same thing." She swept an arm across the shop. "We obviously have a great deal of restocking to do, and as I mentioned earlier, River will be coming over to meet Mama tonight."

At the mention of Carr's name, a little spot in my gut

hardened.

"I could spare five minutes for a cup of tea." Why was I pushing this? I needed to get home and talk to him.

"Not tonight, Jayne. River will be leaving the village after dinner, so we'll have plenty of time to catch up."

She opened the front door. I hadn't even noticed we'd walked across the shop.

"We'll chat soon. I promise." With fingertips on my arm, she guided me out the door. "Blessed be."

I stood on Shoppe Mystique's front porch feeling dismissed. *Schadenfreude*, as I'd told Constance, was when you took pleasure from someone's misfortune. Was there a term for when you got what you asked for but weren't happy because someone else made it happen?

~~~

As the garage came into view at the end of my long driveway, my heart raced at the sight of the Aston Martin. Was I nervous? I couldn't remember ever being nervous to conduct an interview. Maybe I had been with my very first one, but not since. The truth was, for Morgan's sake, I really wanted Carr to be innocent.

I let Meeka out of her cage and crossed the yard to the back patio. Halfway there, I heard people talking. As I rounded the corner of the house, I found our guests sitting back there, Tripp with them.

"What's going on?" I asked when he came over to greet me.

"I thought they could use a bit of a release. Come join Pine Time's first wine and cheese gathering."

The first thought that entered my mind was *I hope you didn't spend too much*. Violet's warning about being open in the winter had been eating at me all afternoon.

"You should go change clothes first," Tripp said. "This is a casual gathering. No need for the sheriff to be here."

"Actually," I began, and his face dropped, "do you know where River Carr is?"

He glanced over his shoulder, checking that no one was close enough to overhear. "He's a suspect?"

"I'm not sure, but I can't rule him out if I don't talk to him. He hasn't checked out yet, has he?"

"No, he's paid through tomorrow. Why would he check out?"

"I just saw Morgan. She said he was leaving tonight."

Tripp's brow furrowed with confusion. "Why would Morgan know that?"

"I told you about them last night, didn't I?"

"About them? No, I'd remember that. What about them?"

I was doing my best to keep sheriff stuff separate from personal stuff. When we discussed how our day went at dinner, I only gave him a quick recap, otherwise, he wanted to help me solve crimes. Not that I didn't appreciate his help, but things were fuzzy now that I was sheriff. There were details I couldn't tell him. Since the Morgan issue wasn't related to the Halpern case, I told him about how she'd gone off the grid yesterday.

"And you're worried that he did something to her. Is she okay?"

His tone and stance said he was ready to rush over and help her if she needed it.

"She's fine," I assured. "I need to talk to Carr because of that exchange he had with Halpern at breakfast that first morning. It was probably nothing, but you never know what will push someone's last button."

Tripp stood straight and shoved his shoulders back, his alpha gorilla pose. "I'm pretty sure he's upstairs. He came down to fill that goblet of his, grabbed a few pieces of cheese, and left." He stared at me until I met his eyes. "You'll let me know if you need assistance?"

That was the other reason I tried to keep sheriff and

B&B separate. He meant well, but when it came to law enforcement, I knew how to handle myself.

"I'm fine. Save a glass of wine for me."

Meeka wanted to stay with Tripp, she could smell the cheese on the table, but I made her come with me. Part of defending myself meant having my weapons, both Glock and K-9, at the ready at all times. We found Carr sitting in the little landing at the top of the stairs.

"The lake is beautiful," he said as he stared out the window. "I understand why the residents like it here so much."

I agreed with him and took a seat. Meeka positioned herself between us.

"Time for us to have a chat?" he asked.

His confident calm didn't sway me if that was his intent. "It is."

"Which topic shall we discuss first?"

"Which topic?"

Carr stood, turned his wingback chair away from the windows to face me, then sat back down. "Your unfortunate deceased guest or the enchanting Ms. Barlow?"

That threw me a little. I hadn't planned to discuss Morgan with him.

"Business first." I turned on my voice recorder and set it on the small round wood table between our chairs. "You and the deceased had an exchange at breakfast."

"We did." He sipped from his goblet before responding further. "I have to say, Sheriff, if a minor verbal disagreement is enough to make someone a suspect in a murder investigation, you must conduct a great many interviews."

"His words clearly upset you. I saw what you did." I pointedly traced my finger down my throat.

He smiled but remained otherwise unaffected by this. "Neat trick, isn't it?"

"Where were you when Nick Halpern died?"

"I'm not privy to the hour of his death so can't answer precisely. If you mean where was I late Saturday night or early Sunday morning, I was here both by myself and talking with Mrs. Halpern."

"Constance? Why were you talking to her in the middle of the night?"

"I tend to stay up late into the evening. Since only my bathroom windows face the lake, I sat right here, in this very seat, in fact, to observe the night lake and sky."

"What time was that?"

"Approximately one fifteen. The house was busy that night. Around one thirty, someone walked past, but I didn't see who. Then perhaps fifteen minutes later Mr. Halpern walked by, grumbling about his, excuse the language, 'bitch of a wife.'"

"How did you know it was Halpern and not Mr. Mandel grumbling about Mrs. Mandel?"

He tilted his head, granting me that. "A fair question. It could have been Mr. Mandel, but it sounded like Mr. Halpern's voice."

"When did you speak with Mrs. Halpern?"

He paused, remembering. "It was around two o'clock when someone walked passed again, returning this time. As before, it was dark and I didn't see who it was. Since I had been under the impression Mr. Halpern had left earlier, I went to be sure everything was all right with Mrs. Halpern."

"You went to their room?"

"I did. I knocked and when she opened it, I immediately noticed that her eyes, nose, and cheeks were red."

"Red as in she'd been crying or red from being outside in the cool night air?"

He shook his head. "I couldn't say. I asked if she was all right, and she mentioned an argument with her husband. I escorted her downstairs to the kitchen and got her a glass of water. We talked for perhaps twenty minutes, about her frustrations over her husband's state of mind, and once she had calmed, we returned to our rooms."

I stared out the window while I analyzed Carr's timeline. The mystery person passed the landing at one thirty. Constance? Kyle? Halpern, supposedly, passed by at one forty-five. A mystery person returned around two at which time Carr went to Constance's room and spoke with her until almost two twenty. That was the approximate time Laurel called me on my walkie-talkie.

"Constance will verify this?"

"I expect she will."

"Did anyone see you sitting here in the landing?"

"It was quite dark that night. If I couldn't see the people passing by, I don't imagine they saw me."

"In other words, your only alibi for the night is Constance, who you saw at two o'clock."

"That's correct."

"Everything else you told me is unsubstantiated, then. Mr. Halpern's body was discovered shortly after two. You could have killed him and then talked with his wife expecting that she'd alibi you."

"That is possible but not what happened." He studied me for a moment. "You have a great deal of anger for me, Sheriff. Since you have no real reason to believe I did anything more than speak to Mr. Halpern, I sense this has to do with me spending time with Ms. Barlow."

Conflict coursed through me. On one hand, I wanted to clear this guy for Morgan's sake. On the other hand, I wanted to nail him to keep him away from her. This was not good police work. He was right, I had nothing to prove he'd done anything wrong.

Holding his gaze, I asked, "Was there supposed to be a question in there, or are you just making an observation?"

Carr's mouth turned in an amused smile and he glanced at his wristwatch. "I have to leave for dinner in ten minutes. Is there anything else you wanted to discuss with me?"

Obviously, he meant Morgan. The last thing I wanted

was to discuss her with him.

"Your dinner date will tell me anything she wants me to know." I stood to leave and added, "Keep one thing in mind: she's got friends who would do anything for her. A few know how to cast spells, so don't hurt her."

Did I seriously just threaten him with woo-woo?

Chapter 29

TRIPP LOOKED UNNECESSARILY RELIEVED WHEN I appeared on the patio, the wine and cheese gathering still in full swing. Excellent. Alcohol tended to loosen people's mouths.

"Everything went okay?" he asked.

"Not sure yet." I went over to Constance and quietly asked her to join me on the sundeck. She followed, glass of wine in hand. I paused at my vehicle to get Nick's file folder and then led her up to the deck. I chose a chair that would let me see anyone who might come up the stairs and indicated she should take the one to my right, facing the lake.

"I haven't seen you since yesterday morning." I turned on my voice recorder and set it on the fire pit table. "I wanted to check in and see how you were doing."

"You mean has the shock worn off and am I crying over the death of my husband yet?"

Still cold as snow. "I've got to say, Constance, your reactions are a little shocking."

"I told you, being married to Nick has been a real challenge for more than a year. If things would have been good between us before that, I could have dealt with the harassment charges more easily."

"A year? You never said anything about things being unhappy before he lost his job."

She shrugged. "It had nothing to do with our discussion. The fact is, for the last two years, give or take, we both worked insane hours. We never had dinner, or any meal, together. The closest thing to a social life were invitations to Kristina and Kyle's house parties. I couldn't tell you the last time we had a date. We had become roommates, and honestly, I was okay with that. Better the devil you know, as the saying goes."

"Are you athletic at all?" My question took her by surprise.

"Athletic? As in do I play organized sports?" She laughed. "I just told you, I work insane hours. The closest thing to a sport, for me, is running on the treadmill. Occasionally I get to run outside; I do enjoy that."

"Do you have any skill with, say, throwing a ball? Or throwing a punch? Do you ever work out with a heavy bag?"

She laughed as though the thought was hilarious. "No, I have no skill throwing either a ball or a punch. I'm not sure I even know what a heavy bag is. Where are we going with this line of questioning?"

I took the file folder from where I'd wedged it between my seat's arm and cushion and pulled out the picture of the bruise on Nick's chest.

"Your husband's autopsy results came in. The preliminary results, I should say. I'm sure you're aware that the full report can take weeks."

Constance shifted in her chair, looking uncomfortable, rather than indifferent, for the first time.

"And what do those results show?"

"Are you familiar with a condition called commotio cordis?"

She appeared to be scanning her memory banks for that information and then nodded. "Yes, it's actually Latin for 'disturbance of the heart.' It's an arrhythmia caused by a blow to the chest or back. There have been reported incidences of people causing the condition while trying to help a choking victim by pounding on their back, which is not advised to begin with."

I turned the picture to face her. "The medical examiner found this bruise on Nick's chest. As you can see, it's rather large so could have been caused by a basketball but probably from some other kind of large blunt object."

"Wait." She snatched the picture from my hand. "This is Nick?"

"It is."

"You're telling me that my husband died from commotio cordis? That's a condition for teenagers, boys in particular."

"According to the medical examiner, while rare, it can occur in adults as well. The truly confusing thing, to me, is that this happened while Nick was walking alongside the road in the middle of the night."

Constance sat there, staring at the picture for a long moment. When she finally looked up at me, there were tears heavy in her eyes.

"As a nurse, I'm trained to deal with life-threatening diseases and death on a daily basis. While I do everything I can to keep my patients comfortable, I'm not supposed to react emotionally. Of course, that's not always possible. There are often patients I become attached to." She wiped away tears that had fallen down her face. "It's never real until there's a diagnosis, you know? I mean, I believed you that Nick was gone even though you didn't ask me to identify the body." She stared at the picture again and then tapped a spot on it. "See this birthmark?"

I leaned in to look closer. "It looks like a little heart."

She nodded, and her tears fell harder. "Back when things were still good, when we were still head over heels for each other, he used to tell me that he loved me so much his heart couldn't hold it all, so he needed a second one."

It was my turn to turn off the emotions as she sobbed. I also witnessed death far too often. Many times, my job, like Constance's, involved turning people's good days into their worst ones. I stepped inside my apartment to get a box of tissues but said nothing until she had herself together again, which also gave me time to center myself.

"You still loved your husband," I said softly, bringing her back to the discussion.

She nodded as she dabbed the corners of her eyes. "I did. I have to say, it wasn't always easy these last eight months." She let out a sad little chuckle. "You think that when you find the person you believe to be your soulmate, everything will be easy. Most things are, but a relationship is never fifty-fifty. Whether a spouse, family member, or friend, one person will always need more than the other. What makes a relationship successful, is that both people accept that and support each other's needs."

"Did you forget about that since his troubles started?"

"I think I did." Her tears started again. "And now it's too late. I should've reminded Nick that I was here for him. I did at the beginning, when the woman first accused him, but then I started to feel the stress of bringing in the only paycheck. I was so focused on keeping us okay financially, I forgot to pay attention to my husband's emotional needs."

"Constance, I need to figure out who did this to Nick. I'm sure you would agree that the chances of this being an accident would be very rare. By which, I mean that someone tossed something out of a car as they drove past and it happened to hit Nick in the chest and cause the arrhythmia that stopped his heart."

"Commotio cordis is rare enough on its own. I agree with you; while it's not impossible, it is unimaginable that this was caused by something from a passing car." She traced the tips of her fingers over the image of Nick's heart-shaped birthmark and then looked up at me. "Am I off your suspect list now?"

For an instant, the question chilled my blood. A question out of nowhere like that, from a highly intelligent woman who had been so cold about her husband's death earlier, struck me as calculated. I wanted to believe her so didn't answer right away. Instead, I observed her body language. She held my eye confidently, but not so long that it felt forced or unnatural. She wasn't fidgeting or demonstrating any other nervous tics. Despite the almost warm temperature outside, her eyes, nose, and cheeks were bright red. She was a rosy crier. The question wasn't calculated. It was a plea from a woman who had suffered almost more than she could take.

"You are off my list." I gave her a moment to exhale before asking, "On the night Nick died, did you speak with River Carr?"

"I did. Nick and I had a fight." She gasped softly, fighting off more sobs. "Our last words to each other were angry ones."

This confirmed that portion of Carr's statement. It seemed safe to assume that Nick was the grumbling man Carr heard walk by. Then who was the second person?

"Did you see anyone else around that time?"

Constance shook her head. "I knocked on Kristina's door. I wanted to talk to someone about my fight with Nick, but neither of them answered."

"Did you find that strange?"

"That neither answered the door?" She considered this question, scanning her memory banks again. "Kristina has always been a heavy sleeper. I can't say for Kyle."

"What about Trevor or Jeremy?"

"I didn't see either of them."

"Is there a direction you feel I should go next?"

She shook her head. "I wish I could offer some suggestion, but I have no idea."

"Don't worry. I will figure this out."

I held out my hand for the picture. She stared like she didn't understand what I wanted her to do. Her world was starting to crumble before my eyes, even more than it already had over the last six months. So she wouldn't have to give it up, I reached out, took hold of the photo, and gave it a little tug, pulling it free from her slack fingers.

I walked her back to the patio. When we were close enough that the lights on the back of the house illuminated Constance's tear-streaked face, Kristina ran over and wrapped her sister in a hug while locking eyes with me.

"It just hit her, didn't it?" Kristina asked.

Everyone grieved differently. It wasn't possible to tell what was going on internally by looking externally.

"It did. You'll stay with her?"

Kristina nodded and brought Constance inside, where they sat together on one of the sofas in the great room.

I glanced around the patio at the guests still there. Alicia and Derek sat talking quietly together, glancing at me questioningly a couple times. Trevor took a long drink from his wine glass. Kyle stared through the window at his wife and sister-in-law inside.

Jeremy seemed the least affected by Constance's emotional response. That could be because he was the newest in the group, or because he was too wrapped up in his own world to care. He had clearly been angry at Nick Halpern for the way he'd been treating women. Had he been angry enough to follow Nick when he went for a walk that night and his anger got physical? Was he the mystery person?

"Jeremy, would you come with me? I'd like to speak with you for a few minutes."

He jabbed his index finger into his own chest. "Me?"

I nodded. "Please. Let's go to the sundeck."

We'd taken our seats, and I just started the voice recorder when he spoke first. "We already talked. Why are we doing this again?"

I matched his aggressive tone. "I'm confused by your attitude."

"My attitude? You're concerned about my attitude after witnessing Nick Halpern?"

He stood to pace.

"Mr. Levine, please, sit." The last thing I wanted was for him to bolt on me. "You seem so angry. Why is that?"

Reluctantly, he returned to his chair. "I'm not angry. I'm irritated."

Semantics. Fine. "Why are you so irritated?"

"Because with the exception of Alicia and Derek, none of these people seem to understand how good they've got it."

"Do you?"

He slouched back in the chair, sulking. "What's that supposed to mean?"

"You don't seem happy with anything. You've got a pretty great boyfriend and good friends."

He flung a hand at the back patio. "You mean those people? They're not my friends. Trevor and I have been together for eight months, and they still haven't accepted me."

"I assume you and Trevor have discussed past partners."

His eyebrows furrowed with confusion, but he nodded.

"Please answer verbally for the recording."

He cleared his throat and shifted positions. "Yes, Trevor and I have discussed past relationships."

"Then you know that he's had a lot of boyfriends. Try putting yourself in the group's position. If you had known Trevor for as long as we have and saw yet another man come into the picture, how likely would you be to get close to someone you thought would be gone in a month or two?"

His cheeks flamed red. "But it's been eight months."

Constance's words about one person always needing more came back to me. "Have you stopped to consider what's been going on in their lives?"

He looked away from me. "Like what?"

"For example, Nick and Constance have been dealing with his job loss and the depression he'd been suffering because of it. Constance said he'd been going to therapy, but it didn't help. Unfortunately, the way he dealt with it was by tearing others down to try and make himself feel better."

Jeremy was listening; I could tell because he didn't reply.

"Alicia and Derek," I continued, "have five children. I don't imagine they have time for each other let alone anyone else. Kristina and Kyle both work full-time jobs and have been dealing with the stress of not being able to get pregnant. Something they both desperately wanted."

He flinched at that one.

"Is there a specific reason that Nick's harassment of people, women in particular, upset you so much?"

He didn't answer, probably hoping I'd let this one go. Instead, I sat back and waited. He shifted positions, again, and exhaled a few huffy breaths. Finally, he said, "My twin sister. She looked a lot like me."

I tried to imagine a female version of Jeremy. I knew that the external package was rarely representative of what was inside, but for most people, unfortunately, external beauty was highly important. It was the first thing they saw, and if they didn't like what they saw, they wouldn't look further.

"I know what you're thinking." Acid filled his voice. "No, she wasn't a beauty. In fact, she was bullied because of her looks since we were little. It was relentless."

He spoke of her in the past tense. I knew where this was going to end and was about to stop him, but he continued telling her story before I could.

"She did everything, tried every beauty tip and trick she came across, to make herself more attractive." He indicated the huge gap between his front teeth, meaning she'd had the same. "She went to a dentist and got crowns." He tapped his nose. "She went to a plastic surgeon and had her big beak of a nose shaved down." He slapped his hands to his face. "She got cheek implants and had her ears pinned back so her face wouldn't look so wide. She had her breasts augmented." He shook his head, disgusted and heartbroken. "By the time she was done, she was an absolute knockout and men noticed her. She was so desperate for attention, she'd go home with anyone who would take her." He looked at me, pain etched on his face. "I'm sure you can imagine the quality of these men's characters."

"She went from bullying to abused?" I asked gently.

"Exactly. About two years ago, there came a night she couldn't take it anymore. She sat in the car in my garage with the engine running." Rather than sorrow, Jeremy's anger started seeping to the surface again.

"I'm so sorry, Jeremy. I really am. No one should have to suffer the way your sister did. What was her name?"

"Justine." He sat quietly for a second. "The saddest part of all is that as she changed the outside, what was inside her changed as well. She had been a really great person. By the end, she was shallow and awful to be around. She started drinking and doing drugs. To numb her pain, I assume." He stared out at the lake, hands clenching and unclenching. "I never used to be so angry."

"Jeremy? Did you kill Nick Halpern?"

He looked me square in the eye. "No, I did not. But trust me, I'm not even a little bit sad he's dead. I suppose when everyone starts talking about him, you know, the way people do when someone dies?" I nodded. "It's possible that once that happens, and I learn about the real Nick, my feelings could change. But right now, all I can feel is anger at the man who could treat people that way."

I could continue questioning Jeremy. I could explain what the autopsy report uncovered and question him more about his own athletic abilities. I didn't need to, though. He was a very angry man, but he wasn't a killer.

"You're free to go, Jeremy."

Rather than shoot to his feet as I had expected, he sat, staring at the ground with his hands on his knees.

"I want to thank you for confronting me the way you did just now. Somewhere along the way, I convinced myself that my problems were because of everyone else. That my anger was justified because of Justine and what I viewed as everyone else being shallow and not appreciating what they had." He glanced quickly at me and away again. "I like these people, especially Kristina and Kyle. I'd like to stick around for a while. I need to step out of my own problems and pay more attention to theirs."

"Have you talked to someone about your sister? A therapist, I mean."

"A few times. But I stopped going."

"I think it would be a good idea to try again. Promise me you'll do that?"

He promised. Rather than following Jeremy down to the patio, I sat there for a minute of my own self-reflection. I had learned two rather large lessons in the past hour, and they both applied to Morgan. First, no relationship was ever equal. There is a constant give-and-take that even friends needed to respect if they wanted to have a truly meaningful friendship. Second, I needed to step out of my own world now and then. I'd said many times over the last twenty-four hours that I was happy Morgan had fun with Carr, but it was surface level. As I stared out at the pine trees that seemed to be standing in judgment over me, I could honestly say that I was truly happy she had found River, even if that meant I got less time with her. I had Tripp, after all. She deserved the same.

Chapter 30

I WENT DOWN TO THE patio for a glass of wine and a few pieces of cheese. Really, I needed to have more cheese than wine because I needed to "keep my wits about me," as Gran used to say, and not imbibe in too much right now. I still had not figured out who had attacked Nick Halpern. Tripp told me once that when he didn't know what to do next, he'd get quiet and the answer would come to him. Since my methods didn't seem to be working, it was time to try someone else's.

Tripp stood at my side, proudly showing off his display of three different wines—white, blush, and red—and a half dozen kinds of cheeses. There were also green and red grapes, and different crackers. Little hand-printed signs labeled one plate *Water Crackers,* another *Rice Crackers,* and a third *Seedy Multi-Grain.*

This had become Meeka's current favorite spot in the yard. She snuffled around the table, gobbling up cracker crumbs and runaway pieces of cheese. She even tried a grape but spit it ouet into the shrubs.

"You haven't taken your uniform off," Tripp noted.

I looked up coyly and returned, "We're not alone yet."

This time, Tripp was the one to blush. Had to say, it made me feel rather victorious.

"I'm still on the clock," I explained. "Which means I really shouldn't be drinking. One small glass won't hurt, though. In fact, sitting back and observing while contemplating the complexity of this"—I took the bottle from his hand—"Moscato might help."

In a tone just above a whisper, he asked, "You still think it was one of our guests?"

"I do, but I can't prove anything."

"What's your next move?"

I looked up with a smile. "Get quiet?"

Understanding what I meant, Tripp smiled in return. He reached for a small plate and filled it with rice crackers and little wedges of cheese. "The lightness of the Moscato requires a cheese and cracker pairing that will complement the wine while not overpowering it."

I took the plate from him and batted my eyelashes. "You're very sexy when you talk like a wine guy."

He pushed back his shoulders. "The proper term is *sommelier*, thank you very much."

Choosing a chair away from the group, so I could see them all at once, I sat and observed. Alicia and Derek were still chatting quietly with each other, both looking far more relaxed than when they'd first gotten here despite the tragedy of Nick. Turned halfway toward each other on the loveseat, they held hands and laughed. A couple that was clearly still very much in love even after five children and plenty of struggles.

In opposition, there was tension between the newer couple, Trevor and Jeremy, that didn't seem to have anything to do with the group dynamics. Trevor was trying to tell Jeremy about something, but Jeremy's attention was on Kristina and Constance in the great room. Finally, Trevor turned away, pulled out his cell phone and tapped on the screen. Making notes for work on Tuesday? Composing an email that would deliver once he had service again? A breakup letter to Jeremy?

Kyle's attention was also focused on his wife and sister-in-law. As he must've been, I wondered what they were so deep in conversation about? I assumed Kristina would counsel Constance on what her life would become now. Except, Kristina was the one sitting back, and Constance seemed to be doing the counseling. Constance held Kristina's hands in hers, and at one point as Constance spoke, Kristina locked eyes with her husband, her expression serious. Then Kristina nodded and said something that made Constance glance over her shoulder at Kyle.

With both women staring at him, Kyle shifted positions, lifting his right foot to prop it on his left knee. When he did, his shorts pulled up and exposed a large bruise just above his right knee.

The condition can also occur during sports where body pads are not worn such as rugby, soccer, karate, or boxing, Dr. Bundy had explained.

He manages the finances for a chain of martial arts gyms. Kristina had told me during our interview. *He loves his job. Too much sometimes.*

Taking my glass and plate with me, I moved closer to Kyle and took the chair diagonal to him. He glanced at me and gave a tight smile.

"It's your last night here," I noted. "Not exactly a relaxing weekend. Are you ready to get back to work?"

Hesitant to turn away from whatever was going on between his wife and sister-in-law, he finally looked at me. "Actually, work will be much more relaxing after this."

"What is it that you do? Don't remember if I asked."

His eyes narrowed slightly. "I manage the financials for a martial arts franchise."

"Oh, yes. Kristina told me." I sipped my wine but didn't even taste it. In fact, my mouth had gone dry. "Do you also practice the sport?"

"I do." His shoulders pushed back. "I'm *Rokudan*, a

sixth-degree black belt."

"Wow. That's impressive. Did it take long to achieve that?"

He smiled like I was a simpleton. "Decades. I started studying karate when I was six."

I tossed back the last of my wine, popped the last cracker with cheese into my mouth, and then set the plate and glass on the table in front of us. Casually, I ran my hands over my shorts, as though brushing away crumbs from my fingers, and confirmed that my handcuffs were in their cargo pocket.

"Would you mind"—I pointed toward the sundeck—"if we went up there? We don't need to disturb everyone else with this conversation."

Kyle had to know what I was doing, he saw me bring Constance and Jeremy up to the deck, but he played along anyway and stood.

As I got up from my chair, I met Tripp's eyes. He'd been standing in the background watching me the entire time. His serious, pointed look said, *Him? Is he the one?* I gave a single nod and assumed he'd watch where I took Kyle.

Making small talk as we walked, I said, "I took kickboxing classes when I worked for the Madison PD. That's kind of like martial arts, isn't it?"

"Some moves are similar," Kyle agreed. "Some of the kicks especially are similar to those we teach in karate."

"We? You teach as well?"

Explaining that teaching was part of his own learning process, Kyle followed me through the yard and up the boathouse stairway. Meeka was right next to me. Ears turned to the side, she was listening to and fully aware of Kyle and any move he might make. Good dog.

When we got to the sundeck, I motioned to a chair for Kyle to sit in, the one that put him with his back to the staircase, the only escape. Unless he went over the rail and into the lake, of course. As I took the chair next to him, I wondered what five foot four me could do against a sixth-degree black belt if he attacked. By the time I drew my Glock, he'd have me on the ground. I glanced at my K-9, sitting dutifully at my feet, and was grateful for her.

As Kyle stared out at the lake, I slid my voice recorder out of my pocket and hit record.

"One of the moves my kickboxing instructor taught us was a knee to the groin."

Kyle turned and studied me, chillingly calm. He settled back in his chair, arms propped on the back, legs spread wide the way men tended to do.

"Knee strikes are among the most effective," he explained in a voice that matched his cool demeanor. "Why don't you ask me what you want to ask me, Sheriff? I assume you eliminated Constance and Jeremy as suspects?"

I pulled out my notebook. "The last time we spoke, you talked about Nick's love for his job and his reaction to losing it. You also talked a lot about the way he treated Constance and Kristina afterwards. I'd like to know more about your relationship with Nick."

"I told you, we weren't friends."

"But as brothers-in-law, you did have a relationship. You mentioned being able to understand 'the devastation' he must've felt losing the job that meant so much to him. Did you talk to him about it?"

"I tried. He didn't want my shoulder to cry on. He and Constance talked about it until she got tired of the drama." He sneered. "So he chose the next best thing, the woman who reminded him of his wife."

"Meaning Kristina?"

He pointed at me and winked. "Right you are. I let it go for a while, but eventually I told her she had to pull away."

"Why?"

This question seemed to surprise him. "Because he was paying far too much attention to my wife."

I didn't like the emphasis he put on *my wife*. Like she

was his property.

"He was around all the time," Kyle continued. "Either she told him to back off and he wouldn't listen, or she was too afraid to tell him. Finally, I stepped in, as I should have from the start, and told him I didn't want him coming around when I wasn't home."

"Did he stay away?"

"He stopped coming to the house but started calling and texting her instead. I saw some of the texts. Disgusting stuff. The same kind of innuendoes he made at breakfast the other day only much more graphic. I told her that was it, no more contact."

"Did Kristina stay away?"

"She said she did."

"You don't believe her?"

He considered this, and his hunched shoulders relaxed a little. "She must have because Nick really lost it after that. Instead of looking for someone else to talk to, like a therapist, that's when he started treating every woman he came across like she was dirt."

I wanted so badly to point out that Kyle's own attitude shadowed this exactly. Character development wasn't what I was interested in at the moment, however.

"Your anger toward Nick seemed to escalate since you arrived here Friday afternoon. Any reason for that?

"Did it?" He paused and rubbed his nose before saying, "Maybe it was being around him again. I hadn't seen the guy in months."

I sat straight, sensing the finish line coming into view. "I'm fascinated by body language."

He frowned, taken aback by this seemingly random change of topic. "Yeah?"

"Yeah. For example, did you know that touching or scratching one's nose while talking can be an indication of lying?"

He froze, his breathing becoming rapid and shallow,

which was a sign of nervousness or stress.

"Did you kill Nick Halpern, Kyle?"

"That wasn't my intention."

I did my best to disguise my surprise. I hadn't expected him to admit it so easily. "Tell me what happened. You saw him leave the house and go for a walk late that night and then what? You followed him?"

"That's about right." Kyle had a white-knuckle grip on the arms of his chair. "I was having a hard time sleeping that night. So I wouldn't keep Kristina awake, I was going to sit in that landing area at the top of the stairs. It was already occupied, so I went down to the great room instead. It was dark that night, and I hadn't turned on any lights, so Nick didn't even see me when he left through the patio doors. It was a spur-of-the-moment decision, really. I just got up and followed him." Kyle chuckled to himself.

"What's funny?"

"I don't know if it's because he walked like such a clod or because he was so deep in thought, but he never heard me behind him. He went up the driveway, past the campground, and all the way to that parking lot. He was heading for one of the trailheads when I finally let him know I was behind him."

"And what happened with the two of you when you were face-to-face?"

"Words were exchanged. Things got heated. Then he turned on his attitude. He said some unforgivable things about my wife, and I couldn't let him get away with it again."

"Let me guess, you hit him in the chest with a knee strike." I pointed at his right knee. "I couldn't see the bruise for the last couple days. It was too cold to wear shorts. Why did you do it?"

"I told you, it wasn't intentional. We argued, words were said, and then he charged at me. I had taken my car keys with me in case I decided to go for a drive. They were rattling in my pants pocket. I didn't want him to hear, so I took them out and laced them through my fingers." He held his hand up, looking at it as though expecting the keys to still be there. "He took a swing at me, and I raised my arm in a high block. The keys caught him in the forehead."

"That explains the jagged laceration on his head. What about the knee strike?"

He looked me square in the eye, his breathing slower now. "After so many years, karate has become less something I do and more something I am. That block was automatic, so was the knee strike. Ninety-nine times out of one hundred I can control my temper even during a heated discussion. I can count on one hand the number of times I have let my training down by allowing my emotions to take over."

"This was that one time in a hundred."

"Nick must've had a heart condition. The exertion and stress were too much for him. I've done that move a million times and can control it perfectly. I didn't hit him that hard."

"The bruise on your knee tells me differently," I said. "Have you ever heard of a condition called commotio cordis?"

He shrugged. "No. What is it?"

I explained what had happened to Nick's heart when Kyle rammed his knee into his chest.

"Well, now." He sat back in surprise. "Talk about your one in a hundred. Although, that's probably more like one in a million, right?"

"Once you realized he was dead, you positioned the body to make it look like a hit-and-run?"

"No," he frowned, a faraway look, like he was remembering the scene, filled his eyes. "Well, sort of. I didn't position his body, just dragged it to the side. Didn't want the guy to get run over. One of his shoes came off while I dragged him, and I left it where it lay. I couldn't turn off the flashlight app so flipped his phone face down. It was blinding on such a dark night." He paused. "I pulled his wallet out of his pocket. Guess I wanted to make it look like he was robbed."

"The empty liquor bottle?"

"Not my doing. It was already there. Not Nick's, far as I know."

Meeka stood from her sitting position. Something had caught her attention.

Watching her out of the corner of my eye, I asked Kyle, "What did he say about Kristina that set you off?"

He broke eye contact and looked past me. "It wasn't any one thing. It was all the little insinuations about how beautiful she was and how lonely she must get when I had to travel, which admittedly has been more than normal lately."

Now, Meeka gave a soft *ruff* and stared at the stairs. A second later, Kristina emerged.

Kyle turned and when he saw his wife, he raised his chin, a defiant gesture. "Here's something you don't know. I had a vasectomy three years ago."

Kristina stood tall, barely reacting to this news other than to grip the handrail.

"You may not remember." Kyle rolled his eyes. "You clearly don't remember, but I told you back when we were dating that I never wanted children. I wanted a career. I was fine with a wife. Children had never been on my to-do list. You slept with Nick Halpern."

Kristina pushed her shoulders back and then laughed, a sound that infuriated her husband. "Here's something you don't know, Kyle. Constance knew about the vasectomy when you had it done three years ago. She just told me about it."

Kyle paled. "Why would she do that? It's illegal to share patient information."

"Not when you sign a waiver giving the clinic permission to tell your wife about any procedures. She kept the secret all this time because she didn't want to get involved in our marriage. Considering my condition, she figured it was time I knew the truth. Are you that arrogant or just stupid? Constance has access to everything." To me, she explained, "He had the procedure done at the clinic where Constance and I work." Back to him, she said, "Constance just needed a little backup these past few months. Like a new mother with a baby, she needed support dealing with Nick's depression. I was that support."

Dumfounded, Kyle finally straightened and cleared his throat. "Speaking of your condition, did he even know that you're pregnant?"

Tears were streaming down Kristina's face. "You killed the wrong man."

Kyle jumped to his feet and made a move toward his wife. Kristina took a few steps closer to me, and I unsnapped the strap holding my Glock in the holster, afraid that his one-time-in-a-hundred loss of control might happen again.

"Maybe you should sit down again, Kyle," I instructed.

His energy seemed to leave his body in a single breath, and he dropped back into his chair.

"What Nick said about me being lonely was absolutely true." Kristina took a tissue from the box I'd brought out for Constance earlier. "It didn't matter if you were traveling or not, you were at the gym all the time. If it's not for your job, you're teaching classes or working on your next belt advancement. We see each other for maybe ten minutes first thing in the morning, and then you don't get home until well after I've gone to bed. Depending on which shift I'm working, we can go weeks without even being in the house at the same time."

"Who is it?" The growl in Kyle's voice was almost animal.

Kristina stood, defiant and mute.

"Who is it?" Kyle screamed at her. "Who's the father?"

"Kyle." I pulled my weapon and prayed I wouldn't

have to take aim. "I don't think you want to lose control again."

I wasn't going to push Kristina to say anything, but I had to admit, curiosity was eating me up.

"Tell me one thing first," Kristina bargained. "How did you sneak out the night you killed Nick without me knowing?"

Kyle looked away and sucked on his teeth. "You sleep like a rock, but just to be safe I put ground-up sleeping pills in your chamomile tea."

"You drugged me? Do you know what that could do to the baby?"

Kyle shrugged. "Not my baby."

The look of hatred on Kristina's face turned to one of smugness. "Did you ever wonder why Jeremy won't look you in the eye?"

Kyle analyzed the statement and then pointed toward the group on the back patio. "Jeremy Levine? He's gay."

Kristina shook her head. "Actually, he's bisexual. And even if he was gay, that doesn't mean he's not capable."

"Why would you sleep—?"

"Okay," I interrupted, "I've heard enough. You two can go over the gory details later."

I instructed Kristina to go back to the group and removed my handcuffs from my pocket. When she was about halfway down the stairs, Kyle leapt to his feet and went after her. When I tried to stop him, he tilted to his left and caught me in the gut with a sidekick that knocked me to the ground. Snarling and barking, Meeka took chase for me. It took me a few seconds to catch my breath and get back to my feet. By the time I was down the stairs, I found Kyle flat on the ground with one of my deputy's knees in his back, Meeka standing guard.

"Told you I've been working out," Reed said with a proud swagger in his voice. "I assume you want me to take him in and book him."

"That would be great. How did you—?"

"Ask your boyfriend," Reed responded.

I waited until Reed had Kyle securely in the back of the station van, handcuffed to the two steel loops soldered to the floor. I held up a splayed hand, indicating I'd be five minutes behind. He nodded and gave a two-finger salute.

I turned and nearly ran into Tripp.

"Are you okay?" he asked and wrapped me in a hug. His heart was pounding, his body shaking. "I saw him kick you. Do you need to go to the health center?"

"No, I'm fine. Just shocked, once again, to find out that people aren't who I thought they were." I had to stop there; I couldn't tell him what Kristina had just revealed. Although, I had a feeling Tripp and the rest of the group would know the whole thing by the time I got back from the station. "You called Reed?"

"I did. I figured you could handle everything by yourself, but you've told me many times how important backup can be."

I let him pull me into another hug. "Thank you. Backup is important. And this time I needed it."

"Well, you know I'm always here for you."

I stepped out of the hug. "I need to get over to the station and help Reed with everything. I'll be back as soon as I can."

He kissed the tip of my nose. "I'll be right here."

Chapter 31

BY THE TIME MEEKA AND I got to the station, Reed had contacted the County Sheriff's Department to send someone for Kyle. We were just finishing up the paperwork when Deputy Evan Atkins arrived. I let Reed handle telling the deputy all that he knew about the case, and I filled in with the details Reed wasn't sure about.

"When I got the call tonight," Deputy Atkins said when we were done, "I figured it would be about the little boy. How did that turn out?"

"That ended happily," I told him. "Just a case of a curious little boy and a grass snake. Fortunately, we've got our own Grizzly Adams and Blue the Community Cat wandering our woods, so little Dustin is safe and sound with his family once again."

"I have no idea what you just said." He held up a hand before I could explain. "Doesn't matter."

"It's all good," I assured. "Standard run-of-the-mill stuff for Whispering Pines."

"I understand that you knew both of these guys?" Deputy Atkins circled back to the Halpern case. "Both the victim and the guilty party?"

"I'd never met the victim before Friday, but I've been good friends with our perp's wife since college. Not sure what the status of that friendship is now."

"You make it sound like it's your fault that you had to arrest him. You were just doing your job."

Besides that, Kristina was no longer the person she used to be. Her lack of remorse over having an affair bothered me a lot. Time for a new subject. "Any progress on Donovan?"

"There was a report of someone who fit his description on Mackinac Island."

"In Michigan? What's he doing over there?"

"No clue. Someone called in the report, but you know how that island is. Cars aren't allowed, so they patrol on foot. By the time they got to the area where he'd reportedly been seen, there was no sign of him. He may have jumped on a ferry leaving the island before they could even start looking. Either way, we're not positive it was even him."

"It was him." I was sure of it. Donovan was easy to identify. Six feet tall, bulky, and a silver ponytail. Changing his hair would be easy, but I didn't see him doing that. He was arrogant and would hide in plain sight with us looking right past him, waiting for the right moment to reappear. "My guess is he's either wandering Michigan's Upper Peninsula or he slipped into Ontario. Maybe we—"

"There is no we," Atkins demanded. "You're too close to this. He escaped on my watch; I'll make sure he's captured." He gave me a pointed look. "Seriously, this guy isn't mentally stable. Promise me you'll leave it alone."

After a few seconds of sulking, I gave him a big cheesy grin. "If I had to have a big brother, why couldn't he be like you?"

He ignored my grin. "Anything else you need from me? If not, I've got a bit of a drive, so I should get to it. I hate driving through these woods at night."

"You can stay." I held my head high and proud. "I have a bed-and-breakfast now, and there's a room available. It's yours if you want it. No charge for a fellow law enforcement brother."

He debated the offer for a long moment then smiled and shook his head. "Thanks, but I think I'll just head out."

"Okay, but you're missing out on a great breakfast."

"Another time." He looked from me to Reed. "You two, stay out of trouble up here."

"Believe it or not," Reed said, "that's always our plan."

Once Deputy Atkins had taken off with his prisoner, it was time for us to call it a night.

"I can't thank you enough for showing up at the house the way you did."

Reed responded with a flip, "That's my job," but quickly added, "You're welcome. I'm glad I got there in time. You should really be thanking Tripp. He sounded pretty worried."

Cozy warmth spread through me with that pronouncement. "He's quite a guy."

On the way home, I paused at the intersection that led up to Morgan's house. It was late, almost eleven o'clock, but after all that talk about relationships not always being fifty-fifty, I needed to go see her. I had acted like such a child, pouting over her date or whatever it was with Carr. I wouldn't sleep well if I didn't apologize, so I turned north instead of continuing west.

As we pulled up to the Barlow cottage, my gamble that she'd still be up was proven right; there were shadows moving around in the garden. I pushed the car door shut quietly and let Meeka out of the back with a whispered warning for no barking. She softly sneezed her understanding and darted beneath the border hedge.

As I stood in the short driveway, debating if I should call through the hedge to Morgan or just go on in, the front door opened.

"Blessed be. What are you doing here? Is everything all right?"

I opened my mouth to answer, but nothing would come out. Instead, I just shook my head.

"Oh, Jayne. Come on in."

Morgan guided me through the house to the garden and over to a chair tucked into a cozy corner where an oil lantern was burning. She went back inside and returned a few minutes later with mugs of tea.

"What's in this one?" I asked.

"This is Comfort—chamomile, clove, linden, lavender, rosemary, and valerian." She sat next to me and waited for me to take my first sip. "You look like you could use some comfort."

"I wanted to apologize to you," I said a few seconds later when I was indeed feeling comforted.

"To me? Whyever for?"

"Because you found someone you wanted to spend time with—"

She cut me off with a crisp shake of her head. "River and I spent a little time together, and now he's gone. His involvement in my life is no longer anything that should concern you."

"You really don't care that that's all it was?"

"Not at all. That's all I needed and wanted."

I studied her expression over my mug as I sipped my tea. She seemed sincere, so who was I to judge? "If you're happy, I'm happy, but that's not where I was going with this. I'm apologizing because you found someone you wanted to spend time with, and I acted like that meant you were kicking me to the curb. If River were to have become a part of your day-to-day life, that's no different from what Tripp is for me."

Morgan waited silently, letting me say all I needed to say.

"In a very short time, you've become a true friend for me; something I haven't had in my life in a long time. I mean, other than co-workers, the only people I had in my world were a mother who wanted me to be like my sister, a sister who wanted nothing to do with me, and a boyfriend who wanted to turn me into his version of the perfect politician's spouse."

"All of that just because I went on a date?" Her tone was teasing yet serious. "That's impressive."

I cringed. "I'm so embarrassed."

"You know that isn't the case, though, don't you?"

"I had a very big revelation today, so now I do." Morgan settled back into her chair and wrapped her sage-green fringed chiffon shawl tighter around her shoulders. "What is this revelation?"

"That relationships are never equal. Or they seldom are. That at any given moment, one person will need a little more than the other. I want you to know that as your reformed-by-revelation true friend, I'm always willing to take a step back so you can step forward if you need to."

Morgan took a sip of her tea and then cleared her throat. "That's a really good revelation. Thank you. Now, what else is bothering you?"

"It can wait. Let's just sit here and drink our tea."

"You came to me in the middle of the night, Jayne, and not just to give me that beautiful apology. Tell me what else is weighing so heavily on your mind."

I gave in and told her what Lily Grace said about being careful not to change Whispering Pines, and how Violet had agreed that maybe Pine Time shouldn't be open year-round.

"The village is changing, isn't it?" I asked.

"The village changes with every passing season, but I understand what you're asking. What you uncovered, Priscilla's death and Flavia's involvement in it, did change things. That secret lay deep beneath the village for decades. Buried things can fester and cause tremendous problems once they're uncovered. Had the truth about Priscilla been revealed at the time, the villagers could have dealt with it then. Now they have to deal with both the event and the fact that they were lied to."

I nodded. "Gran messed up."

"She did," Morgan agreed. "As for what Lily Grace said, you did, in effect, open a wound that now needs to heal. These things have a way of rising to the surface on their own, though. We would have had to deal with it one way or another."

Briar appeared from the shadows, mug of tea in hand.

"Mama, you should be in bed."

"I should," Briar agreed. "So should you two. What are we talking about?"

"How Jayne is not responsible for the sins of the village's past."

Morgan gave a quick recap as Briar settled into a chair. Then I told them both, "Sugar told me that she believes there's a dark cloud hanging over the village."

"And you think that's your fault?" Morgan asked.

"I'm not sure what to think. Sugar did make me wonder about the possibility."

"I agree with Sugar's theory," Briar began, her voice slurring with late-night fatigue, "but not that you are responsible. This cloud started forming forty years ago when Priscilla died and has grown bigger and darker with every negative thing that's happened here."

Morgan nodded. "If you are responsible for anything, it's that you're peeling back layers and uncovering secrets. If your path is to help heal these secrets, then I say, do so proudly."

"You think that's it? You think the reason I'm here is to help heal the village?"

"I think that's very possible," Morgan said, "but you can't rush through it. You have opened a bed-and-breakfast that you call Pine Time, but you have not yet embraced the speed at which time moves in this village."

"That's what I told her yesterday," Briar said. "She's always looking ahead. Right now, she's clear at the end of the next summer season."

"That's because my parents will put everything up for

sale if we aren't profitable. Then what will happen to the village?"

Morgan reached across the little café table and placed a calming hand on mine. "If helping Whispering Pines truly is your path, it doesn't matter what you do, everything will work out the way it's supposed to."

"That's true for everyone," Briar added. "Slow down and listen and your path will present itself."

Or get quiet and wait for the answer, as Tripp says.

"You really believe that, don't you?" I asked.

Briar smiled. "I really do."

Morgan got up from her chair. "I'll be right back."

Either she was going for more tea or she was going to cast a spell for me again. My nightstand drawer would soon be packed full of little charm bags at this rate. Less than a minute later, Morgan came back with a candle, a small bowl, and a glass of water.

"Oh, yes," Briar said when she saw the collection, "good idea."

Morgan placed the candle and the bowl, which she filled with the water, on the table.

"What are we doing?" I asked. "What kind of spell are you going to cast on me this time?"

"No spell," Morgan said. "We want you to learn to live life and enjoy each day for the gift that it is. We're going to teach you to meditate."

I nearly choked on my tea. "Meditate?"

"The candle is a focal point," Briar informed and then looked questioningly at her daughter, who nodded. They were doing their telepathy thing again. "We have some suspicions about how you relate to water."

"How I relate to water? What does that mean?"

"Your dear grandma Lucy," Briar began, "drew strength from water, it energized her. That's why she built that house right on the lake."

"Sugar told me that Gran was a water witch," I said.

"You think that maybe I'm one, too?"

Morgan gave me an isn't-she-cute smile. "No, but I think you get strength from water just like Lucy did."

She could be right about that. The day I arrived here, I sat out on that deck looking out at the lake. A sort of peace that I didn't know was possible spread through me.

"How do I meditate?" I asked.

"You just need to focus and breathe deeply." Morgan lit the candle. "The hardest part is keeping your mind quiet. That's where a focal point helps. I prefer to focus on candlelight. If you want to do the same, don't stare directly at the flame, it will burn your eyes. Look around the flame, if that makes sense."

Just like I had suggested Reed do at the accident site. "Perfect sense. What about the bowl of water?"

"I think since water seems to calm you," Morgan said, "you may want water as your focal point instead. We can hear the stream running past out front. Maybe listening to the water will be enough to center you. Or you can gaze into the water in the bowl. Or position the bowl so you can see the flame in the water."

"How you do this is up to you," Briar added. "There is no proper way to meditate. Your goal is to relax and settle your thoughts, so you can be more in the present like we talked about."

Morgan pulled her legs up onto her chair in a position I assumed was a full Lotus. No way could I do that.

"A simple crisscross is fine," Morgan said, reading my mind.

"Or you can just sit." Briar sat with her feet on the ground and her hands resting in her lap.

"Are you ready?" Morgan asked.

I chose crisscross with my hands in my lap and the bowl of water as my focal point. I inhaled deeply and did my best to clear my thoughts and focus my mind. "Ready as I'll ever be."

Chapter 32

IT WAS WELL AFTER MIDNIGHT when I got back to the house. I wanted to go wake up Tripp and tell him what I'd just learned about taking things slower and settling into our world here. With his unease over the B&B not being full all the time, this was something he needed to learn, too. Waking someone from sleep to discuss living in the present seemed a little ironic, though. Not to mention mean. Besides, I was so mellow from Morgan's tea and the meditation session, I wasn't sure my words would make any sense right now anyway.

Instead, I went to my favorite place in all of Whispering Pines: my sundeck. Morgan was right, I did feel a sort of energy when I was near water. The connection Gran always talked about, the peace she got from being outside in nature, near water in particular, I understood that now. No matter what else was going on in the world, if I could just stand right here and smell the lake and listen to my whispering trees, my world was good.

I decided to believe Morgan, that if being here to help heal the village was truly what I was meant to do, then nothing would be able to stop that. If my parents decided to sell the house and the land, I'd find a way to buy it. Or make the buyer understand the importance of the village.

Or maybe I could make my parents understand that this wasn't just about money. They might have bad feelings about the village, but I loved it and the people here with all my heart. If I could get Mom and Dad to come here and experience the Whispering Pines I knew, maybe they could get past the events that had all but destroyed their marriage so many years ago. That would require getting Dad back in the country first. That could be a challenge. Of course, Mom was only a few hours away, and getting her here would be an even bigger one.

Done with yard patrol, Meeka came upstairs for the night, her claws clacking on each step as she climbed. She sat by the doors, waiting for me to let her in.

As I did, I caught the tiny sliver of the moon out of the corner of my eye and realized that I'd just spent the last five minutes thinking about my parents and the future instead of taking in the night. Living in the present would take practice. I grabbed a blanket from inside my apartment and then curled up on a deck chair and focused on the moon's reflection on the water. Talk about a focal point.

~~~

My chirping birds alarm woke me at five o'clock. I didn't know what Tripp had planned for his day, but I wanted time alone with him before it started. After a quick shower, I crossed the yard and saw that none of the lights were on in the kitchen yet. I didn't have quite the same touch with coffee that Tripp did, but I'd watched him prepare his brew often enough that I should be able to get it close. Such a simple act, making him coffee, but it made me happy to be doing this for him, especially because he did so much for me.

Five minutes later, the door to the bedroom off the kitchen opened, and Tripp peeked his head around the corner.

"What are you doing up already?" His voice was husky with sleep.

"I wanted to be sure I started my day with you."

"That's a nice surprise. You got home late last night. Did everything turn out okay?"

"I had to stop by Morgan's and apologize for being an idiot."

"You? Never. Did she tell you our warlock friend plans to come back?"

My mouth dropped open. "No. In fact, she seemed fine that he was gone. As in, that's what she preferred."

Tripp laughed. "He didn't say when, but it sounds like she'll be getting a surprise visit someday." He yawned big. "Give me a minute to get dressed. I'll be right back."

Before he could return, our guests all came down from their rooms.

"No need to make breakfast this morning," Constance informed me. "We met before going to bed last night and decided we've caused enough grief."

"Not at all," I began, but they kind of did. As a B&B owner, I expected things wouldn't go perfectly; people had issues that they'd bring with them. I had hoped things would go smoothly with our first guests, though, especially because they were my friends.

Kristina stuck right to her sister's side. "We're going to head on out."

I took Kristina's hand, wanting her to understand I didn't hold any of the events against her. "You don't have to go, but if you want to, at least wait for coffee. I just made a huge pot. Tripp and I can't possibly drink it all ourselves."

The tension running through the group was awful. Trevor and Jeremy were clearly not good. I suspected that if they hadn't broken up last night, they would on the way back to Milwaukee. Trevor was obviously avoiding Kristina as well. He had a habit of being able to walk away from people and not look back. There was a benefit to that sometimes, but I hoped he'd get past what Kristina had done with Jeremy. Although that might be hoping for too much.

Alicia gave me a big hug and whispered in my ear, "I'm so sorry for everything that happened. Your grand opening should've been a happy time."

"Can't dwell on that," I said and pulled away. "I did get to see you, and that's a happy thing. Are you heading straight home?"

She shook her head. "My parents agreed to stay with the kids until dinnertime. We're going to take the slow route back and enjoy the scenery."

Tripp came out of his room then, confused to see everyone gathered.

"Good for you," I told Alicia. "Hang on. I'll get you coffee and see if I can dig up some scones or muffins."

Tripp and I filled everyone's travel mugs with coffee and assembled to-go bags. After the last car had pulled away from the house, I led him to the great room.

"Let's have a chat."

"A sitting on the couch discussion," he said. "This sounds serious."

"We need to rethink some things." His eyes went wide with panic, and I laughed. "Not about us. Sorry, didn't mean to start your morning with that."

"Good. Because I'm not going anywhere. I told you that." He took a long slurp of coffee. "What did you mean?"

I explained my discussions with Lily Grace and Violet.

"I don't have a problem making lunch and dinner for people." He got up to let Meeka in the patio doors. "I don't think it's a good idea to close down for the winter."

"Not the whole winter. Just February. And maybe only be open for long weekends in March, like Thursday or Friday through Monday."

He pondered that option. "That would mean a lot of time alone together. Do you think you can handle that?"

"It would be a real sacrifice"—I exhaled a put-upon sigh—"but I'm willing to try."

"I checked for reservations before I went to bed last night. Looks like the party was good promo because there were a half a dozen or so waiting. What if instead of investing money in winter sports equipment like we'd been talking about, we invest in more advertising instead? Then, if people want to stay, we let them stay."

I nodded, working that through in my mind. "Here's a thought. If we're providing three meals, we can charge a little more."

"You figure that out, and I'll start putting together lunch and dinner menus."

"Oh good. Test food," I joked. "How about, we go with this plan and see how things go between now and February?"

"Deal." He held up his coffee mug and we sealed the deal with a little toast.

"One other thing," I said. "Things should quiet down since there will be fewer tourists now, but Reed will be taking criminal justice classes over the fall and winter. That means it'll be just me running the station again."

"I remember."

Taking his cup to refill it, I considered telling him about the black cloud and my path presenting itself discussion I had with Morgan and Briar last night. I would eventually. First, there was something far more important.

"I want you to promise me something."

"Anything," he said immediately.

I handed him his refilled mug. "I didn't even tell you what it was yet."

"Doesn't matter."

I took his free hand in mine. "Promise me that if I'm gone too much, you'll let me know. If you're getting lonely, tell me."

"How could I be lonely with the house full of guests all

the time?" He winked.

"I'm serious about this."

He tucked my hair behind my ear. "I know you are. This has to do with Kyle and Kristina, doesn't it?"

"Yes, but Constance and Nick even more. She started out being there for him but lost track of him along the way. I don't want that to ever happen to us. Even if I'm crazy busy hunting down murderers and you're crazy busy with guests, we should be able to find five minutes to check in with each other every day."

"I like that plan."

"Good. I don't want you to end up in the arms of another woman." I narrowed my eyes and looked sideways at him. "I've seen the way Holly checks you out when she comes to work."

He swatted a dismissive hand at me. "Holly? Arden is the one you need to worry about."

He took the coffee mug out of my hand and set it along with his own on the coffee table. Then he pulled me onto his lap and kissed me long and deep. This time, he was the one to pull away first.

"Hungry?" he asked.

"Starving." I grinned at him. "Oh, you meant breakfast."

He picked me up and headed for the kitchen. "I'll make something for you."

I popped off the barstool as soon as he set me down on it. "Let's make something together."

As Tripp taught me how to make omelets and muffins, we chatted about the upcoming day. That was far enough into the future for me.

Suspense and fantasy author Shawn McGuire started writing after seeing the first Star Wars movie (that's episode IV) as a kid. She couldn't wait for the next installment to come out so wrote her own. Sadly, those notebooks are long lost, but her desire to tell a tale is as strong now as it was then. She grew up in the beautiful Mississippi River town of Winona, Minnesota, called the Milwaukee area of Wisconsin (Go Pack Go!) home for many years, and now lives in Colorado where she is a total homebody. She loves to read, craft, cook and bake, and spend time in the spectacular Rocky Mountains. You can learn more about Shawn's work on her website www.Shawn-McGuire.com

Made in the USA
Monee, IL
19 January 2022